More Than Words

Keren Hughes
&
Jodie Harrold

ISBN 978-1-912768-86-8

Published 2020

Published by Black Velvet Seductions Publishing

More Than Words Copyright 2020 Keren Hughes & Jodie Harrold
Cover design Copyright 2020 Jessica Greeley

Visit us at:
www.blackvelvetseductions.com

Dedication

To the people who think that true love is a myth, may our words bring you hope that it's something that is out there for everyone.

You are worthy, you are loved, you will find "the one" in a place where you least expect it.

***

Let someone love you just the way you are – as flawed as you might be, as unattractive as you sometimes feel, and as unaccomplished as you think you are. To believe that you must hide all the parts of you that are broken, out of fear that someone else is incapable of loving what is less than perfect, is to believe the sunlight is incapable of entering a broken window and illuminating a dark room.

~ Marc Hack ~

Acknowledgements

From Keren:

Firstly, a note of thanks must be given to my co-author, **Jodie Harrold**. This has been our baby from the start, after all.

Jodie, thank you for saying yes when I asked you to join me on this mad adventure. You're the only person I've ever co-written with and with both of us having anxiety, I thought we'd be itchier about control than we were. Instead, we worked in harmony and I believe we worked well.

Thank you for giving us Evie. Thank you for allowing me to be part of your journey as you wrote what is to be your debut novel. It has been so much fun that I didn't want it to end. Alas, it has and now our book baby is out in the world. I hope you're as happy about that prospect as I am. I love you. Always. <3

Nan; you made me the woman I am, and you encouraged me to become the author I am. A little piece of you inspires all I do. Thank you for everything you ever did for me. You were my biggest cheerleader and even though you're not here anymore, I always feel your love surrounding me. <3

Calum, my handsome, witty little boy; thank you for always being you. I'm so proud to be your mum. Thank you for always being proud of me for my writing. You are the reason I do everything I do. Why I wake up in a morning, why I love people the way I do. Being your mum taught me that your heart grows exponentially when you love a child. You'll always be my baby, no matter how old you get, so I'll never allow you to read my books, but I will always thank you for being there for me. <3

Ric, my boss-man; thank you for always taking a chance on my stories. You are truly amazing. I haven't just gained a publisher; I've gained a friend. Thank you for bringing my book babies to life. I am humbled by your support and your patience with me.

My PA, BETA and all-round superstar bestie, Kara; thank you for always being around for me to bounce ideas off, for me to vent to when I can't think straight, and just for being the best friend I could ask for. It's going to be a blast finally meeting face to face when Calum and I come to stay with you at Easter. Canada won't know what's hit it. ;) I love you, boo. Thank you for everything you've done for me over the years and continue to do for me. <3

To the readers, bloggers, and anyone who reads this or any of my other books; thank you for taking a chance on my work. Whether you've been here since the beginning of my journey in 2013 or only just picking up a book by me, thank you. Your support means everything to this girl! Readers truly rock and without you, us authors wouldn't be able to do what we do. We'd have untold stories in our heads, but nobody to tell them to. So, thank you for making this not only possible, but worthwhile.

www.blackvelvetseductions.com

From Jodie:

I first want to thank **Keren Hughes**, my co-author, best friend, and all-around awesome woman. Writing has always been a passion for me, I've always had the thought to write a book, wrote parts to some which will never see the day. Eventually, I gave up on my dream. Until now, you helped make it true. Thank you for believing in me and asking to co-write a book with me, thank you for beginning my journey, for listening to my ideas and allowing me to write from the heart.

Thank you for dealing with my incessant questions… there was a lot of them. You listened to them and answered them all with honesty, with no complaints. Which was more than my nagging could have asked for.

More thanks goes to you for giving us Trey, he's amazing, and now the man of my dreams.

I love you, always.

Second, I want to thank **you**, the reader. I've had all this help from family, friends, and our publisher. But this wouldn't be read if it weren't for you picking up this book and giving it a chance. Thank you for being here for the beginning of my journey, and I hope to make you just as happy in the future. I hope you love Evie and Trey just as much as we do.

Aiden; Thank you for pushing me to do this, for helping me to believe in myself.

Thank you for sitting there as I crazed about a character, for the times where all I wanted to do was write and plan. You listened and endured through all my explanations and didn't do anything but smile and listen. Sorry for putting you through that.

Nan & Grandad Harrold; Nan, you were one of the first people I told, and you were ecstatic. You filled me with nothing but confidence when I told you. You didn't hit me with any scepticism, nothing but full on certainty that I could do this; that I would do it successfully. Grandad, thank you for listening to both mine and nan's chatter as we talked about it, for being interested, and happy for me to be doing something different.

You two have always been my biggest supporters, whether it be art, writing, or my degree. Thank you for believing in me, I love you.

Yet again, I'm sorry for some of the scenes in this book, please skip those pages, promise?

Ric, and everyone at BVS; Thank you for listening and believing in me, somebody who knew nothing of the writing community, and bringing me into it with open arms. You are an awesome bunch of people.

Lastly, thank you to the **rest of my family**. Some I was hesitant to tell, some I wasn't, but no matter who I told, you were all happy for me. Your assurance helped me carry on and allowed me to continue in this new phase of life.

Prologue

I try to calm my shaking hands as adrenaline rapidly travels through my body and up my arms, until my whole body is nearly convulsing in shock. Gasping, I try to take in deep breaths to be able to distinguish what I am seeing and hearing. It takes all my concentration. After gaining the control to slowly take in the blurring lines on the piece of paper before me, I am finally able to form words.

"They left me everything? As in *everything*? Even their house?" I ask in shock as I stare at the solicitor sitting before me. "What about my parents? Did they not leave anything to them?"

I continue my frantic attempt to absorb the knowledge before me as the solicitor sighs in frustration. Having asked him the same question multiple times in a row, I can understand why he's frustrated. I am too.

"No. As you can see, it is written in this will that their sole beneficiary is their grandchild—you. They left you everything for you to do whatever you please."

He pauses as he shuffles through some papers stacked on his desk, looking for something.

"There is a letter addressed to you, which is my reason for asking you to meet me today. Their only request was for you to read it before you make a decision."

He slides the envelope towards me as he talks. I stare at it in fascination. Realising I have been silent for so long, he clears his throat to get my attention.

"I will leave and give you some time to digest what has been brought to your attention. I will be back in five minutes."

After staring at the envelope for what feels like hours—but in reality, is only a couple of seconds—I tear into it. I'm taken aback as a flurry of photos falls over my lap and to the ground.

Bending to pick them up, I gasp in shock as I see all the photos of me with my grandparents as I grew up and some more recent ones.

One stands out the most; there I am with a large grin on my face. My grandad John stands behind me looking worried, and I'm holding a revolting looking cake to my grandma who's behind the camera.

Inside the envelope is also a letter. I begin to shake as I see my name in cursive writing, knowing it to be my grandmother's.

To our dearest Evie,

If you're reading this, we know you're going to be upset and confused. We wanted everything to be left to you, for you to have a future. We remember the joy in your eyes when you used to play in the park as a child, and then how that joy turned to inquisitiveness as you blossomed into a teenager. But then it slowly faded away after university. We wished that there was anything we could do to bring that little girl back, when you were so full of life and weren't afraid to do anything.

Do you remember when we used to bake together? You would get flour everywhere! However, you enjoyed it so much that I didn't mind finding flour in all the nooks and crannies for months on end.

I remember the day you and Grandad tried to make that surprise chocolate cake while I was in town with the girls, buying more ingredients for a special recipe I had found. When I came home, all we could smell was burnt cake, as you had left it in the oven for too long. But the way that your eyes filled with pride as you presented that cake to me, with Grandad trailing behind you looking worried. Oh, the look on his face was priceless! Even though it was burnt, we ate it. We knew how much it meant to you, and over the years you perfected the art and became an amazing baker. You managed to take my recipes and make them better. I hope you keep that passion, that it will live on after me and you. I hope you take that box of recipes and produce some amazing treats with them, and eventually pass them down to your children, with your recipes added in there.

We are proud to be able to call you ours. You were ours, just as much as you were your parents'. Which is the reason why we decided to leave everything to you.

We knew you may need help one day. At first, we didn't know what it was for—I just called it intuition—but as time went past, we had our suspicions. We hope that you can live the life that you are meant to live, without restraints holding you back. We want you to be free.

We love you with all our hearts,

Grandma and Grandad.

I shuffle to wipe the tears spilling down my cheeks as they hit the paper before me, not wanting to ruin the last remains of my grandma's handwriting. I stare in disbelief as I scan the letter repeatedly, trying to make sense of what she meant. I kept what had happened between me and Greg quiet, not wanting anybody to step in and possibly make things worse.

I know immediately that I am going to leave my hometown; I need to get away from my past as quickly as possible. Saying goodbye to my family is going to be the hardest thing, but I need to leave. They may not understand why, but I feel the urge to create distance between me and my past. This money gives me the freedom to do what I could have only dreamed of before—to create a future for myself. I need to take what my grandparents have given me and leave. I smile at the thought of making a new home for myself, of having a place that I can call my own. Where I can leave dishes in the sink for more than five minutes, place my shoes wherever I want them to be, and lounge around the house doing nothing for a day. A life where I can dress how I want, instead of having an outfit laid out for me by Greg. Where I can make friends with other men and not be reprimanded for speaking to someone of the opposite sex. In fact, a life where I can actually have friends full stop.

The opening of the office door pulls me from my thoughts, and I quickly wipe my tears and face the solicitor. He smiles as he makes his way to the desk and shifts paperwork again. The mess that has ensued makes me want to go over and file it all, rather than having stacks of paperwork on top of each other.

"All of your grandparents' assets will be transferred in your name by the end of the week. You will then be free to sell the house and do what you wish."

He extends his arm towards me and shakes my hand as though he's just done a business deal. I wonder if he can hear how hard my heart is beating.

As I make my way out the door, I quickly turn.

"Thank you for having me here and giving me that envelope."

I smile as I briskly walk out the doors to accept my fate.

***

I stare at the numerous pregnancy tests before me as I'm slumped on the toilet seat. It's not possible. I thought the first couple were just defective—is it even possible to get a false positive the way you can get a false negative?—but after the fifth test, I've realised my fate.

They are *all* positive. The thought of bringing up a child in this type of hostile environment terrifies me. I may be stupid for putting *myself* through this, but could I do that to another human being? *My* child. I couldn't—no, I wouldn't—do that. Greg would either beat me the moment he found out or make me abort the unborn baby. Abortion is out of the question; I couldn't do that to a living being. I'm not against it for other people, they have their reasons, but it isn't a possibility for me. I just know that I could give this baby a life, I could bring this baby up. It would be my salvation.

I need to leave. I jump up as quickly as I can, ignoring the excruciating pain that travels up my side from the movement. I run through the house to get the binbags out of the kitchen, and I throw as many belongings as I can into them, only wanting a few tops and the jewellery that my grandma Heather gave me.

Looking at the time, I know I've only got an hour to get out of the house before he returns. I pack as quickly as I can and am about to make my way to my parents' house, but first I turn and race back into the bathroom to grab all the pregnancy tests and boxes. I don't want Greg to have any inclination of what is going on.

After I've locked the door to the apartment, I race down the stairs, jump into my car and reverse out of the parking space. I drive down the road as fast as I dare, not wanting to be pulled over for a speeding ticket at this time. As I make my way onto the motorway, I dial my mother's number.

"Hello, sweetheart. Are you okay?" I hear the muffled voice of my mother through the car speakers.

"Umm … Yeah. I-is it okay if I stay at yours for the night? It's an emergency."

I hear my mum go silent on the other end. I can imagine that she's sitting there scratching her head.

"Of course you can. Are you sure you're okay? Is this about Greg?" I hear her say over a muffled reply from my father.

"I'm fine; I just need to get away. I'll be half an hour. I'll explain everything when I get there. I'll see you soon. Love you."

I quickly end the call before my mother gives my father the phone, knowing he won't let me get away with only half answers.

I knew it wouldn't take long for her to figure it out. I had tried to hide it as best as I could. But I couldn't prevent it.

***

Curled on the sofa, I wait for my mother to come back into the room with a coffee. I wince as I shuffle, trying to get comfortable. I suddenly feel my mother's warm hands gently grasp my side where my top has risen. She pulls it all the way up and gasps at the sight.

"Who did this to you?"

"It's nothing, Mother. Don't worry. I fell down the stairs the other day; you know how clumsy I am." I fake a laugh, trying to make her believe the lie.

"I'm not stupid, honey. I've seen plenty of those. Was it Greg?" She looks me in the eyes.

I nod my head ever so slightly. I don't want to actually admit what happened, and I don't want her to have a tainted view of me or think that I deserved it.

I look up, waiting for a response, and she leans over and hugs me as gently as she can, smoothing my hair as she whispers soothing words, and that's all it takes for me to break down.

***

I shake my head, clearing it so I can focus on my goal. I turn my phone off as I want to make sure that Greg can't get ahold of me—I'll need to change my number soon, so I don't have to be afraid each time the phone rings. It will only take him an hour, maybe two tops, before he figures out that I'm not coming back. He knows that today is usually shopping day, and I always forget to charge my phone, so thankfully, luck is on my side for the time being.

Having known that I'm pregnant for just an hour, the protectiveness that I feel for this unborn baby shouldn't be natural. I'm not the maternal type. After being with Greg for the last four and a half years, I knew I didn't want to bring a baby into this type of life. I did everything I could to prevent it; I secretly had the contraceptive injection so I wouldn't fall pregnant. But he found out and decided to get his payback, trying everything to get me pregnant. Even if it was against my will. *Looks like he succeeded*, I thought. I shake my head, wanting to get rid of that thought before it fully festers in my mind. I won't allow my child to grow up thinking he or she was a mistake or not wanted.

The driver's side door opening startles me. I jump and turn, ready to kick and scream, before I realise it's my father. As I visibly relax, his sharp eyes take in everything; I notice his eyes narrow, then soften. He reaches in and gently grabs me in his arms, cradling me to his chest as if I were a child. The full force of what has happened makes my body shake as I sob into his chest. He whispers soothing words into my ear as he helps me from the car and guides me into the house. I notice my mother standing in the foyer with a hand over her mouth, unshed tears brimming in her eyes.

How I managed to pull into my parents' driveway without realising makes me feel unnerved. I can't have been completely aware of my surroundings like I usually am.

As my dad turns into the living room, I see my uncle sitting there in his police uniform. I start to shake and try to get away, but my father's arms clamp tighter around me.

"You need to finally make him suffer for what he's done to you," he whispers in my ear. "No more hiding."

Reporting Greg to the police has never been an option before. He warned me that if I ever did, he would hurt me so much worse than he ever had before—and that pain didn't have to come as physical beatings or mental abuse; it could mean hurting my parents. So, I never went to hospital with my injuries in case they saw signs of abuse and reported it to the police, as they are duty-bound to do. I never dialled 999. I always dressed to cover myself from head to toe, sometimes using makeup to cover bruises—something I became an expert at doing.

I instantly feel overwhelmed. Do I really want to report him? What if it goes to court and I don't have any physical evidence of what he did to me? He'd get off and then come after me ten times as hard as before.

My heart races in my chest, feeling like it's trying to burst free of its constraints. I try to swallow past the lump in my throat as I feel tears sting the backs of my eyes.

I *can* do this. I *will* do this. I *have* to do this. For myself, but more importantly for the innocent life inside me. My child deserves the best start in life, and that can't happen with Greg walking free. He has to pay for what he's done. I can't live my life constantly looking over my shoulder, in fear of every street corner, every dark alley …

The blows he dealt me over the years made me feel weak. But I know now that I'm not weak. I am strong. I am willing to fight back. For my life and for my child to grow up without him.

If he isn't behind bars when my baby comes into this world, I dread to think what he would do if he found out. He's not a real man, so he could never be a real father. But he'd want access, and he'd fight me for it. It would go to court, and if they found in his favour, I'd have to allow my child to see that piece of shit on a regular basis.

Over my dead body.

I sit on the sofa and am instantly squashed with my mother and father on either side of me. My mother's hand reaches into my lap and takes hold of my hand. As I look up at her, she gives me a reassuring smile.

I can do this. I know it will hurt my parents to hear my story, but they need to know the truth. I need to stop lying and covering up for that bastard. He's the one to blame in all of this and it's about time I stopped blaming myself for making him hurt me.

That's one thing he always said, "You know I'm only giving you what you deserve. You brought this on yourself. I wish I didn't have to do this, but you give me no choice. *You* make me hurt you."

I'm sick of being petrified of my own shadow and I won't let my child—my innocent, pure child—be tainted by a life with that man in it.

Steeling myself for what's to come, I close my eyes and take a few deep breaths, drawing it in through my mouth and out through my nose.

Opening my eyes, I face my uncle sitting opposite me with a tender smile on his face. I open my mouth and suddenly, the dam breaks and everything comes pouring out. I can taste the salty tears on my lips as I tell him the truth, but I don't care. For once, I'm going to cry it out and let it wash over me, taking my pain with it.

My life as a victim is over. This is the first day of the rest of my life as a *survivor*.

Chapter One

Evie

6 years later

"Mummy, wake up," I hear Maya say as she squeezes my arm.

Trying to conceal my grin, I wrap my arms around her and pull her into the bed, yanking the covers over us in the process. I make her giggle and thrash around as I tickle her.

"Morning sweetheart." I yawn as I hug her.

"Are we making cupcakes and pies today, Mummy?" Maya says, staring at me with her large grey doe eyes, "because I really want some Rose specials."

They're Maya's favourite. A concoction I made up when I was pregnant and craving something sweet, I had eaten that much that she has been addicted to this day. As it's a chocolate and vanilla swirl cake with mint and orange ganache on it, I don't blame her. It's basically a fancier version of a chocolate orange.

"Of course; it's Sunday." It's become our tradition to bake on a Sunday, typically because I would always bake with my grandma on a Sunday, and I want to keep that little bit of tradition running through the family.

"We'll go to the bakery after we eat breakfast, but try not to get flour everywhere this time. We trod it in the house last week." I look her in the eyes and start to tickle her again, so she knows I'm just playing. She insists on measuring the flour every time we go on a Sunday, so we usually end up wearing more then we put into the recipe.

Pulling the duvet from over the top off our heads, I pull us both up. With Maya in my lap, I sit there and welcome the comfort that she brings. Then I put her down, and we make our way down the stairs and into the kitchen. I place her on the worktop. Immediately, she opens the cupboard and pulls out her cereal of choice. I laugh at her hair, which closely resembles a mane this early in the morning. With her long wavy brown hair and grey eyes, we look very much like mother and daughter. Thankfully she took after me in that department.

"Mummy, I need a bowl," she says impatiently as she shakes the cereal box in front of my face.

I pull her down from the work surface, and she makes her way to the table in the corner of the kitchen-dining area. I follow her and place the bowl and milk next to each other.

"Remember not to make a mess this time. Pour the milk carefully," I warn as I eye her picking the milk up.

I make my way to the coffee machine and turn it on. I can't function throughout the day without a coffee. I think that was one of the main reasons I added a small coffee shop into the bakery—everyone needs a coffee with a cake or tart. *Queen of Tarts* is probably one of my greatest accomplishments, after my daughter of course.

***

I laugh as I watch Maya dump icing sugar into the standing mixer and a plume of sugar-smoke, as Maya calls it, hits her in the face.

Giggling as she inhales the sweet smell, she exclaims, "Look, Mummy! Look at how high that went!"

"That one did, sweetie. Let's be careful, though." I eye the mess on the floor, a mix of flour and different types of sugar. "We still need to ice these cupcakes before we go home."

I take the tarts and large cakes into the walk-in freezer and place them so they're easily accessible to be put in the display case tomorrow morning. As I walk back into the decorating room, I see Maya adding the last ingredients into the icing. I have always been impressed with how she knows the recipe for the icing; she never gets it wrong. It brings me comfort that she will be able to keep the bakery going when I can't anymore.

"Okay, let's ice the cupcakes then." I pull a separate rack for Maya to decorate.

I always let her decorate her own. She usually takes them to school to give to her friends and teachers, but with it being the Easter holiday, we're going to take them home and gorge on them. I continue decorating the cakes that I make for the Easter season and add little chocolate eggs to the top, making them look like little nests.

Just as I finish putting the cupcakes for tomorrow away, I see that Maya has finished hers.

"Wow, sweetheart. They look delicious, I can't wait to have some later." As I look into her eyes, I see them brighten and pride take over her face.

"Thank you, Mummy. I can't either! Are we going home now? I'm hungry."

"Of course. Are you going to help me make spaghetti and meatballs tonight?" I grab her and place her down on the floor.

Maya holds the box of cupcakes in her arms, and we make our way out of the shop. I always try and make simple things for tea, so she can help me, usually just by stirring the sauce or pasta.

She nods her head as we make our way home, too absorbed in watching the birds fly around the sky.

***

Just as I finish placing the icing on the last tier of a wedding cake for Mr and Soon-To-Be¬-Mrs Smith, my friend and employee, Ryan, bursts through the door.

"Oh! My! God! That hot hunk of a man just came in. Oh how he makes me swoon," he says, over-exaggerating every word as he plonks himself down in a chair. "Sadly, he doesn't bat for this team. You really should get to know him."

Rolling my eyes at his usual tactic to get me with any man in this town, I close the door to the freezer just as Maya walks in.

"Mummy, look at the drawing I've just finished in my colouring book!" Enthusiastically, she shows me a colouring of a giraffe.

"Wow, sweetheart! You're getting so good." I watch as Ryan quickly nods his head in agreement. "I hope you have been good for Ryan at the till." I raise my eyebrows at her.

"I haves been good! Just ask Uncle Ry!" She skips towards him and flings herself into his awaiting arms.

"Of course. You have been amazing, my little fairy!" He stares at me in mock annoyance, then starts playing a hand game with her to keep her distracted.

I always have Maya with me at the bakery in the holidays; she alternates sitting back here with me, or sitting at the till while Ry is here, colouring in one of her new colouring books.

As I start to get the decorations ready to place onto the cake, I hear Ry take Maya out, muttering something about leaving me in the zone. I make quick work of stacking the tiers for the Smiths and adding the sugar flowers that I made late last week. Thankfully, I didn't need to come in on the weekend to finish the cake, as they are having a late wedding.

Once that is finished and has been picked up for delivery, I make my way to the front part of the shop. I love that the front of the bakery is set up almost like a restaurant, so customers can stay in and have a cup of coffee or a cake, but still have the choice to take things away. The back is reserved for baking or making a cake if I have an order for an event through my website. I notice that Maya is in her usual spot, with Ry standing next to her, talking to the last customers of the day and, as usual, being a flirt to anybody who listens. Chuckling, I go and stand behind Maya.

I watch as Ryan locks the front door after everybody has left. "Want me to put all the things from the till into the safe?" he asks.

"Yes, please. I'm going to move all the cakes from the display cases and put them back in the freezer. I'll be making fresh ones tomorrow anyway, so they can go out while they're baking."

"Can I help with the cakes tomorrow, Mummy?" Maya asks as I'm making my way to the display cases.

I turn and see her looking at me with hope in her eyes. "Of course. I need my little helper." I grin as I give her a cupcake from the display case. "This is a treat for being so good today."

She smiles, and just as she goes to take a bite Ry runs in and jokingly cries out "Where is mine? I have been good today too, haven't I, Mummy?" He pretends to fall on the floor and cry as he keeps up this façade.

Maya sits there and bursts out laughing at his acting. "Yeah, Mummy. Uncle Ry has been good too! It's mean not to give him a treat."

I play along, as it is our usual routine. "Well, looks like we'll have to have Ryan over then and cook him dinner, huh?" I say, looking at Maya.

Ryan stands up and, with the biggest grin, gives me a hug. "I think tea is the perfect treat."

Maya shakes her head as we make our way out of the shop and towards home.

***

Curled on the sofa, with a glass of wine in my hand, I wait for Ryan to come back downstairs. After we'd eaten our takeaway—I was too lazy to cook—and after watching Snow White, Maya demanded that her uncle Ry took her to bed and read her a bedtime story. With the length of time he's been up there, I guess he's been roped into reading more than one, but then the thump of feet on the stairs brings me to the conclusion that he has managed to get away.

***

Thumping travels throughout the flat, shaking the bathroom, as Greg tries to get into the room. He's been on one of his drinking weekends again, he always comes back either extremely happy, or like this, wanting to do anything to frighten me. I shouldn't have provoked him really. I should have just cleaned the dishes last night. But I thought I had more time; he wasn't meant to be back until late tonight. Not at nine in the morning.

"You can't lock me out forever, Evelyn! You'll let me in eventually." The pounding on the door ensues.

Panic consumes my whole body as I hear the door creak and groan, about to give way. I try and find a more substantial barricade to place in front of the door separating us, but there's nothing. Only the bending door separating me and him. Finally, I feel the door give way, and I jump back to prevent myself from getting crushed. I see Greg's red face, reminding me of …

***

"Hun, where'd you go?" I'm snatched out of my memory by Ryan crouching before me, shaking my shoulders with a concerned look on his face.

Only then do I realise the tears streaming down my face, some landing in my empty wine glass.

"Oh, nowhere. I'm fine." I shrug off his hands and try to act nonchalant.

I've only given small bits of information about my past to Ryan, and he knows not to push me. Instead, he sits next to me and pulls me into his arms, giving me the comfort he knows I need.

"I think it's time you move on darlin', try and make a life for yourself, instead of living in this shell that you've created. It's obviously not helping you. I know you struggle to sleep; I see the bags under your eyes at work." The more Ryan talks, the thicker his voice gets with emotion.

"I have made a life for myself! I have Maya. I have you. I have a business that's successful! I don't understand how that's not living," I ramble, as quickly as my lungs will allow.

"I don't mean that; don't get upset." He looks into my eyes with sorrow. "You haven't given anybody a second glance since you've been here, and trust me, I tried to test you. I thought you just weren't interested in men, but even women didn't catch your attention. And I've seen some women flirt with you who are so hot they could make me straight, if that was possible."

Giggling, I lean back and lean into Ryan.

"You know that I love you, right?" I ask as I snuggle in closer, enjoying his warmth.

"I love you too, you sap. I just think maybe trying to go back into the dating scene might be a way for you to finally heal." Suddenly, he gets this glint in his eye. "Like that hot hunk of a man earlier!"

Confused, I try to shuffle through the events of today in my brain.

"The one you came in the back raving about?"

"Yes! You'd go perfectly together, plus he lives for your pies."

Winking at me, he pulls me up and leads me into the kitchen.

Leaning against the work surface, I watch as Ryan pulls two cups out from the cupboard and fills them from the coffee machine.

Turning to me and handing me my cup, he cocks his head as he asks, "Why are you so afraid to date?"

"I hate answering that question," I reply, mumbling into my coffee. "You obviously know some of what happened." I look at Ryan and he solemnly nods his head. "I'm afraid that it will happen again. I'm not ready to be hurt like that again, to go through that again."

"But how do you know that you'll be hurt again if you don't just try? You'll never know what the future holds, but you can never let the past hold you back. You can't stay hostage to something that happened years ago; you need to let go and live."

He looks at me with his eyebrows raised.

I huff, knowing he's right.

"But how will I know I won't be hurt again?" I whisper as I try to keep the tears at bay. It's a futile attempt, because a few slip out anyway.

"You won't know if you don't try." Ryan turns on his heel. "Come on, you've got to be up early for tomorrow. Mind if I stay tonight?"

Looking at the time, I gasp in shock.

"It's midnight? How did that happen? Yeah, of course, it's alright. The spare room is made up for you as usual."

Ryan walks towards me and smiles, giving me a kiss on the top of the head, before making his way to the spare room. I'm grateful for having a friend like him; he knows when I've drained myself mentally. Turning in the opposite direction, I head towards my bedroom.

I stare at my large queen-sized bed as I walk in and notice for the first time in years how lonely it feels. How lonely it is to go to bed by myself and not have someone to keep me warm and safe for the night, for somebody to love me—truly love me—and only me.

Chapter Two

Trey

If I've said it once, I've said it a thousand times: life can be one big clusterfuck of epic proportions. Today has been disastrous from start to finish.

First, there was the hot water not working for my morning shower; it turns out I need someone to come and take a look at the boiler. Then I discovered that I've run out of my—rather expensive—favourite coffee. After realising I was running late for work thanks to the boiler problems, I made some toast as I prepared to leave, but didn't keep an eye on the toaster and it came out like a slice of charcoal.

As if that wasn't enough, you can pile on the stress of the current case I'm working and my own pent-up sexual frustration. Bobby is out of town until tomorrow morning, so I won't be able to see her until tomorrow evening.

My workout at the gym was the only thing all day that actually went to plan. Cross-country running, lifting weights, kettle bell routine, the rotational cable chop—which can be pretty gruelling on its own—and then the barbell straight-leg deadlift. All done to a playlist I compiled on Spotify that I've labelled *Beast Mode*.

After the exhausting morning I've had, I feel I'm entitled to indulge in my dirty little secret—a flat white and a slice of pie at a great little bakery called *Queen of Tarts*. I work hard to keep my physique in shape, but I can't deny myself the odd slice of pie or cake, whichever takes my fancy or is the special of the day.

The barista, who I've learned is called Ryan, offers free samples of indulgent cakes when the owner is trying out a new recipe. Indulging may make my workouts a little more gruelling, but they're so worth it.

When I order my usual flat white, Ryan offers me a piece of lemon torte garnished with fresh strawberries and a little sprinkling of lemon rind and icing sugar. I might be going straight to hell for the decadence and the sheer number of calories, but who cares? It looks bloody delicious.

There's a little girl sitting behind the counter. I see she's colouring, and it's taking all her concentration. She's such a pretty little thing, with long wavy brown hair. She's dressed in a pretty little yellow sundress with bunnies on it, which I'm assuming is because it's close to Easter Sunday.

Looking away from her colouring, she looks directly up at me and smiles.

***

"Look Trey, I'm dressed all pretty," Leah says as she twirls in her yellow sundress. Her long brown hair is curled today, courtesy of our foster mother.

We're ready to go to church for the Easter service. Our foster parents like to go to church every Sunday, and for what they call important services throughout the year. I don't believe in God, but I daren't tell our foster parents. There'd likely be a form of punishment for not being a God-fearing Christian.

"You are so pretty, Leah. Your yellow dress is the prettiest thing, apart from you, of course," I say as I tap her on the end of her nose playfully.

She blushes at my compliment and bats my hand away. My beautiful sister has always been the most important thing in my world. I couldn't see my life without her in it.

We've had a bad run of foster parents; growing up in care has been particularly difficult. Leah is so impressionable, and even though I'm only one year older than her, it's on my shoulders to make sure she is looked after properly. And she isn't. Well, the Dearings look after us okay, I guess, but they are only the latest in a long line of foster parents we've had.

"Remember to put your cross on, Leah," Mrs Dearing says as she walks through the lounge.

"I'll help," I say as I take her hand and walk to her bedroom.

She takes her cross out of her jewellery box and hands it to me, and I fasten the chain around her neck. Normally, she's made to wear it every day, but she took it off this morning before getting in the bath.

I don't have to wear one because I'm a boy, so they gave me some saint or other on a sort of coin pendant to wear instead. It feels like it chokes me sometimes, but I wear it because otherwise they'll see fit to punish me.

Leah looks up at me with her grey eyes and I feel a protective instinct within my chest. It's in every fibre of my being. We've had our share of crap, but the Dearings actually treat her okay. Better than they do me. I'm only guessing, but I think it's because they always wanted a daughter. They didn't really want the package deal Social Services lumbered them with—the two of us, instead of just Leah.

Social Services didn't want to break us up, because Leah doesn't do well for long periods without me.

Our real parents died a long time ago, I don't even really remember them, and our grandparents were deemed too old to take us in.

Our long line of foster families have never seen fit to let us see our grandparents. I've fought against that because we love them and they love us, but nobody seems to care what we want.

"Are you two ready to go?" Mr Dearing calls up the stairs.

"Yes, sir," I reply as I grab Leah's hand and make my way to the staircase.

***

I shake my head to clear the cobwebs. My past has a way of creeping up on me when I least expect it. This time it's because the little girl looks so much like Leah. Same hair colour, same eyes.

The little girl waves at me and gives me a bright smile. I wave and smile back.

"Isn't she a darling?" Ryan asks as he hands me my coffee and lemon torte.

"She's gorgeous. Is she your daughter?"

"No. She's my little angel, but I bat for the blue team, if you know what I mean," he replies with a wink and a smirk.

I don't know what to say to that, so I hand over my money and take a seat at the bar across the back wall of the bakery.

My briefcase is spilling over with the amount of paperwork that needs my attention, but I can't find it in me to care while I enjoy my precious few minutes of peace. My clients mean a lot to me, of course, but so does fifteen minutes of heaven as I enjoy the tartness of the lemon on my taste buds.

***

With my Mac out on the table in front of me and papers piled high, I pull out my Dictaphone and record some notes for my most pressing case. It's domestic abuse, which hits a little close to home.

The quiet in the house is perfect for working on sensitive cases, but tonight it feels oppressive. It's a feeling that follows me, no matter where I go or what I do. I just can't shake it. The only time I don't feel it pressing down on me is when I'm working out at the gym, hence why I spend a lot of free time there. There's none of this "my body is a temple" crap—I just like to stay in shape.

As a child, I was overweight and got bullied no matter what school I ended up at, and there were plenty of those, considering how many times Leah and I bounced from home to home. A different set of foster parents, a new school, new peers to be bullied by. I hated it with a passion.

So now, I like to keep in shape, even if that means busting my balls at the gym a few times a week—which it often does.

Struggling to keep my eyes open after working into the early hours, I decide to head to bed and tackle the problem tomorrow. The guy has appealed his sentence and may even be let off on a technicality. I have to make sure that doesn't happen. I sent him to prison in the first place and I did my due diligence. He will stay behind bars where he belongs, if it's the last thing I do.

In my en suite, I turn on the shower—thankful that the man called to fix the boiler earlier this evening—and grab a towel from the heated towel rack. Hanging the towel over the top of the glass door, I step into my luxurious walk-in shower. It isn't enclosed, which gives me more space. Far removed from the shitty houses I was used to living in as a kid, my home is my castle.

When my grandparents died, they left me an inheritance in trust until I turned twenty-one. They knew that, growing up in care, Leah and I had nothing, so they left us a ridiculous amount of money in their estate. As sole executor of the will, I was trusted to give Leah her share. They sold their house and cars as well as their holiday home in Devon. All the money went into trust for us, to give us a better future. A future Leah never got to realise.

***

Her ashen skin is the first thing I notice. The needle is second. I let out a piercing cry as I rush to my sister and place my fingers on her neck to check for a pulse. She's eighteen; she can't die. She has so much to live for.

Turning her over, I give her mouth-to-mouth followed by chest compressions and keep repeating the pattern. I have 999 on speakerphone and they keep giving me instructions until the ambulance can get to me.

I suspect it's a heroin overdose. She turned to drugs as an escape from the miserable existence we share. I've seen her high so many times that I can't count them all. Why she turned to drugs and I turned to hitting the gym, I don't know. Well, no, I do know why she'd want to escape, I just don't know why she chose an induced high.

***

I don't even notice as the first tear falls, nor the one that follows it. I only notice when I look at myself in the mirror through the glass door.

As the door steams up, I lose sight of the tears and I step under the jets of hot water. Fuck! My heart clenches in my chest like someone is clutching it in a vice.

Leaning my head back, I allow the water to wash away the tears and relax my taut muscles.

Later, as I'm drying myself off in my bedroom, I grab my phone off the nightstand. Opening a new text thread, I send a message to Bobby.

>Hey! You still coming home tomorrow?

I continue to get ready for bed as I wait for my phone to chime. Bobby knows how to make me relax. If I can't get to the gym for a good workout, Bobby gives me a pretty vigorous private workout session.

>Yes. You do know it's two-thirty in the morning, right?!

Shit. I didn't even think about the time. Selfish dick. She was probably fast asleep.

>Sorry, I didn't think. Been working all hours on this case.

I see three dots showing she's typing back.

>Don't worry, I wasn't asleep. I've been binge-watching *Secret Diary of a Call Girl*.

>WTF? Why would you watch that? It's not like you need any tips. Not that I'm calling you a call girl, shit, my words are coming out wrong.

>Don't sweat it, I'm not insulted. Takes more than that to piss me off. You must be worked up if you're texting me instead of trying to sleep at this hour.

>Totally. Sexual frustration all pent-up.

>Don't worry, we're still on for tomorrow night. Unless you want to FaceTime and get dirty enough to need a shower?

Her text makes me laugh. She's certainly a little wild. I've never been one for anything other than instant gratification, but she's been teaching me things I never ventured to do before. Lying down on my bed, I throw the towel to one side and completely expose myself and my already hardening cock.

Dialling Bobby for a FaceTime call with one hand and gripping my cock in the other, I work myself over as I wait for her to answer.

"Hey," she purrs through the screen.

"Hey yourself."

"Naked already?"

"Damn straight. I've not long come out of the shower."

"Well, let me return the favour and get naked," she says as she leans her phone against something and stands to strip.

My cock is rigid as I watch her peel her negligee away from her creamy skin—skin that I know feels better than silk.

***

After getting my rocks off with Bobby last night—or should I say this morning—I felt the pent-up frustration leave my body somewhat. She always knows how to make me relax.

Seeing her touching herself and calling out my name in a hotel room isn't a new thing. We've been doing it for the last few weeks whenever she's out of town.

I met Bobby about a year ago, when she came in as a solicitor at a rival firm. I've never been one to mix business with pleasure, but as she doesn't work for my firm, I say it's no harm, no foul. The partners might disagree with me sleeping with the enemy, so to speak, but what they don't know won't hurt them. Bobby is the soul of discretion, and I've learned how to keep a secret or two in my time.

She was like a siren song, luring me in. Her lithe body, her full pink lips, those beautiful amber eyes … everything about her is divine. Especially the feel of her skin against mine or the way her mouth stretches around my cock and takes me deep … God help me, now all I can think of is sex. I need a cold shower.

Getting out of bed, I walk to my en suite, my cock bouncing against me thanks to my stray thoughts of Bobby.

The cold water hits me, and I am sure if it was any colder, my balls would shrivel up and crawl back up inside me. It does the trick though. Now I can quickly shower and get ready for work.

***

Parking in my designated spot, I get out and lock my car. As I head towards the office, my mind turns to the most important case I have on at the moment. This bastard will rot in jail; I'll make damn sure of it.

Ever heard the saying "Can't do the time, don't do the crime"? Well, he definitely shouldn't have beaten his poor ex-wife so badly if he didn't want to suffer for it. All because she got sole custody of their son after telling the police and Social Services about the abuse and torment she'd suffered at his hands. And what did he get out of doing that to her? A stint in jail.

Poor little Keane is the reason I took this case. Well, him and Angela, his mother. But, in reality, it hit so close to home for me that I decided to offer her my services pro bono as she had left him with nothing more than the clothes on her and Keane's backs. She couldn't afford a good solicitor, and the duty solicitors they assign these cases—well, I shouldn't speak badly of anyone in the same profession as me, but let's just say some of them aren't worth the piece of paper their degree is printed on.

***

After a gruelling day in court advocating for Angela and her son, I decide to hit the gym, and I mean hit it hard. His attempt to get out of jail on a technicality didn't work, but that didn't mean the asshole didn't try.

I know his solicitor was only doing what he was paid for, but I stood there and wondered how in the world he could sleep at night when he's actually defending scumbags like him and trying to keep them out of jail.

I hit the punchbag like it's Angela's ex's face. Beating the crap out of the bag makes me feel a bit better, but not enough.

My trainer takes me through a gruelling regime, as per my instructions, but my body is really feeling it now.

Heading for a shower in the locker room, I grab my shower gel and a clean towel from my bag. It's nowhere near as good as my shower at home, but I simply can't wait to shower the stink off me. I swear I've been sweating more than I ever thought humanly possible.

After towelling off, I dress in my indigo jeans and a maroon t-shirt. I know exactly where to go right now, and my car can't get me there fast enough. I'm craving a sugar high, even though it'll undo some of my hard work at the gym. I've always had a bit of a sweet tooth; it's my one weakness when it comes to my diet. But I know the calories I consume this afternoon will be worked off tonight when Bobby arrives.

Never one for small talk or other trivialities, we always go straight to bed. She never stays the night or oversteps her boundaries. Sometimes we'll share a bottle of wine, make idle chit-chat for a few minutes if one of us has had a hard day, but there's no pressure, no relationship, just a healthy and active sex life.

Pulling up outside *Queen of Tarts*, I shake all mental images of tonight with Bobby and head in for my usual flat white and whatever cake Ryan wants to tempt me with.

I haven't been coming here long, but Ryan knows me well enough to know I always cave into his temptations of something decadent. He can't persuade me to bat for his team, as well he knows, but he can persuade me to try out the new recipes the bakery's owner concocts.

The aroma of something I can't quite place permeates the air as I open the door. The bell above it jingles, announcing my entrance, and Ryan's eyes are automatically drawn to me. He waves as he serves another customer and I offer him a smile and a nod in return.

Taking my place in line, I read the specials board.

"What can I get you, handsome?" Ryan practically purrs as he looks me up and down.

"I'll take a slice of the pineapple, Malibu and coconut decadence cake and a flat white, please."

"Sure thing. Take a seat and I'll bring it over."

I hand Ryan the money and leave a tip in the jar. Waving at the beautiful little girl who's colouring again, I earn myself a smile and a wave back.

"Now, be careful with that plate, sweetie," I hear as Ryan approaches.

"I will Uncle Ry. I'm always careful," a sweet, melodic little voice says.

The girl from behind the counter hands me my cake as Ryan sets down my coffee.

"Why, thank you, young lady," I say as she hands me a fork.

"You're welcome. My name's Maya. What's yours?" she asks as she bounces on the balls of her feet.

"What a beautiful name fitting of such a pretty young lady. My name is Trey. It's nice to meet you."

Maya holds out her hand, so I extend mine and shake it.

"I helped Mummy make the cake," she says excitedly.

Her energy is infectious and so is her big toothy smile.

"Did you? Well then, I'm sure it will taste amazing."

"My Mummy is the bestest baker everrrr," she says, drawing out the word in a sing-song voice.

"Oh, I know. I have been here several times now. I can't get enough of her cakes and pies."

"What's your favourite?" she asks as she takes a seat opposite me.

"Now, now, come Maya," Ryan says, taking her hand. "We don't want to bother Trey, do we?"

"It's okay, Ryan. You go back to the counter. I want to talk cakes with Maya, if she wants to stay and talk to me."

He gives me a look as if to ask if I'm sure, and I nod. Walking back to serve his next customer, he whistles the tune to a Disney song, "Whistle While You Work", from *Snow White*.

It reminds me of one of my sister's favourite cartoons as a child. A bittersweet memory.

Maya doesn't allow me time to get lost in my own head as she asks again what my favourite cake is.

"Well, this cake actually has to be one of the most awesome," I reply with a grin.

"Of course. That's cos Mummy soaked the sponge in Malibu, which she says keeps the cake moist. She says I can't have any cos it's alcohol and I'm too little. But she did make me a pineapple and coconut cupcake with extra frosting."

"Well, then your mummy must be awesome."

"Oh, she is. She's so pretty too. She tells me I look a lot like her when she was my age."

"In that case, she must be very beautiful, just like you."

My response earns me a face-splitting grin. She really is a stunning looking little girl. I can only imagine how beautiful that makes her mum, who I have yet to meet. Every time I come here, I see Ryan. Maybe she's too shy to show her face in the bakery, or just too busy. But Maya has me wondering what her mum looks like.

"Maya-Rose, are you bothering our customers?" a voice asks gently.

I look up and see an older version of the little girl before me. She's stunning. Literally jaw-dropping. I have to consciously remind myself to close my mouth.

"She's not bothering me," I say before Maya can speak. "She simply asked me what cake here is my favourite."

"Still, you have your colouring book, Maya. You should be sitting behind the counter with Uncle Ry."

"Sorry, Mummy."

The poor girl's face looks crestfallen.

"Oh, sweetie," says the lady whose name I have yet to learn as she takes her daughter's chin in her hand. "I'm not telling you off, my darling girl."

Kissing Maya on the head, she looks up at me and smiles.

"Trey," says Maya, "this is my mummy who bakes all the cakes."

"Hi," I say, and I suddenly have the urge to cough, so it comes out funny.

She's utterly gorgeous. Beguiling. I doubt I've ever seen a woman as attractive, outside of paintings in the finest galleries.

"Hi," she replies as she extends her hand, "I'm Evie."

"Nice to meet you, Evie."

"It was nice to meet you, Trey," Maya says as she gets down from her chair.

"It was lovely making your acquaintance, Maya. Thank you for keeping me company."

She beams a grin at me as the pair wander back behind the counter. Evie smiles back at me over her shoulder, her long dark hair framing her face. And those beautiful eyes … oh those eyes could be the undoing of any mere mortal.

Chapter Three

Evie

I can't help myself—I have to take one more look at the beautiful man. I toss a look over my shoulder, giving him a smile. As he smiles back at me, I get a look at his perfectly straight, white teeth. I look away before he thinks I'm a creep. As I continue my way to the counter, Ryan is standing there with a grin that could top the Cheshire Cat's. I glare at him as I approach him with Maya holding my hand.

"Are you mad, Mummy?" Maya tugs me to a stop, as she looks up at me with a question in her eyes.

Confused, I crouch down on the floor before her, holding her tiny hands in my own.

"Of course I'm not. What could I ever be angry at you for?"

"For sitting with Trey when I should haved been colouring with Unc-Uncle Ryan instead." She stutters as she talks, trying to prevent herself from crying.

I lean in towards her and give her a cuddle, trying to prevent the sobs I can feel making their way through her body.

"Oh, sweetheart. I could never be angry with you for doing that; you made a new friend. I was just worried when I came from the decorating room to bring you a cupcake and I couldn't find you."

I sit on the floor, not caring that I'm in the middle of the bakery, and I rock her back and forth and whisper in her ear.

While I'm down there, I see a shadow loom over the both of us. Flinching, I look up quickly and try to shield Maya from whoever it could be. I relax just a fraction as I see Trey standing over me with question in his eyes. He squats down until he is almost eye level with Maya, which is difficult as her head is now tucked into my chest.

"Now, what could ever be wrong with a pretty young lady?"

He glances down to his hand in a question and then back up to me. Confused, I lift my eyebrow. He repeats the action, and I see a cupcake in his hand. I nod, giving him the go-ahead. Maya's head shifts to see who is there, and her tears begin to dry.

"I brought a cupcake for the happy little lady I was talking to earlier. I don't know where she's gone though. Could you help me find her?" Trey asks, trying to make Maya smile.

Her eyes instantly brighten at the word cupcake, and she gives him her beaming smile.

"I can help you find her! I'm amazing at finding things."

Maya wiggles out of my grasp as she makes her way to Trey.

"Why, thank you, Maya; you've found her!" he exclaims as he gives her the cupcake.

Maya looks at me for confirmation. I smile and nod my head at her. She snatches the cupcake from Trey's hand and runs towards Ryan.

"Maya," I call, and she skids to a halt and turns. "What do you say?"

She quickly runs back, barrels into Trey's legs and hugs them.

"Thank you for the cupcake, Trey."

"It's okay, Maya." He pats the top of her head with a smile on his face.

As she runs back towards Ryan, no doubt to brag about the cupcake she has been given, I realise that I have been sitting on the floor this entire time. Just as I go to stand up, a large hand appears in front of me. Looking up, I see Trey looking down at me with a smile. I grip his hand and smile as he pulls me up.

"Thank you." I look up at his tall frame, realising just how large he is compared to my five foot seven inches.

I'm not small by any means. I have curves. I have never been the type of person to have the energy to go to the gym or work out. I've tried, trust me. However, I ruined it by eating cake too much. I like to think that I'm tall compared to most women, but with Trey before me I feel tiny. As I'm standing there, I notice hints of a tattoo peeking from under the short sleeves he's wearing. Subconsciously, I lean towards him, trying to make out the markings on his arm.

I'm brought out of my bubble when I hear an amused voice down my ear.

"Have you found something interesting?"

I look up quickly and notice how close I am to Trey. I can feel his warm breath on my cheek and faintly smell the lingering scent of Malibu.

I pull back quickly, trying to create as much distance between us as I can.

"Sorry, I, umm … I've never seen a tattoo like that before. I-I didn't mean to intrude." I feel my cheeks flush in embarrassment as I realise what I've just done.

"Don't worry about it, honestly." I see a glint in his eye as he chuckles. "Most people are intrigued by the tattoos."

"Do they have specific meanings?"

I find myself asking him questions just so I can hear his voice, a perfect mix of husky and sultry.

"No, I just see what I like and get it."

I notice that my question has made him uncomfortable, and he looks away. When he looks back at me, I notice how his features have started to harden and his jaw starts to tick.

I try and change the subject, knowing that I've hit a nerve. It hits me that I don't want to see that expression again or see him upset.

"What's your favourite cake here then?"

"I actually don't have a favourite." He smiles at me. "I always order a flat white and then a slice of whatever Ryan tells me is the special of the day. I like trying different things. Do you have a favourite of any of your creations?"

"My favourite has to be the Rose special. I always serve it with a scoop of homemade ice cream, however, I usually add a shot of bourbon into the ice cream for me or Ry. It makes it more flavourful, and boozy, of course."

I chuckle as I remember when Ryan sneakily poured a shot into the ice cream mixture when I was making it years ago.

"And I made it so much better darlin'," Ryan shouts from across the bakery. "Probably the only thing I've managed to add taste to."

He hustles his way over, with Maya trailing behind him while she makes her way through the cupcake. Ryan drapes his arm over my shoulder, tilting me from side to side as he chuckles. Maya looks up at us and giggles as she stands beside Trey. It strikes me how comfortable she is with Trey. The only man she has ever been comfortable with is Ry. However, he's been there for all of her life. She's always had a problem with men, never knowing if she's able to trust them. I partially believe that's my fault. She may not have known Greg, but I know she notices how I sometimes flinch or jump when a man gets too close, and how I have only let Ryan touch me over the years.

I feel myself being shaken slightly. I look up in confusion and see Ryan looking down at me with a worried look in his eyes. I shake my head slightly, not wanting to say anything in front of Maya or Trey. I look over to them, and my eyes instantly lock onto Trey's. I see something that I can't make out in his eyes, almost a protective look. I look down towards Maya and see that she is oblivious to the events that just took place. Instead, she's staring up at Trey with a smile on her face, and some chocolate icing round her mouth.

"Would you like to come and colour with me, Trey?" she asks, with hope in her eyes.

Just as I go to tell Maya that he probably has things to do, Trey butts in.

"I would love to come and colour with you Maya, not for too long though. I need to get home soon." He smiles down at her and grabs her hand.

"Can we go into the decorating room, Mummy? I lefted my colouring things back there."

She looks at me hopefully.

"Of course you can. I'll be going back there soon because some cakes need to come out of the oven." I look down at my watch and notice the time. "Sugar!"

I shake Ryan's arm off, run towards the decorating room and make a beeline for the oven.

"Shit! No! Sugar. Oh crap," I mumble to myself as I pull the cakes out. "Oh, thank god!"

I release my withheld breath as I look at the cakes and see that they are fine and not burnt. I was worried as I had left them in the oven for ten minutes too long.

I hear a giggle behind me.

"I just heard Mummy swear!" Maya sings as she giggles and runs towards Ryan and Trey who are standing in the doorway of the room.

Ryan has a shocked look on his face. With me having only sworn a couple of times in the six years that I have lived here, I'm not surprised. Trey is leaning on the doorframe with a smirk on his face and his arms crossed, his bulging muscles on show. I give a sheepish look towards Ryan, needing his help to try and get myself out of this mess

"Oh no! Mummy has been naughty, hasn't she?" Ryan looks at Maya with an over-exaggerated look of shock on his face. "Should she be put on the naughty step?"

He looks at Maya for validation. Maya has a thoughtful look on her face, obviously contemplating what my "punishment" should be.

"I think she shouldn't be allowed a cake later!" she replies as she looks at me with a mischief look in her eyes.

I gasp in shock.

"You wouldn't take that away from me, would you?" I fall to the floor dramatically. "You wouldn't be that cruel."

Ryan runs towards me and crouches on the floor next to me, cradling me as he does so.

"That's mean, Maya!" He continues to play along.

Maya runs towards us and crawls into my lap.

"I'm sorry, Mummy. I don't want to upset you!"

I giggle as she looks up at me, wrapping her arms around my neck and squeezing as she does so.

"It's okay, sweetheart. I shouldn't have sworn; that was very bad of me."

I look down into her eyes as I cuddle her. I feel Ryan move from beside me as he chuckles. Movement from the corner of my eye makes me swivel towards it. I notice that it's Trey; he has moved closer and is now standing next to Ryan. I see a hint of sadness flash through his face, then, in the blink of an eye, his face changes and he laughs at our exchange.

Ryan turns to Trey. "This is a regular occurrence, just in case you're wondering." He's probably explaining so he doesn't think we're weird.

"I was guessing so, with how dramatic you guys acted. By the way, you should consider acting—you'd probably win an Oscar … for the hammiest acting of course," he adds with a wink.

At the sound of Trey's voice, Maya jumps out of my lap and goes to get her colouring book. Pulling two stools out from under the large, kitchen island, she puts her colouring book down with her pencils and looks up at him expectantly. He makes his way over and sits next to her; as he does so she shoves some coloured pencils towards him and points to a picture he can colour in.

Knowing that she's occupied, I turn and get the ingredients to make a meringue icing for the lemon cakes. Ryan trails behind me and helps me carry the ingredients to the standing mixer, which is opposite Maya and Trey.

"What you making?" Ry asks as he plonks himself next to Maya and proceeds to eat some extra icing that was left in a bowl in the fridge.

"A cake version of a lemon meringue pie." I shrug my shoulders as he looks at me in confusion. "I wanted to do something different, and this was the first thought that popped into my head."

Ryan laughs as he finishes the icing off. I see Maya look at Ryan in question.

"Why are you just eating the icing like that, Uncle Ryan?"

"Because it's heaven."

Ryan looks at her bug-eyed, knowing it creeps her out.

Chuckling, I look through the window and see that there is a regular customer at the counter.

"Ry! Customer!" I can't go and serve them as I'm beating the egg whites.

He jumps from his seat and jogs out of the room and towards the counter. I flinch as I hear his overly pitched apology. Hearing a deep chuckle, I look up and see Trey looking at where Ryan was once standing.

"Is he always that perky?"

"Yep, especially if he's had too much sugar. It's like having an extra child."

I chuckle as I pour the sugar into the mixing bowl.

"At least you'll never have a dull day." He looks at his watch and puts the crayons down, "I'm sorry, sweetheart, but I have to go."

He looks at Maya and gives her a sad look, and she looks up at him and pouts.

"But I'll see you tomorrow for another colouring date?"

At the mention of him coming back and being able to colour again tomorrow, she gives him a huge smile and hugs his side.

"Okay, Trey! That would be really fun."

As he walks out the room, he stops beside me, and touches my arm.

"Thank you for having me, Evie. It was lovely finally meeting you and putting a face to the name of the talented lady that makes these amazing cakes."

"It's no problem, Trey. The cake will be on me tomorrow."

I smile up at him, then watch him walk through the doors. I look at Maya and see that she was also watching Trey walk out.

"I really like him, Mummy. He's nice."

She looks up at me and then continues colouring.

As I turn the mixer off, it finally sinks in what she said. I know not to read too much into what she says, but Maya's very intuitive when it comes to people and what she said is unusual. I smile and realise that I've had a day where I wasn't looking at every corner or looking to see who walked into the bakery with fear coursing through my veins. I've felt relaxed and safe, secure even. I'm confused, because I don't know why. No—scratch that. I don't want to *believe* the reason why. Surely one person couldn't make me feel safe, like he does? But what stays with me the most is that I didn't flinch when he touched me.

Chapter Four

Trey

Arriving home, I throw my keys in the bowl on the side table before removing my shoes. There's a feeling that settled over me today, and I'm finding it hard to name. Peace, maybe. Maya is the sweetest little girl. Are all children like that, or is she special? I have a feeling her mother has something to do with that. She seems like a real sweetheart herself.

What's with me? I don't normally pay any attention to how sweet women are. It doesn't normally matter. So why does Evie play on a loop in my mind, occupying my thoughts?

Deciding to take a long hot shower, I make my way to my bedroom and get undressed. Noticing the time on the clock on my bedside table, I realise Bobby's arrival is imminent.

I turn on the shower, grab a towel and wait for the water to heat up before stepping in. As the water beats down on me from several different jets, I close my eyes and picture those innocent grey eyes. The laughter in them as she joked around with her friend and daughter. They're an unusual colour, for sure. A deep grey, but under the lights of her bakery, you can see a blue tinge in them. Her perfect lips are full and pink. What would it be like to kiss her? Would they feel as soft as they look? And would they feel even better somewhere other than my lips? My cock begins to twitch.

No! I can't think like that. She's a friend. And I'm not interested in offering any more than I give to Bobby. A woman like Evie wouldn't be happy being a guy's fuckbuddy, friend with benefits, whatever you want to call it. A woman like her wants strings, surely? She has a kid. That makes a woman's priorities change.

I'm not good enough for a woman like that. My past made sure I was fucked up good and properly. Permanently too.

That doesn't mean we can't be friends though.

The knock at the door startles me from my thoughts. That shower must have taken longer than I thought. Getting out, I wrap a towel around my waist and make my way to the stairs.

Another knock makes me hurry my steps. Bobby isn't normally this impatient, and she can see my car on the drive, so she knows I'm home.

I open the door to see her looking like she just stepped off the front page of some glossy magazine. Only this magazine might be found on the top shelf.

She places a kiss on my cheek as she hurries past me.

Closing the door, I turn to take in the sight before me. Long dark hair, a heavily made-up face, a long, beige—what they call a flasher—mac. My eyes trail down, and I see black, leather, knee-high boots with what must be stockings underneath them.

As she undoes the top two buttons of her mac, I see the lacy top of a red bra.

My cock twitches at the sight, and I see hunger flash in her gaze as she looks at me, covered only in a towel.

With my blood singing in my veins, I pull Bobby flush to me. Her lips claim mine in an intense kiss. She smells like expensive perfume and tastes like honey. What an odd combination, but somehow, not an unsatisfactory one. My cock stirs as Bobby slips her hand between us and frees it from my towel.

Here I am, naked and at a disadvantage. More than anything, I want to see what she's wearing, wondering why she rushed through my door so quickly.

No words are spoken as she sinks to her knees and takes me in her mouth. My groan is almost feral, and I close my eyes as she grasps the globes of my ass in her hands and pulls me closer to her, and my cock further down her throat.

I cradle the back of her head in my hand as her mouth moves up and down my stiffening cock. It feels so good I can't even think straight. Bobby has been my fuckbuddy long enough to know what I like and how I like it. She sends desire through me in waves.

Standing suddenly, she strips out of her mac and lets it pool around her feet. It wasn't a red bra I was seeing, it was a corset, complete with G-string, stockings and suspenders. Wow. Now I know exactly why she didn't want to be standing on my doorstep too long. She might be brazen and bold in bed, but she isn't one to carry off that confidence outside the bedroom. I think that's one of the reasons I'm attracted to her. She's meek and unassuming in the street, but a freak between the sheets.

I look her up and down, over every inch of skin. She's sex personified when dressed like this. Watching me for a reaction, she begins to peel away the corset, freeing her ample breasts. I'm watching her like a hawk, not wanting to miss a single moment.

Once free of the corset, she's standing before me in just her G-string, stockings, suspenders and sexy boots. She turns around, allowing me a chance to take all of her in.

My cock yearns to be buried inside her, and my heart hammers in my ribcage as I look at the perfect globes of her delectable ass and the dainty floral tattoo that trails up her spine. Lust overpowers me as I reach out my hand and trail the path of the tattoo, my hand lingering on her ass. She leans back into me and turns her head so I can kiss her.

Tracing a line of feather-light kisses from her earlobe to her shoulder, I feel her shudder underneath my touch.

I reach around her and dip my fingers between the red lacy material and her skin. She's wet already, turned on from the way she went down on me, combined with our kisses. How is it women can get turned on from giving as well as receiving? I don't know the answer, but nobody will find me complaining.

Little breathy moans escape her as I touch her sensitive nub. Her arms come up and wrap around my neck. Her lithe body looks sensational from this angle. Her breasts bounce up and down with her short, fast breaths. My fingers dip inside her and she clenches around me. Her breathing grows faster as I push her to the brink. When she tips over the edge, she calls my name and I have to hold her steady as her legs weaken.

"Fuck, that was … incredible," she says breathlessly.

"Bend over," I command, my eyes on her as she does as she's told.

Bracing herself against the side unit in my hallway, she spreads her legs so I can stand between them.

I pull down the scrap of material between me and her pussy. Slapping her ass, I smile as she yelps.

"Fuck, no condom!" I berate myself as the realisation dawns on me.

"Coat pocket," she whispers.

Turning around and grabbing her coat off the floor, I scrabble around to find the pocket and pull out the little foil packet.

Once I've got it open, I sheath myself in it before standing in my previous position behind her.

Her long dark hair spills over her shoulders and I take a moment to appreciate how good she looks.

"Brace yourself," I whisper in her ear and watch as my breath across her skin makes her shiver.

**

Once Bobby went home, I poured myself a large whiskey and lit a cigar. I don't smoke them often, but as I stand on my bedroom's Juliet-style balcony, I allow myself this one small vice.

I did something previously inconceivable. As my orgasm thundered through me, I had shouted out one word: Evie.

Bobby assured me it didn't matter, that we're nothing to each other but frequent good sex. But I knew it mattered. The crestfallen look on her face as she pulled away from me and wouldn't even look me in the eye—that cemented my feelings of wrongdoing.

How many men call another woman's name during sex? More to the point, how many have lived to tell the tale afterwards? I contemplate this as I feel the whiskey burn down my throat.

What the hell was I thinking?

As Bobby scrambled around to gather her things and fled to my downstairs bathroom to get herself dressed, I just stood there, jaw slack with shock.

When she came out fully covered, I tried apologising, but she batted me away like it meant nothing. I might not be a steady relationship kind of guy, but I'm not stupid. Nobody would relish being called by somebody else's name. Especially during sex.

I let Bobby go without trying to talk more about it. She seemed flustered and embarrassed enough, like she couldn't wait to get away from me, so I didn't prolong her pain.

Since then, I've been berating myself for being such a douche. I don't know what possessed me. Since when am I the kind of person who does that kind of thing?

Pouring myself another whiskey, I walk to my study and sit in my favourite leather wingback chair. Surrounded by the smell of leather— from the chair and my leather-bound books—and another smell I can only name as "old books," I feel a measure of comfort.

My law books are arranged neatly on one side of the room, while fiction books line the other, with a few autobiographies on a small shelf at the bottom.

If I'm not working—which is hardly ever these days, it would seem—I like to read.

With an upbringing like mine, fictional worlds were my only escape. I didn't have many books back then, I didn't have many belongings whatsoever, but I had this dog-eared copy of *The Hobbit*. I took it with me wherever I went. It moved home with me every time Leah and I moved to a new set of parents. I lost it some years ago, but the memories remain.

Every time something bad happened, I took myself back off to the fantasy world of Middle-earth.

***

"Don't take it out on her, punish me," I shout, trying to protect my sister from our evil foster father.

He grins his stupid, dangerous, drunken grin at me, his teeth all rotten. If I could smell his breath from here, I'd smell his tipple of choice—White Snake cider. His favourite, because it's cheap. And so is he.

"Why would I do that, boy?" He snarls as he pulls her by her hair. "I can make this little bitch cry with the things I'll do to her."

I shudder at the thought of him touching her. Leah is innocent, pure, a seven-year-old who likes playing with Barbies and styling their hair. She's not some toy he can play with.

"Because I promise I won't fight back this time," I sigh as I scrub my hand over my face.

I'm only a year older than Leah, and this guy likes his kids young. He doesn't care whether they're boys or girls, he just enjoys toying with them in a way no adult—no person—ever should.

He likes to threaten to hurt Leah, knowing I'll stand up for her. He's given me beatings before, left me with cuts and bruises where nobody can see them. He might be an asshole and a drunk, but he's not an idiot; he knows if anyone saw the evidence of his abuse, he'd be locked up. Even his wife doesn't know what he does to us.

"Nah, I think I'll take the girl. Thanks anyway, boy. Now get the fuck outta here."

Leah screams as he yanks her hair and drags her to her bedroom. He stops as he opens the door and flashes me another dirty grin.

"I'll tell your wife," I shout.

He freezes in place.

"You wouldn't dare."

"Try me!"

He drops Leah and rushes towards me. Grabbing me by the throat, he pins me against the wall of the hallway.

"You little fucker," he spits in my face. "You can take your sister's beating. But I swear, I'll do worse to you than I would have done to her."

I can't answer him; his hand is gripping my throat too tight. I can barely breathe, never mind speak.

"O-okay," I gasp out as he loosens his grip.

I'd take a beating for Leah any day of the week. I don't know what he'd do to her, and I don't want her to find out.

"Get to bed," he yells at Leah.

She lies still on the floor, crying hard.

"I said—"

He stops speaking as I boot him in the gut.

Gripping my throat tighter, he gets right up in my face.

"You deserve a special treat for that, boy."

And don't I know it. Whenever I fight back, he hurts me worse. But I want him to leave my sister alone.

"Get to bed," he shouts at her again.

Leah scrambles up from her place on the floor and almost trips over as she struggles to get into her room and close the door.

Once it's closed, the prick looks at me, releasing his hold on my throat.

Trying to take some deep breaths, I try to fight off the panic attack I've been keeping at bay. I feel a warmth trickling down my leg. The smell of urine permeates the air.

Looking at me, Paul, my foster father, sees the wetness on my trousers. He glares at me and grins triumphantly.

***

Shaking off the memory of my least favourite foster father, I gulp my remaining whiskey. Paul was a wicked, wicked man. He was cruel for the sake of it. He knew he could do whatever he liked to me and Leah. Sometimes, I'd beg for him to take me in her place, and he'd have this wicked glint in his eye as if it had been exactly what he wanted all along. Other times, his dark gaze focussed intently on me as he dragged Leah away. God only knows what he did to her behind closed doors.

I'd tried to ask my baby sister more than once about the things he did to her, but she'd never tell me. She just clung to that damn bunny of hers with tears in her eyes.

Opening my desk drawer, I pull out the much-loved bunny. Its soft grey fur has seen better days, and it's missing an eye, but I can't bring myself to fix it or to throw it away. It's exactly the way Leah left it the day she left me.

Lifting the soft toy to my nose, I inhale deeply. My olfactory senses don't pick up anything much, but it does stimulate my memory.

***

It's a beautiful sunny day. Rhys, our foster brother, is having a birthday party later on, but first we are going on a family day out to the beach.

When we first moved in with this family, we thought we'd find ourselves in a similar situation to last time. But Rhys has looked out for us from day one. He's only a little older than me, but he's tall and built well enough that kids at school don't mess with him, which is good for me and Leah, because they steer clear of us too.

We're about ten minutes into our road-trip to the beach when Leah shouts at our new dad to stop the car. He does, thinking something bad has happened. But Rhys and I have been sitting next to her and I haven't seen anything.

"What's the matter, sweet girl?" Dane asks as he crouches down by the back door of the car.

"Rabbit isn't here," she replies, her bottom lip trembling.

"Did you have him with you when you left the house?"

"Yes. I must have dropped him. I need him."

The first tear falls and is soon followed by a cascade of others.

"Don't worry, Leah, he'll be at home waiting for you when we get back," I say, gently squeezing her arm.

"I can't wait. I need him."

"Sweet girl, we're already on our way to build sandcastles. Do you really want Rabbit to get sand in his fur?" Dane says soothingly.

Leah shakes her head, but her tears still continue to fall.

"I need him, Dane. Please?" she replies in a cracked voice.

"Wouldn't you rather wait until we're home, sweet girl? Rabbit can have a day of fun, with the house all to himself. Then you can get home and tell him all about your sandcastles and how you buried Rhys in the sand. That way Rabbit stays clean and you get to tell him about your adventure."

Leah doesn't reply for a moment. Her body is still as she sits there, just thinking.

"I'll let you bury me in the sand and make a tail like I'm a mermaid," Rhys

says, offering Leah a small smile.

If there's one thing she loves other than Rabbit, it's mermaids. Her eyes light up at the suggestion and she nods her head.

"Okay then, let's get back on the road."

After returning home from a long day on the hot sand, I see Rabbit on the driveway. Leah must have left him behind when Dane strapped her into the booster seat. I pick him up and take him in the house. He's seen better days; his fur isn't as clean as when she first got him and he's missing an eye from where our last foster father pulled it out to hurt Leah when he said she'd misbehaved. But even though he's a bit battered and worn, she loves this rabbit with everything she has.

Leah's eyes light up as she notices what I have in my hand. She rushes over and wraps me in a hug, squeezing me as tight as her small arms can.

"Thank you, Trey."

"You're welcome, sis."

She runs off in the direction of her bedroom, no doubt to fill Rabbit in on her day.

Rhys had done exactly what he promised and let Leah bury him up to his neck, while Leah, Dane, Anne and I had all shaped him a body and tail like a mermaid. He hadn't complained when he got sand everywhere, and I am grateful for that. He's so good to my little sister, protects her the way I try to.

***

I don't feel the first tear fall, nor the second. I only notice when Rabbit's head is a little wet. Then I wipe my cheeks and try to dry my eyes. How did my sweet baby sister end up the way she did? There are so many possible answers, yet I'll never know which is the truth.

Leah is why I busted my balls at school and got good enough grades to get into college and study law. She's the reason I'm a solicitor, and she's the reason I try to help people pro bono when they have domestic abuse cases or something closely resembling anything we went through as kids. Of course, I have many paying clients too, but they are what allows me to actually take on the few pro bono cases I do each year.

The partners at the firm have always been one hundred percent behind me since I suggested that side of the business. There are many people out there who can't afford the best legal representation, but they deserve it all the same.

Looking around the now-dark room, I switch on my desk lamp. I've never been scared of the dark, but every so often I'll catch myself thinking about the monsters that lurked after dark when I was a child.

I put Rabbit back in the drawer and close it. It's my last remaining link to my once carefree beautiful sister. The sister who became withdrawn and shied away from me in the end. She felt like she couldn't confide in me after Rhys turned on her. He'd always been so kind and loving, but when he got older, he turned into a manipulative monster. That time, it wasn't our foster parents we ran from, it was him.

Social Services tried to take us back to them, but Leah was kicking and screaming all the way. That was when I found out he'd touched her inappropriately.

Rhys had been our brother. He never hurt us; he always protected us from bullies at school. But then he became the very definition of a monster. He'd touched my sister and told her it was okay because he was her brother. He would never hurt her, he just wanted her to touch him, to let him touch her. He touched my sister in a way no person ever had, and she didn't understand he was bad. And he turned her against me, making her think I would do the same because I was her brother too.

Over the following few years, Leah turned to drugs and alcohol to numb her to the world. If everyone she trusted was a monster, then she couldn't trust anyone anymore. I was oblivious at first, too busy studying to notice her sneaking out at night. But eventually—albeit way too late—I found her passed out at a party. She was as high as a kite. I carried her home, crying all the way. I got her to the front door, and Mrs Perry opened it wide, her eyes wide with shock at the state of Leah.

Once I got her inside, Mrs Perry called an ambulance, something I couldn't do before because I didn't have a mobile phone.

Leah was as angry as I'd ever seen anyone when she came around in the hospital. She refused to speak to me because I'd got her in trouble.

Mrs Perry had called her husband, and the two of them sat by her bedside as I sat at the foot of her bed with my head in my hands, crying and wishing I'd seen the signs sooner.

Alone in my study, I mirror that position from long ago, as I sit with my head in my hands and cry. I miss my sister so much that it physically hurts.

She became a rebellious teen, promiscuous, with a proclivity for alcohol and an induced high. But I loved her with all my heart. She's the only woman I've ever truly loved. And she is the reason I protect my heart to this day by not getting involved with women on a personal level.

Sex is all I have to offer women these days. I can't give them my heart, because I know eventually they'll break it. Whether they mean to or not, they will break it, and I'll be left alone picking up the pieces. So I decided to build walls around my heart. It's an impenetrable fortress made of Kevlar. Nobody can scale those walls, nor tunnel underneath. It's a sad truth. I've never known the love of another, other than familial love.

I used to wonder what love felt like. But the sceptic in me says it's not even real. Love is the biggest myth of all. Forget fictional stories and myths and legends, love is the biggest work of fiction besides God.

Why is God a myth? Because my sister wouldn't be dead if he really existed. No God would ever take my beautiful sister from this world and leave me feeling cold and empty. He wouldn't have let us go through so much shit as kids, wouldn't have let those families neglect or abuse us. He would have loved us and kept us out of harm's reach.

As my tears subside, I stand and stretch out my tired limbs. Making my way up to my room, I decide to take another shower to try and rid myself of the feelings inside me. I feel dirty, the way I did back then.

The water cascades over my body and I welcome its heat. Scrubbing myself with the shower gel in my palms, I try to rid myself of the dirt of my past. It's something I know I'll never be free from entirely, but it's my mind that holds me captive.

***

After a quick breakfast of black coffee and toast, I make my way to the office. I have my gym bag ready for later, but for now I'm suited and booted for a day of hard work.

As I get into my car, I turn on the iPod connection and select one of my favourite albums, *Lifehouse*. Singing along to the first track, "Come Back Down", I make my way through the busy morning traffic to the office.

Pulling into my designated spot, I turn the engine off and grab my briefcase from the passenger seat.

The lock beeps, and I make my way into the imposing glass building with my briefcase in one hand and my travel mug of coffee in the other.

"Good morning, Peter." I greet a colleague as I make my way to my office.

Once safely ensconced, I shut the door and boot up the desktop computer. Today isn't going to be an easy one. I have a lot of paperwork to go through ahead of a particularly gruelling court case.

Jennifer Lewis is a victim of particularly brutal domestic abuse. I hate that word. *Victim.* I prefer the term survivor. But then I'd much prefer the need for neither of those words to exist. Bastards like her ex should be chemically castrated, if you ask me.

A knock at the door pulls me from my thoughts.

"Come in," I call.

"Sorry, boss," says Leanne, my assistant, as she opens the door. "I know you're working the Lewis case and asked not to be disturbed, but there's visitor in reception for you."

"Who is it?"

"A lady by the name of Roberta."

Scrubbing my hand down my face, I sigh deeply. I didn't want nor expect to see her or hear from her so soon after yesterday. I was hoping for a little distance until I was ready to face the music.

"Could you tell her I'm in a meeting and ask her to maybe make an appointment?"

"I told her you weren't to be disturbed, boss, but she's quite insistent."

"I'm sorry, Leanne, but I really don't have the time for this shit," I bark a little too loudly. "I'm up to my eyeballs. Tell Bobby—Roberta—to make an appointment or give me a call sometime."

I don't mean to take my frustration out on her, she's a really good assistant, but I can't help my rising temper.

"Will do boss. Again, I'm sorry."

"No, Leanne. I'm sorry. I'm an asshole. A highly-strung asshole, who hasn't had enough coffee for this shitstorm. I really am too busy for whatever Roberta needs, and she knows she can just call me. But I'm sorry for snapping at you."

"No worries, boss."

Closing the door softly behind her, Leanne retreats from my office.

A couple of minutes later, my phone buzzes on my desk. I'd put it on silent so as not to be disturbed, but I pick it up and look at the screen anyway. Bobby. Just as I thought.

I don't decline the call; I just leave it to go to answer machine and get back to work.

Five minutes later there's a knock at the door, and I really want to tell whoever it is to … insert an expletive and go away, but I don't.

"Yes?" I shout curtly.

"Sorry, boss. Thought you might need this," Leanne says as she walks in with a steaming mug of coffee in hand.

"I'm sorry, Lee. I'm being an asshole this morning."

"All in a day's work, boss," she replies as she smirks at me.

"Are you trying to say I'm always this asshole-ish?" I ask in as jovial a tone as I can manage.

"Not at all, boss. You're just tightly wound when it comes to cases like Mrs Lewis."

"That's too true, Lee. I'm sorry. I really am."

"No problem, boss. I'll try to make sure you aren't disturbed for the rest of the morning."

"Thanks, Lee. I appreciate it."

"Her face was pretty scary," she adds before walking out.

"She's always pretty scary. She's a very aggressive prosecutor."

"Well, you know me boss. I never back down. She didn't like being told no, but I lied smoothly and said you were in a meeting, like you asked."

"Thanks, Lee, I appreciate it."

I pick up my mug and take a sip. The perfect antidote. Caffeine.

With a smile, Leanne closes my door behind her and leaves me in peace.

I notice my mobile says I have an answerphone message, but I ignore it and indulge in my coffee before diving back into the case. The only thing that could make this better is a slice of something heavenly from *Queen of Tarts*.

Closing my eyes for a moment, I picture those perfect grey eyes and her long dark hair. She's beautiful. Too light to be touched by my darkness. If she absorbed any of that, she'd be scarred for life. But I can't help but picture her full pink lips and wonder how they'd taste. Would they be as sweet as the delights she creates?

***

After a day of paperwork and being exceptionally pissed off, I head to the gym. The rotational cable chop is just what I need right now. The perfect distraction.

Slipping my ear pods in, I select a good workout playlist on my iPod and slip it into the band around my arm.

I head out of the locker room and make a beeline for the cables. They give me a bloody good workout, but boy do my arms ache afterwards.

On second thoughts, maybe it isn't best to actually start with those, because I might not be able to lift weights and stuff for a bit afterwards.

I head over to the small area for warm-up exercises and watch as others lift weights, run on the treadmills, and use the rowing machines, all oblivious to the inner turmoil of others.

As I work through my routine, my body begins to ache. It's a delicious feeling that spreads throughout my entire body, making me feel it from the tips of my fingers to the tips of my toes.

After a hot shower, I change into my jeans and a t-shirt, then spray some deodorant and a little aftershave. I don't want to walk in and make the place smell like sweat and body odour.

As I've been working out, I'm craving something sweet. I don't know whether that means the cake or the woman that creates it, but …

Sitting in my car outside *Queen of Tarts*, I watch as Evie changes her window display. It looks like she's decorating for Easter this weekend. The cakes look sensational, and I can tell she takes a real pride in her work. They're also highly calorific, but that's what the gym is for.

Looking at the baskets overflowing with eggs of every conceivable colour, the bunnies posed here and there around them, makes me think of Leah. There's a pang in my gut as I see a grey bunny that looks just like Rabbit, only with both eyes intact. Tears sting the backs of my eyes, but I take a couple of deep, steadying breaths to keep them at bay.

I promised Maya a colouring date, and I fully intend to keep my promise. I am a man of my word. But sitting here looking at Rabbit's doppelgänger, I want to turn the car around and go home.

My knuckles are white as I grip the steering wheel. I let my head drop to the wheel for a few moments before pulling myself together.

As I get out of the car and head around to the boot, Evie notices me and offers me a smile and a wave. I feel a grin spread across my face as I wave back.

Opening the boot, I take out the small bag I just picked up on my way over. I couldn't help it; I'd been driving when something had caught my eye. I just hope Evie doesn't mind.

"Hi," she greets as I walk through the door, setting the little bell off.

"Hi, Evie."

"Your date will be happy you're here," she says with a small smile.

"Can I get a flat white and a slice of cake?"

"Of course. Your table is ready for you," she says as she points in the direction of the prettiest little girl.

I see a table littered with colouring books and colouring pencils. At the table sits a gorgeous little girl who is busy colouring and doesn't notice me watching her.

"I'll bring your order to you," Evie says as she walks back behind the counter.

"Thanks."

I make my way over to Maya, and she looks up as I approach.

"Trey, you came," she says with a toothy grin.

"I most certainly did. I keep my promises. May I sit with you?"

"Yes. Mummy said if you came, we'd need more room, so she letted me set this table up with all my stuff."

"It's vastly more spacious than the decorating room," a voice behind me says, making me jump. "Sorry, I shouldn't sneak up on you."

"You nearly gave me a heart attack," I reply as I take a seat opposite Maya. "But I'll let you off, because you have coffee and cake. The perfect remedy to an otherwise rubbish day."

"What's a rememdy?" Maya asks.

"It's, umm …" I scrub my hand over my face trying to come up with an easy explanation.

"It means that after a day of working, it will make Trey feel better, sweetheart," Evie supplies for me.

"Oh. Okay."

Maya happily goes back to colouring in as Evie hands me my coffee and a slice of what can only be described as heavenly looking indulgence.

"I hope you don't mind, but Ryan says you normally order the special of the day."

"I don't mind one bit."

"It's not technically today's special. It's one I've come up with for Easter and, well, I need a second opinion other than my daughter and best friend who are obviously biased."

Her smile is sheepish as I look up at her.

"You mean you need a guinea pig?"

"Umm …"

"It's okay, I really don't mind."

"It came to me in a flash of inspiration last night and I kind of got up at about five to make a trial run."

"It's really good, Trey. Mummy gave me some after my dinner."

"If it gets a thumbs up from you, Maya, then I'm sure I'll love it."

"I'll umm … leave you to it," Evie says.

As she goes to walk away, I stand and close the distance between us.

"Before you go, is it okay to give Maya something?" I whisper as quietly as I can.

"You shouldn't be spending your money on her, but yes."

"I couldn't resist, sorry. I didn't plan it; I just saw it as I drove through town."

I open the bag to let her peer in.

"Oh, my gosh; you'll have a friend for life."

"I'm not trying to bribe her to be my friend. I just thought she might like it."

"I didn't say you were trying to bribe her, silly," she replies with one hand on her hip. "I just meant that if she wasn't already, then she'd definitely want to be friends with someone who walks in with awesome gifts just to make her smile."

Evie beams a beautiful smile at me and I can't help but mirror it. She has that effect on me. My heart feels like a jackhammer in my chest as I inhale her scent, all sugar and spice and something I'm sure is uniquely her own.

"Your coffee is probably going cold, you know."

"Oh, yeah, I should …"

"Let me know if she gets too much. I only allowed her a small slice of cake, so she won't be on too much of a sugar high. Trust me, six-year-olds don't need sugar to be bouncing off walls."

"I'm sure we'll be just fine. Now, go create!" I shoo her away with my hands.

Sitting back down, I gulp back my coffee. It's lukewarm, but Evie's smile is worth it.

"I'll keep you topped up," Ryan says as he walks past the table.

"Thanks."

I clear my throat and look over at Maya colouring. Her hair keeps falling in her eyes and she keeps flicking it back. She's so intent on colouring, it's like she doesn't notice me here.

"Maya."

She looks up at the sound of her name, and her gaze lands on me.

"I bought you a little present. Would you like to see what I got you?"

Her face transforms into an enormous grin.

"Yes, please," she answers, clapping her hands in glee.

Chapter Five

Evie

I'm standing here peeking around the edge of the front door, too far away for Trey or Maya to notice me, but close enough to watch her face as she opens up the present he bought her. I have this weird feeling in my chest, having had nobody but family buy anything for Maya before. But here Trey comes, whisking up Maya's heart and then bringing her presents. *Presents.*

I wasn't expecting him to show up today. I knew he said he would be here for another colouring date with Maya, but when do men do anything they say they will? I mean, I don't have the best experiences with men, so I didn't expect this tall and tattooed male to just appear and act as though he's known us for years. It brings me comfort knowing that Maya will have another person to look after her, to protect her. The way he looked so unsure of himself when showing me the presents, but then looked delighted when I said she would love them; that's what family do, not friends. Can I even call him a friend? The fact that he's brought such a smile to my face and Maya's, even though he's only been here for ten minutes, says a lot.

I look up in time to see Maya peer into the bag and squeal with delight.

"Oh, wow!" she exclaims, "I love them, Trey"

She looks up at him and beams, then runs around the table, climbs into his lap and wraps her arms around his neck, squeezing him. I walk more into the shop, forgetting the display that I was doing in the window as I watch Trey wrap his arms around her. I look up and lock eyes with Ryan—who is mirroring the facial expression that I'm sure I'm sporting— then we both whip our heads back towards Maya and Trey.

"Thank you!" Maya says.

"It's okay, pretty lady." He looks down at her. "I saw them in the shop, and it reminded me of that pretty dress you were wearing the other day."

She jumps down off his lap and scans the store for me. Her eyes lock onto where I'm standing with Ryan and she skips towards us. In her hands, she's holding the Barbie that was in the bag. It has a yellow sundress on, almost identical to the one she was wearing the other day.

"Look, Mummy. Look at what Trey brought me! Isn't he so nice?"

"Oh, wow! It's so pretty isn't it?" I crouch down so I'm eye level with her. "Have you said thank you?"

She looks at me for a moment, as if she's trying to remember if she used her manners.

"Yes, she did."

I look up and see Trey standing behind Maya with a smile on his face.

"Okay, that's good then."

"He also got me a new colouring book and pencils! Wanna come see, Uncle Ry?"

She doesn't give him a chance to respond before she pulls him towards the table she set up earlier. I stand up and chuckle as I watch Ry gushing over how amazing her new colouring pencils are. I turn towards Trey.

"Thank you for coming by the way. You didn't have to feel obliged to come, much less bring her something."

"I wanted to. I told her that we had a play date, and then I saw them earlier. I hope I didn't offend you by buying them?"

A concerned expression mars his face.

"Oh no! You didn't offend me, don't be silly. I appreciate it. Did you see that smile on her face? That's what I live for, and you made her happy by bringing them."

I look up at him and smile. I place my hand on his arm as I turn to look back to where Maya and Ry are standing. Maya looks back at us and waves, wanting us to come closer.

"Mummy, look! There's Disney princesses in this colouring book!"

I peek over her shoulder as she flips through the book.

"Wow, Maya, you don't have that one. Are you going to colour this one in today?"

"Yep! Trey can have any pick; I want to colour in Ariel!"

Trey chuckles and slides back into the seat opposite Maya.

"I think I'm going to colour in …" He looks thoughtfully around the table. "What about this princess? It's Cinderella, right?"

He looks at Maya when she gasps in horror.

"Cinderella? No, that's Rapunzel!" She shakes her head in disgust. "Have this one; it's so good!"

Maya looks up at him, smiling as she slides a flower colouring book towards him. He chuckles as his face turns red with embarrassment.

"I'll leave you two to it then. I've got cakes to make."

Just as I turn to leave, I hear Maya behind me.

"Can you colour with us for a little while?"

I turn and see Maya giving me the puppy-dog eyes, knowing that I can't resist them. I hear Ryan walk off quickly, mumbling something about a customer. I laugh because I know if it was directed at him, he'd be sitting down in a heartbeat. I go to sit beside Maya.

"You can't sit there, Mummy! My Barbie is sitting there." She gives me a "duh" look and shakes her head. "You're sitting next to Trey."

Trey shuffles over as he tries to conceal his laughter at Maya's sassiness. Sitting down, I realise how small these booths actually are. With the whole of my left side pressed up against Trey, I feel a slow tingling sensation travel down my body. Maya pushes a colouring book towards me, and then becomes engrossed in colouring her princess. I clear my head and reach towards some colouring pencils, knowing that if Maya notices I'm not colouring she'll give me a disappointed stare.

"What are you colouring, then?" Trey asks me in a hushed tone, not wanting to disturb Maya.

"Looks like"—I flit between the pages—"a family of otters."

I shrug my shoulders. With Maya throwing a nearly full colouring book about animals towards me, I had little choice in what to colour in.

"What about you?"

"I think I'm going to do the calla lilies."

I pear over his arm and look at the picture; it has a bunch of wild calla lilies with a couple of butterflies around.

"Cute. Calla lilies are my favourite. Plain, I know. But there's something beautiful about their simplicity."

"They are beautiful flowers. Very alluring."

He looks me in the eye, and for some reason I get the feeling he isn't talking about the flowers.

"I really liked the cake, by the way. What was that in the middle? It tasted like a cookie."

"It was! It was a chocolate cake with a gigantic cookie in the middle, with mint buttercream. I added broken-up mini eggs to the cookie and for decoration, so it's more appropriate for Easter. I'm glad you liked it. Sometimes the cookie can make it a funny texture and people don't like it."

I shrug my shoulders and try to conceal my rambling as I start on the next part of the drawing. I feel Trey's shoulder bump into mine; looking up, I see him smile.

"Well, I for one think it tasted amazing. I'd quite happily eat a whole one to myself."

I chuckle as I look towards Maya, who, instead of drawing, is looking at us with question in her eyes. Just as I go to ask her what's wrong, Ryan appears at the table.

"I've put everything away, hun. You've just got to sort out the cakes."

He plonks himself next to Maya, with her new Barbie on his lap. I look down at the time and realise that the shop has been closed for fifteen minutes now, I don't understand how I didn't realise.

"Sorry, Ry, I didn't realise the time. Why didn't you come and get me when you were closing? I'll do those cakes now." I start to ramble as I realise I got lost in Trey.

"You were having fun. I only needed to put the cash from the till away; it'll need banking later in the week, don't forget," he says as he gives me a knowing smile.

I get up and make my way to the back room. There are just a couple of items that need to be put away, so I'm finished in no time. As I walk back through the doors, I see Trey standing next to Maya, who's still holding her doll. All of her colouring items are in her princess bag on Trey's shoulder, while he's holding her hand. Just seeing them standing there, I wish Trey was part of this family. Since he only met her a couple of days ago, he's acted how a family member should. How a father should. I give a tentative smile, feeling like I'm intruding as I make my way towards them. I look around for Ryan, noticing that he isn't standing beside either of them.

"He said he'll meet you at yours; he just needed to run home to get something," Trey says to me, obviously knowing who I'm looking for.

"Okay, that's fine." I look down towards Maya as she goes to grip my hand. "You ready sweetheart?"

"Yup, I'm alls ready, Mummy. Trey helped me put my colouring books away, so you didn't have to do it."

She smiles and looks up at Trey.

"Thank you." I look up towards him and smile. "You didn't have to do that."

"I wanted to."

We make our way out through the doors. Maya stays beside Trey while I press the button for the shutters to close the shop up fully.

"How are you getting home?" Trey asks.

I jump a little, not realising how close he was standing.

"Umm." I look around and notice that our cars are the only two left in front of the shop. "I brought my car today, because I came here so early."

"You don't usually bring your car here?"

He gives me a puzzled look.

"No, we walk down." I laugh at his puzzled expression. "We only live down the road, and Ry usually comes back with us anyway."

"Oh, that makes sense. I'm guessing that one is yours then?"

He nods towards the only other car in the car park besides his.

Maya runs towards her side of the car and climbs in after I've unlocked the door. I make my way over and buckle her in as Trey leans against the side of the car.

"Yup, It's Mummy's car! I have my owns seat."

She points down at the car seat she is sitting on and grins.

"Wow, you do have a very special seat, Maya." Trey leans into the car and smiles at her. "I'll see you soon, Maya. I'll be back for another colouring date. I promise."

She beams up at him and nods as I close the door.

"Thank you for coming today, Trey. It was fun." I smile up at him. "I hope you know she's never going to put that doll down now, though."

"It's fine; I really enjoyed our colouring date. I'll be over again tomorrow. Can't miss being a guinea pig for one of your new creations."

He winks at me and makes his way towards his car.

I slide into the driver's side, giving him a smile and wave as I reverse out of the parking space.

***

I look over at Ry and laugh at the compromised position he's in, with a sleeping Maya lying half on his chest, and with her legs draped over my lap, he's struggling to see me over her head. I have no idea how she's comfortable like that.

"So, what do you think of Trey? I noticed you were getting on well." He looks at me and smirks over Maya's head.

"He's nice." I shrug my shoulders. "Maya really likes him."

"Let's not dodge the question. You like him, don't you?"

"No, I just think he's attractive. Anyone with eyes would think that."

I stare at the fireplace intently, knowing that I've started to feel something for Trey. But how could this happen in such a small amount of time? It's not possible—this is the sort of thing that I read about in books, not something that actually happens in real life.

"No, I see those little cogs in your head turning. You feel something, but you're—what? Scared?"

I glare up at him, hating that he can read my mind so easily.

"Yes, I am scared, but who in their right mind wouldn't be? A man *isn't* that nice; it's not possible. They're either hiding something or they just want a one-night stand. Nobody can just appear out of nowhere and then do things like earlier! He just bought Maya something, just because."

I look up towards Ry, feeling my eyes sting from unshed tears.

He shifts slightly, trying to move closer to me but not wanting to disturb Maya.

"Oh, honey. It's not your fault. Just because he's being nice doesn't mean that he's got an agenda. He hasn't just appeared; he's been coming to *Queen of Tarts* for years, but you're never out front much so you just don't see him. Why do you think he's got some sort of an agenda? Is this because of Greg?"

"Is it bad if I say yes?" I ask, shaking my head. "He was overly nice to start off with, and he had an agenda. But it's my fault; I just assume automatically that when somebody is nice, they want something. I can't accept having anybody in my life right now; I've got Maya to care for. I can't think about *my* future; I only care about *Maya's*. She's six now. They soak things up like a sponge at this age. I can't afford for her to be heartbroken; she needs to have a normal childhood. Without something getting in her way. You've seen how she is around other men. That's because of me. *Me!* She sees how I act with other men, and she's—"

"Now, hold up. It isn't your fault! How could it be? What he did to you was *his* fault, and he's paying for it; he'll never be able to get to you or Maya. What happened isn't your fault. You can't view yourself as a victim; you are a survivor! You survived the pain you endured, and you moved across the country when you were four months pregnant.

You've made a life for yourself. Look at what you've got now. You have a successful business, a lovely daughter and a home—not many can say that at twenty-eight years of age. Why can't you move on? It's been— what? Six years since the case closed?"

"It's my fault because I stayed. It took my grandparents dying for me to leave. My nan wrote me a letter, and that was what brought me out of it and made me leave. It's my fault because I would antagonise him. I don't feel like a survivor. I'm constantly living in the shadows; I'm scared that he's going to appear." I shrug my shoulders as I take in a shuddering breath. "I know it sounds stupid, but I can't help it. They said life imprisonment, but they also said that there is a chance that he will be eligible for parole after ten years if he displays good behaviour. I've already had six of those years. I've only got four left, then, if the worst comes to the worst, I'll have to leave. I don't want to leave. I've got the business, which is doing amazingly. I don't want to upheave my life just for one man who ruined my life. *I* shouldn't be punished for *his* actions. *Maya* shouldn't be punished either. She's comfortable here. Imagine the problems it would cause for her, trying to get situated in a place she isn't familiar with, trying to get new friends. I can't do that to her; I want her to be happy. I don't want her life to be ruined for what happened to me, but it's a sacrifice I'm willing to make to keep her safe. It's not fair! This all just isn't fair."

The thought of only having another four years in this lovely town before having to move again brings tears to my eyes.

"It's not your fault. I know it's a horrible thought, but when your grandparents passed, it flicked a switch inside you. It made you realise your worth, made you realise that you deserve a better life. And you may think it's your fault, but it's not. I see you looking around every corner when we go out, how you flinch whenever you hear a door slam. This isn't living. You're just *existing*, and you can't carry on like this for the rest of your life. It's not healthy—not just for you, but for Maya, either. You need to live for both of you, not just for her. It's sad to say, but life does suck, it sucks donkey ass. But if you leave, I'm coming with you. You're the only family that I have now. You're not leaving; I won't allow it. Leaving will just prove to him that you're scared of him, and that he's still affecting you six years on. I'm not saying move in with Trey straight away—he'd probably think you're a stalker—but go on a date with him. Test the waters; at least try and make an effort to move on with your life. Let yourself be open to love again."

I try and take in what he's said, knowing I should probably take his advice. I'm just too scared to. After all, he has first-hand experience in running away. With his family being devout Christians, he was cut out of their life when he told them he was gay. Which is why we both have such a strong bond—he's the family I need, and I'm the family he's never had. The thought makes me decide to pull up my big girl panties and voice what I'm truly afraid of.

"But what if I don't deserve love? What if I'm not worthy? I've never felt worthy, not since what that *thing* did to me. He systematically broke me down and made me believe that he was the only one who would ever want me, that I would never be worthy of love from anybody else."

I take in a deep breath, trying to keep the oncoming tears at bay. I feel movement; as I look down, Maya turns and crawls into my lap. She looks up at me sleepily.

"Why you sad, Mummy?"

"I'm just being silly." I roll my eyes, trying to not upset her. I try and come up with an excuse, not wanting her to actually know why I'm upset. "I don't want Uncle Ry to go home."

"Well, he can stay tonight, can't you, Uncle Ry?"

Ryan turns and gives me a sympathetic look, while nodding his head.

"How about I take you up to bed, huh?"

He extends his hand towards Maya. She nods her head and leans into him, and he picks her up and carries her up the stairs. Knowing he won't be long, I go into the kitchen and pour us both a glass of wine. By the time I've put the opened bottle in the fridge and made my way back into the living room, Ry is sitting on the sofa with a throw blanket around his legs. I hand him his glass and he nods his head in thanks.

"Shall we discuss the stupidity that came out of your mouth then? Or should we ignore it?" He looks at me with his eyebrows raised. "Because what just came out of your mouth was so ridiculously idiotic, I can't fathom it for a second. You deserve to be loved, just like anybody else in this world. You. Are. Worthy. And anyone that can't see that, doesn't deserve you. I can't think of anybody who is worthier of love than you are. After all the shit you have been through, you deserve to be loved, cherished and worshipped. Hell, the ground you walk on should be worshipped. You are more than words. So, when are you going to get it through your thick skull that you are worth more than you think you are? Because I'll drill it into your head if I have to."

I look up at him and see his eyes burn with sorrow. I lean into him, and his arms come around me as he leans his head on top of mine.

"I'm sorry; it's just hard. I don't feel like I'm worthy. I'll try. For you, I'll try; for Maya, I'll try. I know that I've got to at least make an effort to get out of this bubble I've created; I just haven't had the confidence to do it."

He squeezes me to him.

"Thank you, you won't regret it. I know you won't regret it."

I nod my head, knowing that, more often than not, he's right. I look up at the mantlepiece and see the time.

"We should go to bed." Sighing, I stand up. "I can't believe I'm still awake."

"Yeah, we really should. I can't, either. You were at the bakery at what? Five this morning?" he asks as he stands up.

"I think that's correct, yeah. I just couldn't sleep."

I shrug my shoulders as we make our way through the house, not wanting to tell him that I haven't been sleeping very well lately.

"Well, goodnight, darlin'. Love you."

"Goodnight, Ry. Thank you. I really appreciate it. Love you too."

I make my way up the stairs and into my bed. This is the first time in days that I've gone to bed feeling like a weight has been lifted off my shoulders.

***

I walk through the front door, my arms laden with bags from going grocery shopping. I immediately place them on the table, which is situated in the divide of our living room and kitchen. With it being just one large square, I'm able to see from the kitchen into the living room. Greg is sitting on the sofa.

"Hi, babe," I call through the kitchen, knowing he's seen me.

I'm making my way around the kitchen, placing the groceries away, when I feel him behind me.

"What are you wearing?" he slurs in my ear, turning me around.

I look down, confused, not being able to see anything wrong with the jeans and vest top that I'm wearing. Before I have a chance to say anything in response, he carries on.

"I hope you know that this isn't acceptable. You're mine. You aren't some prostitute that can walk around flaunting their goods. You cover up. Only I am allowed to see this body—my body."

He pins me against the counter, grabbing my hips hard. I wince, knowing that there will be bruises there tomorrow morning. As he gets closer, I can smell the faint tanginess of whiskey on his breath. I try to calm myself, knowing that if I make a comment, he won't hesitate to knock me around, especially since he's drunk.

"Well! What do you have to say for yourself?" he bellows in my face.

"I-I-it's just so hot, I thought it was okay. I'm sorry. I won't make the mistake again."

"You're damn right you won't."

That's the last thing I remember before I black out.

I wake up suddenly, realising that I'm on the kitchen floor. I look around and see some glasses and mugs shattered around me. Amidst it all is a note.

This all better be cleaned up before I get home. Change out of those clothes. –Greg.

I jump up, not knowing how long I have been out for. As I stand up, I double over at the pain in my ribs, knowing that they're at least bruised. I try to make quick work of cleaning all the shattered glass and pottery off the floor, trying not to manoeuvre too much, as I don't want to cause more damage.

After the kitchen is all clean, I go into the bathroom and take my vest off, trying to get a good look at my side. I gasp as I see black and blue bruises adorning my entire side. I walk into my bedroom and grab an over-sized shirt from my drawers, then I make my way into the kitchen and get some ice to place onto my side. While walking through, I pick up some empty food packets and the large Jack Daniels bottle from the coffee table. Throwing them all in the bin, I settle onto the sofa, knowing that the house is clean, and it's only five o'clock, so I can rest for a bit.

The front door rattles, making me jolt and wince at the movement. I see Greg walk in, noticeably more sober than earlier. His eyes instantly meet mine and he walks towards me. I see his eyes taking in my awkward sitting position and the bag of ice stretched along my side. His face crumbles as he falls to the floor in front of me. Placing his head into my lap, he cries.

"I'm sorry, baby, I'm so sorry. I'm going to change, I promise. I'm going to stop drinking. I'll do better—no, I'll be better. Please don't leave me, you know I love you. That's why I get like this, because I love you so much. I don't mean to hurt you."

His body shakes as I stroke his hair and speak soothing words to him, wishing with all my heart that he's capable of change. But I know, somewhere deep inside of me, that that's something he's incapable of.

***

I gasp as I shoot upright, tears streaming down my face. I try to conceal the sobs. Flinging the covers off me, I run to my adjoining bathroom and heave into the toilet. Once I've flushed the toilet, I make my way into the shower. Sobbing as I get the soap, I vigorously scrub it all over my body, not stopping until my skin is red raw.

Once I get out the shower, my sobs have subsided, with just a few tears trickling down my face every so often. I numbly go through my morning routine, and by the time I'm finished it's five o'clock in the morning. I make my way down the stairs, knowing Ry will be awake soon.

I turn on the coffee machine and look out of the kitchen window, focusing on the rose bush in the corner of my garden. I stare at it and wish that the woman I used to be would appear in front of me, the woman that was strong and confident, that didn't take any shit. That I wasn't this broken mess who will taint everyone who comes into contact with me. Wishing that somebody could break me out of this dark shell I have cocooned myself inside.

Chapter Six

Trey

My colouring date with Maya was a surreal experience. I don't have much experience with children, only Leah when we were young, and she was only a year younger than me—even though it felt like more sometimes when things were really bad. But it didn't feel wrong. If anything, it felt natural, and that's a pretty scary thought. I don't know whether it's working with women with children—clients of the firm—that has gradually rubbed off on me, or whether it's something that's always been inside me. Something I haven't tapped into until now.

It took me by surprise when I saw that Barbie in the shop window and instinctively went and bought it for a little girl I barely know, a beautiful little girl who reminds me of a younger Leah. Is that why I feel drawn to her, because she reminds me of my innocent sister before she was tainted by the darkness? Hell if I know.

Maya has the same innocence Leah once possessed. My sister was once pure of heart and soul until the darkness tainted her, breaking her and crushing her spirit. This world can be a rotten place and I always wonder, if Leah had lived, what she'd be doing now. Would she have broken free of the underbelly of this world that sucked her in little by little until, one day, all that was left was a strung-out teenager, desperate for her next fix, something she said kept the darkness at bay? She said it kept it at bay, but I believed then, as I still believe now, that it dragged her further in.

I'm sitting in my favourite wingback chair with a book in hand, something I haven't done for a while. I've never been one for romance novels, not believing in their "happily ever after" endings. That's not real life. Real life is ugly. You come into this world innocent and pure, but you rarely leave it the same way. You get to a fork in the road and you have to decide which path to take. One false move and you're damned.

Leah taught me that. It's one of the reasons I fight so hard with the pro bono cases I do. It's hard seeing women who come to me broken and fighting for their lives. They're true survivors. The darkness held them for so long they didn't know if they'd ever find the light again. Unfortunately, the statistics show that far too many women never find that light, but I'm willing to fight tooth and nail for those that do.

Trying to lose myself in the world of fiction for a while—too many things on my mind in real life that I don't want to overthink—I open to where I last left off. *A Dance with Dragons* is a book I've read a couple of times in the lead-up to the final book in the series. I've also watched every single episode of *Game of Thrones* multiple times. I can't wait for the final series, but I wish it didn't have to be over. It's something so far removed from reality that I can actually enjoy it. All this time we thought Jon Snow was the bastard son of Eddard Stark. Oh, how wrong we were. That's what I call a plot twist.

Curled up in my chair with a hot cup of strong black coffee, I lose myself to the words of George R. R. Martin, a true master of fantasy writing. He is a literary genius.

My phone rings, distracting me from the gorgeous, fierce Daenerys, mother of dragons. How dare someone try to tear me away from her.

Looking at the screen, I see Bobby's name and decline the call. She's tried to contact me several times, and each time I have either left it to go to voicemail or flat out rejected the call. I don't care if she thinks I'm being rude. Storming into my office and trying to bully my PA into letting her through to see me—thank goodness someone gave me a PA with sass and spark. She's a spunky little firecracker. If I didn't rule out mixing business with pleasure, I might have bedded her the moment I met her. Thankfully, I draw a line at office romances. And also thankfully, she's the kind of person that would have rejected my advances anyway, given that she's head-over-heels in love with her girlfriend. Yeah, I didn't see that one coming when I interviewed her. But it's even more of a deterrent for office romance.

I've always had a rule of never mixing business with pleasure. What's that saying … don't shit where you eat? Something like that anyway. It can get really ugly, really fast, if you aren't the type to settle down and all they can think of is either sleeping their way up the ladder, or of their biological clock, their ingrained need to procreate.

When Leah died, I made her a promise that I'd never have children unless I was one hundred per cent guaranteed able to give them the kind of life they deserve. No child deserves to fall through the cracks the way we did. Goodness knows, I know well enough how it feels, and I'd never want to do that to someone else, someone as innocent as Leah and I were back then.

Some people think I'm the eternal bachelor because I am just the playboy type. I love them and leave them. Well, not love. I don't like one-night stands, but I did in my heyday. There is a list of women as long as my arm that would say I'm a bastard. They want more. They want something I can't give.

Having lost interest in my book, I get up and pour myself a fresh coffee. I sit back in my office and open the bottom drawer of my cherrywood desk.

Pulling out Rabbit, I look at him before bringing him to my nose to try and inhale the scent of the only woman I've ever loved. Leah. Her scent has long since faded, just like the colour of his fur. But that doesn't matter. The memories I associate with Rabbit and Leah are all that matter.

Looking at him, with his one eye missing, I feel a pang in my chest as though someone is squeezing it as tightly as they can. My eyes mist with tears and I close them, letting my head fall back against the top of the chair.

***

I had just turned thirteen the previous month and it was almost Leah's twelfth birthday. We were finally settled in a better foster home. The Georges made us feel welcome, loved, wanted. Everything we'd never had before. They threw me an awesome party for my birthday; all my friends from school came and we played laser tag before heading back to the house for something to eat.

I wished we could live with the Georges forever. They didn't hit us, didn't lock us in our rooms, they didn't do any of the horrible things some of our past "families" had done.

Leah caught a bug from school and was off for a week, so I brought her schoolwork home, so she didn't fall behind. That week turned into two, then into a month. She wasn't getting any better. I was so worried about her.

Our foster mother, Mia, took her to the GP, then they referred her to the hospital for tests.

The day her test results came through was the day that changed all of our lives. Leukaemia. I didn't know what it was or what it would do to my sister. All I knew was she was looking sicker every day.

Mia and her husband Darren sat us down and explained how poorly Leah was and why. She had a form of cancer. It was something to do with bone marrow and white blood cells. I was told that there was a way to try and save her, but it meant me donating my bone marrow. I did some research on that and it turned out there was only about a twenty-five per cent chance that it would work.

*** *

My hospital nightgown hangs open at the back as I lie on the bed. They have us in a side room of our own, so Leah is in her bed next to mine. Our arms are outstretched between us, our fingers linked.

I have never been more scared in my life. Not even when Paul beat the crap out of me. I knew in time my wounds would heal, but this … this is something I can't guarantee my sister can recover fully from. They've told me this is going to hurt, but I don't care. I would take the pain a million times over if it meant saving my sister. She can't die. She's too young, too innocent. She has so much to live for. Her future cannot be taken away from her. I won't let that happen.

Her dark hair lies greasy on the white hospital pillow, her grey eyes have bags around them, and her skin is pallid. I wish she didn't look so unlike herself. She's so beautiful when she's well. I just want my beautiful, innocent sister back with us where she belongs.

*** *

The pain in my chest pulls me from my thoughts. I sit bolt upright and wipe my eyes with the heels of my hands. Scrubbing my hands over my face and my five o'clock shadow, I feel the pain of losing Leah as though it was only yesterday. We all thought it would be the leukaemia that took her life, but it didn't.

My bone marrow donation helped her, and eventually they said she was in remission. There was lots of treatment and lots of time off school. Her schoolwork was sent home, so she didn't fall behind in her studies. She was fiercely determined she wouldn't fall behind her peers. I helped her with her homework as much as I could, and Mia and Darren looked after her the best they could.

At the age of thirteen, I thought I'd lose my sister. It was the toughest thing I had ever experienced until her death five years later.

A knock at the door startles me for a moment. I take a couple of deep breaths, knowing I'm going to have to have the conversation with

Bobby that I don't want. I know she won't take it well.

She said she wasn't mad at me for calling her Evie, but I'm not stupid. Her pride took a knock, and judging by the fact she left as fast as humanly possible, I know it hurt her more than she cares to admit.

Bobby knew full well who I was before we started anything. I told her I couldn't offer love, stability, a real relationship. All I had to offer was sex. And she agreed that she wasn't looking for anything romantic either. It was an arrangement that suited us both … until it didn't.

I don't know what happened, but meeting Evie was like someone flicked a switch. Just the smallest touch of her skin feels like electricity humming through my veins.

She's beautiful. Her dark hair and stormy grey eyes, her slender physique—that she somehow manages to keep even though she bakes the best sweet treats, those guilty secrets—her full pink lips … I won't lie and say I haven't imagined what she'd look like naked. What her full breasts look like, what her skin feels like to touch. I won't say I haven't fantasized about what I would do to her if she allowed me. I've done all that and then some. But it's her inner beauty that draws me to her. Dangerously close, like a moth to a flame. She is the fire that could burn me, but together we could be explosive.

Making my way to answer the incessant knocking at the door, I turn off the light in my study and look at myself in the hallway mirror before opening the door. I give myself a mental shake and pull it open, fully expecting a slap. When it doesn't come, I look at my visitor and see it's not Bobby after all. Inwardly I sigh in relief.

"What's up, dude? Expecting to see someone turn up and jump your bones the second you open the door? Sorry to disappoint, bud, but I brought pizza, wings and beer," Joe says as he barges past me.

"Beer on a school night, Joe? You been dumped or something?"

"Screw you. I was the one who ended things with Natalie and that was last week," is his reply.

"Sorry to hear that, buddy. So, what's brought you here with beer during the week?"

"Does there have to be an occasion? Can't it be that I missed your sparkling wit and sharp tongue?" he asks as he sits in the recliner in my lounge, taking a slice of pepperoni pizza and extending the box to me.

"Aw, you missed me too? I thought I was the only one pining for my soulmate."

I take a slice and set the box down on the coffee table as I take a seat.

"Seriously, dude, I just haven't seen you in a while. Thought I'd come and see if you were still alive," he chuckles before stuffing his face.

"I'm still here. Just been busy. You know how it is."

He nods as he finishes his slice of pizza in record time. I should look up in *The Guinness Book of Records* to see how fast a person can devour pizza. I'd lay odds on Joe beating them hands down.

"So, what's new in the world of Mr Work Myself Into An Early Grave?" he asks as he opens the box of chicken wings.

"Not much. Working hard, busting my balls as usual. Been hitting the gym in my spare time. Which reminds me, I haven't seen you there in a while."

"It doesn't take much to keep me looking this divine," he says as he waves a hand up and down his body.

"And if your head was any bigger, it wouldn't fit through the door."

"True. But honestly, I haven't been around. I've been working out of town the last couple of weeks. Only came home at the weekend."

"How come you ended it with Natalie?"

"Oh, you know, just wasn't working out. We wanted different things. She wants marriage and babies, and I'm just not there yet. I was working towards it, but she gave me an ultimatum, and you know I don't do well when that happens. Shit got real and I told her I couldn't give her what she was looking for."

"I'm sorry, man. That sucks."

"I'm hoping to meet a woman who does."

"You're a pig, you know that?" I jest as I take another slice of pizza.

"I know it. You know it. It's no big secret. Plus, since when did you do anything other than screw Bobby?"

I shake my head and stand, walking to the kitchen to grab a bottle opener.

"That's been over for a few days," I say as I settle back down on the couch.

Joe gives me a surprised look, widening his eyes and raising an eyebrow in disbelief.

"Seriously, man, we're done."

"How the hell did that happen? Did she grow too attached?"

I take a second to ponder if I should tell him the truth.

"Nothing like that. It was actually my doing."

"Dude, she was hot as fuck and sex on tap. What could ever make you end that?"

Deciding to be blunt, I open my beer and take a swig before replying.

"I called out someone else's name."

The silence deafens me for a moment as Joe takes a few seconds to let that sink in.

"What the hell man? How? When? Where? I want all the details."

"She came around here wearing a stripper mac and sexy underwear. I let her in, and we didn't make it past the side table in the hall before she was sucking me off. After that, I was taking her from behind, and as my orgasm shook me, I cried out another woman's name. Bobby said she wasn't bothered, but she raced out of here as fast as her legs could carry her and I've been avoiding her since."

Jeez, since when did I become an over-sharer?

Joe almost chokes on his beer and ends up spraying it a little.

"Dude, what the ever-loving fuck? Bobby is as hot as any woman has a legal right to be. She's insanely goddamn sexy. Since when could another woman turn your head enough to make you fuck that up? I mean, seriously? Mr I Only Want A Fuckbuddy actually met a woman who held his attention for more than a nanosecond? Who is this woman?"

"Her name is Evie. You should see her, Joe. She's strikingly beautiful, made all the more attractive by the fact she doesn't seem to know how beautiful she is. She's creative, smart as a whip, owns her own business …" I sigh as I think of Evie's face. "Honestly, man, I don't know how or when it happened, but for the first time in a very long time—if not *ever*—I've met a woman who makes me want to stop and enjoy the little things in life. She's everything I've never wanted or needed, Joe. I don't know why, but I feel drawn to her. And no, before you ask, it's not just carnal desire."

His face is a picture as he digests my words.

"Man," he says as he scrubs a hand over his beard. "You're like … like a different person. Who the hell are you and what have you done with my best friend? Did an alien beam you up and probe you? This chick has to be smoking if you're fucking Bobby but thinking of her instead."

"It's not about how smoking she is," I reply, air quoting the word for emphasis. "It's about her as a person. Spending time in her company brings me a kind of peace I've never felt. She's like a breath of fresh air in a polluted world."

"Jeez, you really got probed by an alien, dude!"

We both laugh, and it feels good to actually get things off my chest. I've known Joe since college, and he's been nothing but a loyal friend ever since. We shared a dorm, and there's nothing he doesn't know—except my forbidden past.

He was there when I went through a string of women and never saw the same one more than once. He thought that, like most college guys, I was just enjoying the freedom it provided and just enjoyed sex.

Most of the guys in our year were getting laid left, right and centre, just using women and discarding them like trash, so Joe just thought I was a normal college student, whatever *normal* really means.

It wasn't until later in life that he realised I wasn't growing up and settling down. I was still the same guy I was back then, in the body of an older guy. But he's never judged me for it. He doesn't know my reasons, because hell if I can actually explain them to myself, much less another person, but he accepts that I am who I am.

"I seriously can't explain it, Joe. Evie just crawled underneath my skin. I didn't mean for it to happen, but being with her and Maya is like nothing I've ever known."

"Maya?" he asks, his eyes bugging out as he throws the crust of his pizza back in the box. "Is this a threesome kind of deal or something? If so, I can see why that appeals more than Bobby."

"No, man. Maya is her daughter."

"Oh, shit. Now I sound like an insensitive asshole. But a kid, really? You're not only actually more than vaguely interested in a woman for more than one night, but you're interested in a woman with a kid? What's up with you? I thought you didn't do emotional baggage?"

"I don't. Or I didn't. But maybe I'm finally growing up."

"Stranger things have happened … I guess. No, screw that, this is the strangest thing I've ever heard of."

"Yeah, well, like I say, I don't even know how to explain it to myself, never mind you. There's just something about her. I'm going to ask her on a date, if I can muster the nerve."

"A date? Jeez, bro!"

"I know, I know. Unchartered territory. But how do I know if I don't try?"

"And here I was thinking you were just going to remain Peter Pan."

"Yeah, well, I guess even Peter Pan had to grow up eventually."

***

Joe left an hour ago and I'm sitting back in my study with a tumbler of whiskey in hand. His words of wisdom for the evening—follow your heart instead of your head—are still rattling around in my head.

I can't deny my past, whether it's the past with women, or the past that's haunted my every waking and sleeping moment, always hot on my heels, me barely able to keep ahead of it. But maybe I can change the future. It isn't set in stone. Like I told Leah many years ago, you get to a fork in the road and you have to choose wisely which path you're going to follow. I'm at the fork in the road. It just took me a little longer than most people to get here.

If I go one way, I'll likely continue to be the man I have been to date. If I go the other, into unchartered territory, I don't know what awaits.

Always liking to be in control of every aspect of my life, fear of the unknown grips me as I take a swig of my whiskey, allowing it to burn deliciously down my throat.

Leaving my empty glass in my study, I head upstairs to take a shower.

I grab a towel and throw my clothes in the washing basket in the corner of my room before heading for my shower.

Stepping under the hot jets, I close my eyes. Images of Evie play out like a movie in my head. She's beguiling. There's something about her that seduces me without meaning to. That's possibly what's so alluring, the fact that she isn't even trying to seduce me. In fact, although she's not sending me the vibes of "stay the hell away from me" she also isn't sending any kind of messages, subliminal or otherwise.

I've seen her look at me when she thinks I'm not looking, but she never gives anything away. She has a great poker face. Maybe I should invite her to play the next time the lads are round; she'd make a killing.

Thoughts of her grey eyes fill my mind as I lather up the shower gel and run my hand down my abs. Wishing it was her hand instead, I explore the hard planes of my body as though I've never touched it before.

With a mind of its own, my hand strays to my stiffening cock, gripping it firmly and stroking it up and down. I lean my head back against the tiles and let the water wash over me as I daydream of Evie touching me. I envisage her hand around me, pumping hard, taking me to the brink of the abyss before taking me in her mouth.

My chest moves up and down quickly, my breaths coming faster now. I'm so close to the edge, and all my pent-up sexual frustration comes pouring out of me as my orgasm rolls through me from my head to my toes.

***

Fully aware that she may say no, I walk across the car park to meet my fate, one way or the other.

There were so many first date ideas online that I got a headache just browsing through them. Suggestions like go to an aquarium, go to a concert, visit the theatre, go out for a meal, take a wine-tasting tour … they were all wrong.

Having never been one to date, I shouldn't have any preconceived ideas about the suggestions I was met with. But I do anyway. A theatre: too dark to see each other, and all your concentration is on the play rather than each other. A concert: too loud to hear each other, and I don't know what kind of music she likes. A meal: some women don't like to eat in front of men on a first date. Even I know that.

I thought a picnic in the park might be an idea, until I realised that I don't know if she's gluten intolerant or vegetarian or something, plus the whole "eating in front of someone" thing too.

How to win her over without splashing my cash and leaving a lasting impression on her that I'm materialistic, which I totally am not—that was the real question. One I very nearly didn't have an answer to.

"Hey, Ryan," I greet as the bell chimes over my head and his head whips up in my direction.

"Hello, handsome," he replies, his hand on his heart.

"Oh, Ryan, I didn't know we'd got to this point in our relationship," I sigh dreamily with my stance mirroring his.

"Well, if McDreamy won't answer my phone calls, then I'll settle for someone like you whisking me off my feet à la *Officer and A Gentleman.*"

"Sorry, but I just don't think I could carry you, what with all the cake you eat."

A short, sharp burst of laughter leaves his mouth and I can't help but chuckle.

"I'm not even going to dignify that with a response. Take a seat, and I'll go grab your date. As you can see, your table is set."

I look to where he's gesturing and see there is indeed a table set up with colouring books and pencils galore.

Walking to my allotted seat, I see a sign on the table, it reads *Reserved for Trey & Maya.*

I can't help but laugh, knowing exactly who wrote the sign. Her handwriting is pretty neat for a six-year-old. Or at least it is going by standards I can remember from primary school.

Maya comes running to the table and wraps me in a bear hug. I return the gesture, holding her to me and inhaling her sweet scent. She smells like coconut and flour, probably from the macaroons I saw in the display case.

"Hey, sweet girl. How are you today?"

"I'm good. How are you?" she asks as she takes a seat opposite me.

"I'm good too, thank you. Have you been baking macaroons with your mummy?"

"How do you know dat?" she asks, surprise lacing her tone.

"I have special powers. I know lots of things."

"Really? Like what?"

"Your favourite Disney princess is Ariel, and you get hopping mad when someone confuses Cinderella with Rapunzel. You like to eat cake mix straight out of the bowl, and I'm betting Mummy lets you lick the spoon when she's done with it."

"Mummy does! How you know these things?"

"Like I say, I have superpowers."

"No, you said special powers, not superpowers. Der is a difference."

I love how perceptive this kid is. She's a ray of pure sunshine.

"Okay, I'm sorry, I got it wrong. Shall I let you in on a secret?"

"Yes." She gasps as she claps her hands together in glee.

Looking past me for a moment, she beams a big grin over my shoulder.

"Mummy, Trey gonna tell me a secret."

"Is he now?" Evie asks as she rests her hip against the booth beside her daughter.

"Well, I was. I can't tell Mummy. Only Maya gets to know my secret."

I make a motion of zipping my lips, which makes Maya giggle. I swear I haven't heard such a beautiful sound in a very long time.

"Oh, well, in that case, you don't want the delicious special of the day and a flat white?" Evie asks as her gaze locks onto mine.

"Oh, but I do. I can never say no to cake. And caffeine is my addiction."

"Well, I'll go and get them … *after* you spill your secret."

Evie winks at me and I swear my heart skips a goddamn beat.

"You have to promise not to tell anyone else."

They make the motion of zipping their lips in unison. I can't help but chuckle at the adorable pair. If Maya is anything like her mother when she grows up, Evie is going to have to lock the doors and the windows and sleep with a baseball bat under her pillow, just to beat the boys away from her baby.

"I was telling Maya how I know things. She was asking how I know, so I said I had special powers. But then I slipped up and let my real secret out; I have *super*powers."

"Oh, you do? And what would they be?" Evie asks, trying to keep her face straight.

"I can't tell you all of them. They're a secret. But one of them is knowing things without being told."

"Really? And what would those things be?"

I reiterate what I told Maya a couple of minutes ago and Evie chuckles. Her laughter is melodious.

Melodious? Who the hell am I becoming? Maybe Joe was right, and I really was probed by aliens.

"I'll get you that cake," Evie says and slips away, still laughing.

Maya hands me a colouring book and tells me that if I can remember which one Cinderella is, I may colour her in.

When I get it right this time, I am given some colouring pencils. But before I can start to colour her, Maya looks at me.

"What colour is her dress?" she asks.

"Blue," Ryan whispers as he bends down to place my coffee beside me. "Evie will be back with your cake, she just had to take a call," he says, this time at a normal volume.

"Thank you."

***

After a lovely colouring date with a delightful little girl, I decide to pull up my big boy pants and ask her mum on a real date. Well, sort of.

Ryan is helping Maya pack her things away while I ask Evie if I can talk to her alone.

"Here's the thing, Evie. I'll be totally honest. I'm not generally good at this sort of thing. I wondered if you might like to go on a date with me? But not any date. I wondered if you would consider teaching me how to bake one night when the store is closed?"

My heart beats a staccato rhythm in my chest as I wait with bated breath for her answer.

She doesn't answer right away, which leads me to think it will be a no.

I watch as her chest rises and falls with her rapid breathing. I'm not sure if she realises, but she looks utterly gorgeous dressed in a soft pink dress that falls just below the knee. The cut of the top of it doesn't show too much cleavage, but I can't help but wonder what underwear she's wearing or what her skin feels like. Is it as soft as it looks?

Chapter Seven

Evie

I just stare as I try and fully digest what Trey said. It keeps repeating in my head like a mantra. Ryan said he was into me, but I thought he was just joking. I try to form an answer as I get lost in his beautiful blue eyes. I shake my head ever so slightly, trying to clear the fog that has entered my mind. I notice his features start to droop at the sight of my shaking head.

"It's alright, don't worry; I don't want to pressure you," he says softly.

He turns on his heel to make his way out of the bakery.

"No! I didn't mean no, I was just moving my head. I do it quite a lot, especially in situations that it's not appropriate to do so." I give a sheepish grin as I realise I'm rambling. "I would love to go on a date with you. You want to learn to bake? That I can definitely help you with."

His face instantly brightens, and his posture visibly relaxes. He beams a gorgeous smile at me.

"Really? That would be great! When are you free?" he asks, his voice is more cheerful than moments ago.

"Well, I'm busy the next couple of days with it coming up to Easter weekend, but how about Friday? Are you, umm, free then?"

I look up at him hopefully. Knowing that he has an attraction in some way towards me calms me. I hold my breath as I await his answer.

"Yes, I'm free Friday. That would be great."

My shoulders relax and I smile up at him.

"I've got to go, but I'll see you Friday, at six? For our date."

He smiles at me and touches my arm.

I nod and smile as he waves back to Maya and makes his way out the front door. I turn and see Ryan doing a happy dance; his imminent squeal follows.

"Oh my god, Evie! I told you he liked you. You going to get all dressed up and sexy, huh?" he waggles his eyebrows.

I chuckle and shake my head as I grab Maya's hand. I stop and widen my eyes as I realise that I've got no ideal clothes for a date.

"I've got no clothes, Ryan. I only have my work attire and sweats. What am I going to wear?"

I spin and face him. Almost instantly, a huge grin spreads across his face and he claps his hands.

"Looks like we're going shopping."

Maya smiles as I groan; shopping with Ryan means a million different shops and the smuttiest clothing he can find. I'm more of a run into a store, know what I want, and run back out again shopper, but Ry likes to make me try on anything he can find.

***

I trail behind a skipping Ryan and Maya as we're finding an outfit for Operation Get Evie Into The Dating World, as Ryan has officially called it.

Having been into numerous stores and finding nothing that is suitable for a baking date, I've officially given up hope. Everything that Ryan has picked out has been too slutty, or what I would think is too dressy, and everything that I have picked up has been given a hard no from the both of them. Even Maya is on his side. A sundress in a shop window catches my attention as I'm trying to catch up with Ryan and Maya. Stopping, I turn to look at it. I'm mesmerised as I make my way towards the white beauty; it's a knee-length white sundress with red roses cascading down. It's the bottom that caught my attention, with fallen rose petals layering on top of each other mixed in with some rose gold swirls. It's perfect. I hear Ryan and Maya rush up behind me.

"This is where you ran off to," I hear him say breathlessly. "Oh, wow. That is beautiful. You need to try it on *right now.*"

Grabbing my hand, he pulls me into the store, with Maya on the other side of him. His eyes scan the shop, trying to find the dress. Not being able to find one, he huffs and makes his way to an assistant.

"Excuse me, do you have any more of the dress that's in the window?" he asks.

I shake myself out of my stupor and smile at the lady.

"I believe the one in the window is the only one, sir. Would you like me to get it for you?" She smiles at him, eyes slowly appraising his body.

"If you wouldn't mind." He follows her through the shop.

I chuckle as I see him try and deflect the woman's advances. I mean, I'm not surprised; with his dark brown hair and hazel eyes, along with the stubble he's got going on after not shaving for a couple of days, he can be captivating when he wants to be. He's always deflecting women left and right. He makes his way towards me with the dress, loops his arm through mine, and pulls me and Maya towards the dressing rooms.

"Go and get changed, then!"

He shoos me with his hands, placing the dress in my arms as he does so. I chuckle as I make my way into a cubicle.

I make quick work of getting out of my clothes and into this dress. I turn and look in the mirror. The way that the dress hugs my small waist and then flares out below gives me a nice hourglass figure, and the top has a sweetheart neckline, showing some cleavage but not so much that it's distasteful. It's perfect. I make my way out from the cubicle and see Ry and Maya sitting on the chairs outside the cubicles. Ry's eyes instantly widen, and he smiles.

"Well, I think you look beautiful. I mean, that dress is just—wow. If he doesn't fall on his knees and grovel for you right then and there, I'm turning straight for you."

I laugh, knowing he's joking. Maya makes her way towards me.

"Mummy, you look beautiful. You look like a princess." She fingers the bottom of the dress. "No, you *are* a princess."

I smile as she giggles up at me. Her giggle never ceases to amaze me; just that little sound brings me so much joy.

"So, this is the one then?"

"Darlin', of course it is. Look at the way it hugs your figure. You look magnificent."

Shaking my head, I make my way back into the dressing room. It doesn't take me long to get changed.

Ry and Maya follow me as I make my way to the till to pay. As we're leaving the store, Maya tugs on my hand and looks up at me hopefully.

"Mummy, because we're here, can we get a McDonald's pleeease?"

She draws out the last word while giving me her doe eyes. I pretend to think about it for a minute, wanting to make her wait before giving her an answer. I pull her forward, as I find it amusing that she hasn't realised that we were already making our way there.

"Of course we can. We were taking you there anyway."

I nod my head towards the big sign, and she squeals and jumps about.

"Come on then, sweet pea," Ry says as he loops his arm through mine. "We've got nuggets awaiting."

***

I'm standing in the kitchen, nursing a coffee as I wait for Ry to appear for his movie night with Maya. The front door opens, and I peer around to look at him. I chuckle as I watch him struggle to close the door, his arms laden with bags.

"I thought you were only having a movie night?"

Ryan jumps at my voice and curses at me as he drops a bag.

"Yes, we are. But I have brought snacks and food, and a Disney movie that I know Maya doesn't own."

He awkwardly places all the bags onto the table and pulls out each item. The table quickly becomes filled with numerous bags of chocolate and popcorn, and I laugh at how over the top he has gone.

"I also brought some Easter eggs for Sunday. Now, go and get ready for your date! Time is of the essence." He pushes me out of the kitchen.

I make my way up the stairs and into the bathroom, then I turn on the shower and jump in, letting the water wash over me.

Taking a shower in record time, I make my way to my dressing table to get ready. I go through the actions of drying and straightening my hair, only wanting a simple look as I don't want to look too overdressed. I apply simple makeup, putting some light foundation on, along with a coral blush, then a coat of mascara and some lip gloss.

I'm ready in record time. I turn and look at the dress I bought the other day, hanging on the door of my wardrobe. I pull it on over my matching underwear—I know that nothing will happen, but just knowing that I'm wearing a matching set brings me a sense of confidence.

I slip my feet into a pair of red dolly shoes, knowing that I'm going to want to be comfortable when cooking, but I still want to make an effort.

Making sure that the dress falls properly, I smooth out the invisible wrinkles as I'm looking in the mirror. Standing there, I look at myself, at the steady rise and fall of my chest. As I sweep my eyes up my body, I make sure that everything is perfect.

Feeling more nervous than before, I turn to make my way down the stairs, knowing that Ry will be able to bring me the confidence I need to carry out this date. As I round the corner to the living room, I see Ry and Maya snuggled on the sofa with a plethora of sweets on the coffee table before them. Ry's head instantly swivels towards me; he grins and nudges Maya.

"You look beautiful, darlin'." He moves away from Maya. "You need a pep talk?"

He makes his way to the kitchen and I trail behind him.

"Don't worry or stress about it. You look beautiful; let's not get anything else stuck in your head. You look amazing, and Trey will think the exact same of you. How are you feeling?"

He looks at me expectantly, obviously using his sixth sense to know I'm feeling stressed. He leans his hip against the counter.

"Fine. Nervous, but fine. I know I need to get out there soon, I think I'm just more worried about how to act. I haven't been on a date in years; the last time was in college. Greg never took me out or anything, so it's been a long time. It's nerve-wracking. What if I say the wrong thing, don't act like I'm interested, or don't flirt enough? Why are dates so hard?"

I look down, feeling embarrassed that something as simple as a date has me flustered.

"You'll do fine. A date isn't hard. You're baking. This is your forte; you'll do fine. You just need to have confidence in yourself. Just act like yourself. He's already proven that he likes you for you, so you won't need to pretend to be something that you aren't. He will enjoy the time with you. Whenever he's playing with Maya, he always talks to you, and you can see the chemistry from a mile off. Don't push yourself to flirt, just do what you feel is natural, act like yourself, and it will go perfectly"

He clasps my hand and gives me a reassuring nod.

"Okay, thank you, Ry." I lean up and kiss his cheek. "I need to get going, anyway. I want to set up all the ingredients for tonight. I haven't decided on what we're doing yet, so I've made sure we've got enough of everything, I'll let him choose."

"I'm not surprised. You always want to be prepared for everything possible, you little control freak. You better have fun. I'll go and get Maya so she can say goodbye."

As he goes to call for her, she appears in the doorway.

"I hearded you say my name. You going, Mummy?"

"Yeah, sweetheart, Ry is looking after you, and I'll be back later, okay?"

She comes over and hugs my legs, and I lean down wanting a proper hug.

"Have a good time, Mummy. We're watching a new movie that Uncle Ry brought! I can't wait."

"I will. Be good, baby. Don't have too many sweets, otherwise you won't go to bed."

I kiss the top of her head and hug Ryan.

"I'll see you later, and before you say it, yes, I will call if anything happens. Don't worry about us, Mummy Bear. Have a good time."

He winks and pushes me to the door.

I jump into my car, not wanting to walk home later tonight, although Ryan tried to persuade me to walk there so Trey had an excuse to drive me home. But I immediately shut down that idea. It's not that I don't trust him, I just don't want people knowing where I live.

I pull up in front of *Queen of Tarts* and quickly make my way to the shutters. I jump from one foot to the other as I wait for them to open. Ducking under the shutters when they're open enough to open the door, I leave it unlocked so Trey can just walk straight in. I turn the lights on and make my way through to the back.

Just as I have finished setting up all the equipment and turned the oven on to preheat, I hear the jingle of the bell above the door. I smile and breathe a couple of times before I head through the doors to the front of the shop.

I stop dead in my tracks as I see two large men standing in the middle of my shop. One of them is huge and looks like a tank; the other is smaller and scrawny looking. The smaller one's eyes travel up my body and he gives me a menacing grin as he takes a step towards me. I back up until my back hits the counter.

"Umm, I-I'm sorry, but the shop is closed right now."

I slowly make my way around the counter, trying to create some distance between us.

"It doesn't look like its closed. Why would a pretty lady like you leave the door open so any random thug could walk in? Seems a little bit stupid don't ya think?" the scrawny one says as he makes his way towards the counter.

"Y-you need to l-leave right now." I try and sound stern, but the shakiness in my voice gives me away.

"Oh, we aren't leaving, *babe*. We've been ordered to give him back what he's owed."

He sneers and tries to grab my arm.

"Give who back? W-what are you on about?"

I press my back flat to the wall. I look around to see if I can escape, and I realise that the door to the decorating room isn't too far. As I make my way towards it, I see the large man take a slight step forward as he continues to watch me with wary eyes.

"You think you would know who we're on about, huh? You owe the man you put into fucking jail."

I immediately feel all my bones lock up, and I shake my head. Why would Greg try and come looking for me now? And how did he manage it? I thought I was safe. I'd moved as far away as I could so he wouldn't find me, changed my phone number, changed *everything* so he couldn't find me. I'd made sure of it. Or at least I *thought* I had. My vision goes dark and I feel my chest start to tighten as a wave of pure panic washes over me. I hastily try and find a way to get away but stop my appraisal of the room when I notice the smaller guy has stepped closer to me.

"Greg wants back what he's owed. You shouldn't have run away, bitch. Now we'll make sure you'll never get away again."

He stands at the end of the counter, in front of my only escape from the bakery. I'm too far away from the door to try and slip into the back and make some sort of escape. Just as he goes to grab my arm, the bell jingles. They turn and see Trey. One of the men grabs my arm in a tight grip.

Trey stands there with his arms crossed, covering the entire doorway, with a murderous expression on his face. I feel myself instantly relax at the sight of him, but I tense and whimper as the unknown male drags me forward, while sneering at Trey.

Just as he goes to pull me through the back doors, I hear Trey speak in a quiet yet frightening voice.

"I wouldn't do that if I were you."

Chapter Eight

Trey

The menacing look on Iain Pierce's face is obviously meant to frighten me, but I'm not easily intimidated. Especially not by a two-bit thug like him or his scrawny little brother Jake.

Exactly what these two fuckers are doing here, I don't know, and I don't care. All I care about is the frightened expression on Evie's beautiful face.

Did they break in with the intention of robbing the place? That's not usually their style. They both have long rap sheets, but never for breaking and entering. Theft, yes. But usually cars. Their main charges have been ones of assault.

I don't immediately act, knowing anything rash would bring Evie more harm.

"What do you think you're doing, Iain?" I ask in a barely contained growl.

"What business is that of yours, pretty boy?" he sneers. "We aren't here for you. We're here to collect on what's owed."

"I'm making it my business, dickhead."

I pull my phone out of my pocket ready to dial 999.

"We don't want to hurt you, but we will," Jake chimes in.

"Oh, will you now? Why don't we see about that?"

Iain releases his grip on Evie's arm and lunges at me at the same time as Jake tries to rush me.

I sidestep them both and Jake crashes into the door behind me, carried by his own momentum. Coming around Iain, I grab him in a full nelson. He might be large in size, but he doesn't have the muscle I do, and he isn't skilled enough to fight me off.

Hearing Evie yelp, my heart races. I want to get to her, get her safe. But that isn't happening until I dispose of these two wankers.

Jake tries to hammer on my back, pull on my arms, anything to get me to let go of his brother. I don't let go. Fearing for Evie's safety, I tighten my grip on Iain.

"What say you gents get the fuck out of here and leave this woman the hell alone?" I growl into Iain's ear.

"Like hell. We're here to collect a debt and we won't leave until we get it."

"And what debt would that be?"

"None of your business, pretty boy."

He tries to break free of the hold I have on him. Too bad for him that I'm the one in the position of advantage.

"Get out of here now and I won't report you to the police," I say as Jake stands looking at me holding his brother in place.

"Let's go, Iain. We can come back to collect what he's owed."

"Oh no, you won't. You'll leave here and never darken this lady's doorstep again, because if you don't, I'll talk to someone who'll talk to Mal and get you fuckers beaten to within an inch of your life. You might not be scared of me, but you're damn well frightened of him. You'd piss your pants the second he looked at you, and he'd enjoy every fucking second of tearing you limb from disgusting limb."

"Yeah, like you know Mal," Iain sneers.

"Oh, but believe me, I do. He's ... a friend of a friend, you might say. I got him off charges and he owes me a favour. I'm going to call it in unless you are wise enough to go to hell and not come back."

"Let's go, bro. She ain't worth getting shit from Mal Hudson for."

"Ah, Jake. The wise one as always."

"I might not be smart, but even I know you don't fuck with the Hudson family," he says, his voice small and truly frightened.

"So, what do you say boys? This is your last chance. Leave now, don't ever come back, and I'll pretend this didn't happen."

"Let's go, Iain. I ain't getting ripped to pieces for her or Greg. He isn't that good of a friend that we owe him our lives."

"Oh, so Peterson sent you here, huh?" I ask, this news sudden and surprising.

"What's it to you?" Iain chokes out as I grip him tighter.

"Well, let's see ... This lady here, she's my friend and she's under my protection, and all it takes is one phone call and she'll be under the Hudson family's protection too. The favour Mal owes me isn't small."

Jake opens the door and looks back at his brother.

"I'm outta here, man. Ain't nothing worth this. Peterson's in prison and he can rot. I don't owe him jack shit."

"Maybe not, but I do."

Iain tries with all his might to struggle free of me, but I'm not letting go until he's out of that door and far enough away for me to call the police.

"You don't owe him your life, bro. What you owe him is small fry compared to what Mal could rain down on you."

Jake may not be smart, but he's wise enough to piss his pants at the sound of Mal's name. Everyone in their criminal world is wise enough to know that you don't mess with the Hudsons. Their family is tight, and anyone they see as crossing them gets brought back to earth with a resounding bump.

"You have three seconds to decide," I whisper to Iain.

"Bro, come on. Dude, let's bounce."

Jake looks to his brother one last time before walking out of the open door. Iain whimpers as I choke him. I'm not even using an ounce of the strength I could be, and I think he knows it. If I were to unleash the strength I'm withholding, he'd be unconscious now, at the very least. At worst, he'd be battered, broken and hog-tied, waiting for the police to arrive.

"I'd follow in your brother's footsteps if I were you, Iain. Three … Two …"

I pause for a beat as I let him go a little.

"One."

He breaks my grasp and runs out of the door as fast as his legs can carry him.

I don't know what the fuck just happened, or why, but I'm damn glad I was here. I dread to think what they would have done to Evie. Jake was once arrested for an alleged rape, but they couldn't prove it, so he went unpunished. I don't know whether he did what he was accused of or not, but it doesn't bear thinking about.

Spinning around, I see Evie on the floor by the counter. I turn on my heel, rush to the door and deadbolt it.

"Where are the keys?"

Evie takes a moment to register what I've said before throwing me the keys to the front door.

"Can you put the shutters down from the inside?" I ask as I lock the door and stand looking through the glass to watch as the brothers leg it out of sight.

I dial 999 and tell them I need the police. While I wait to be connected, I rush over to Evie's side. Sliding down next to her, I pull her shaking body into my lap and wrap my arms around her. I stroke her hair and whisper soothingly, trying to calm her down.

"Please, Trey, don't call the police."

"Why not?"

"I don't want any trouble."

"But ..."

"Please?" she all but begs.

I tell the person on the other end of the line that it was a false alarm and apologise before hanging up.

"Th-thank y-you," Evie stutters as I hold her in my lap.

Suddenly her arms are wrapped around me and she buries her head into the crook of my neck. Her breathing slows down to a more regular rhythm as I stroke a hand up and down her back.

"I don't want to ask this, Evie, but are you connected to Greg Peterson?"

"I-I ... I ... oh Trey, please ... I don't want to talk about him."

"Okay, sweetheart. Okay. But we will return to this subject if I have my way. Remember what I do for a living? I can make his life hell on the inside if he sent those twats to hurt you."

"Please, Trey, let's leave it for tonight. I just need to ... to bake and take my mind off it."

"You still want to bake?" I ask as she begins to stand.

"Yes, it's therapeutic. Especially if I'm making bread, where I get to really pummel the dough."

"Don't you knead the dough gently?" I tease, trying to lighten the mood.

"Most of the time, but if I'm frustrated ... well, let's just say, sometimes I have to start a fresh batch after the beating I've given it. Nobody wants to eat overworked bread."

She stands and smooths out her dress. It's then that it catches my eye. It's white and gives her a stunning hourglass shape. I take in the detail of the roses and the fallen petals. Swirls of rose gold catch the light as she moves. She looks breathtaking. I think my heart just skipped a beat.

I stand and brush the seat of my jeans. Not that the floor was dusty, I just want to stop them from reaching out to touch her.

Walking around the counter, I follow Evie into the baking room. I make sure the door is secure and wander over to where she has a mountain of sumptuous ingredients. Easter eggs, chocolate bars, mini chocolate eggs, chocolate chips—I'd say someone has a sweet tooth. There's also cream cheese, a packet of digestive biscuits, butter, flour, and an array of other goodies to choose from.

"Are we baking to feed the homeless here? It's enough to feed an army," I jest.

Evie's shy smile makes me feel weak in the knees.

"I thought I'd get all sorts of things out because I don't know what you want to learn to bake."

"Oh, umm …" I hadn't got one specific thing in mind, if I'm honest. "I don't know. A Victoria sponge?"

"That's a bit more basic than I thought," she says quietly.

"Well, I'm game for something more adventurous if you are. But I'll warn you, I can cook, but I don't have a clue about baking. I don't know plain flour from self-raising or why there's even a difference. Isn't one type of flour enough? Unless you're gluten intolerant; that bit I get."

Evie's laughter pulls me up short. The sound is so soft and beautiful. Just like her.

"I won't bore you with all the types of flour, if you don't bore me with a bunch of legalese. Deal?"

"Deal. I hate talking about my job anyway. It can suck ass sometimes."

"From what I know about you, based on what you eat here, how about we start off with a cheesecake and work our way up from there? There's an easy no-bake cheesecake we can make. I brought a packet of biscuits from home for you to crush to use as the base. I usually do it differently, but I had a feeling I should take it easy on you. All you have to do is melt some butter to bind it together in the bottom of the pan."

"I can manage to melt butter. I just hope I don't burn it."

Evie passes me a rolling pin and a large resealable bag.

"What am I doing with these?"

"Nothing without an apron," she says as she slips her own on.

I grab an apron from the table in front of us.

"Okay, so … grab the packet of digestives."

I pull on my apron and grab the biscuits.

"Put the biscuits in the bag, seal it up, and crush with the rolling pin. I'll melt the butter."

Her warm smile doesn't show any trace of the shit that went down earlier. I'm actually surprised she still wants to go through with tonight, but with what she said about it being therapeutic, it might be the perfect way for her to unwind.

I meant what I said: I'll only let it drop *for now.* We will return to the conversation at some point.

I open the biscuits and put them in the bag as instructed. When I set about bashing them with the rolling pin, Evie laughs at me as she grabs a pan and the butter.

Once the biscuits are down to a fine powder type thing, Evie tells me to stop what I'm doing and pour them into a bowl. She passes me the melted butter and tells me to pour as she stirs it in. When the mixture is combined, she passes me a round tin and instructs me to spoon the mixture in and press it flat.

"So, did you always want to be a baker?" I ask as she opens the tubs of cream cheese.

"Not always. It's something my grandma gave me a love of. The first cake I made her was a chocolate one, but even with all the chocolatey goodness, you couldn't cover the burnt taste of the cake. It was awful, but my grandparents ate every bite."

There's a softness in her eyes as she looks at me with a small smile. She's obviously very fond of her grandparents. Her expression is wistful as she combines lemon juice with icing sugar and cream cheese in a bowl.

"But you've obviously perfected the art over the years. Everything you serve here is exquisite."

"Well, thank you," she says as a blush warms her cheeks. "I practiced a lot. Practice makes perfect, after all."

Handing me a bowl, a whisk and some cream, she cuts open a vanilla pod and opens a small bottle labelled "vanilla essence".

"You need to whisk these together to form stiff peaks," she instructs as she puts the seeds into the cream I poured into the bowl.

"Stiff peaks? Umm …"

"Add the vanilla essence and I'll tell you when you get to the right consistency."

I think she's taking pity on me.

"How about some music while we bake?" she asks as she watches my every move.

"Sure. But no crap. I don't want to hear Eminem or 50 Cent or whatever. My taste is eclectic but doesn't expand to rap."

"Gotcha. How about this?"

Music flows quietly from the iPod dock and I recognise it as "Wake Me Up" by Avicii. Not a bad choice of song.

"Not bad taste, for a girl," I tease and watch her huff in indignance.

"I'll have you know I have extremely good taste. What do you usually listen to?"

"Well, my workout playlist has all sorts on, from Kaiser Chiefs to Killers, Editors to Imagine Dragon … my car playlist is usually upbeat to wake me up of a morning or cheer me up after a long day, so … I guess there's some AC/DC on there…"

"Thunderstruck," we both say at the same time, before laughing.

"Girl got taste," I say with a wink. "I also have a bit of Panic! at The Disco on there. You have to love 'High Hopes', 'Say Amen', 'Hey Look Ma, I Made It' and older stuff like 'Sins' and 'Lying'."

"I Write Sins Not Tragedies"—shortened by most people to "Sins"—plays next and I can't help but sing along.

Evie tells me to stop whisking.

"We mix the cream cheese and this whipped cream together, making sure to fold it all in so it's fully combined."

I help her do just that before scooping the mixture out and spreading it out over the biscuit base we made before.

"Now it chills in the fridge for about an hour before we can decorate it. So, pick your next project."

I look at all the ingredients and my mind boggles. I don't know anything about baked goods at all except how to eat them.

"You're the *Queen of Tarts*," I say with a smile, "so why don't you tell me."

"Hmm," she says as she scratches her chin. "How about a tart with cream cheese filling and sliced fruit on top?"

"You like cream cheese or are you just taking it easy on me?"

"Both."

Lifehouse begin to play through the speakers and I let the words to "You and Me" wash over me.

Evie takes me through the steps of making a tart, doing what she calls blind-baking, and though I don't understand the term I don't ask what it means.

When she looks up at me, she steals my breath. Her grey gaze penetrates mine and I see a storm swirling in her irises.

She really is beautiful. Captivating. The epitome of pure beauty. She isn't heavy-handed with her makeup, and I like the fresh, natural look. So much nicer than how Bobby was, all smoky makeup and fake tits. *God, how did my mind go there?*

My eyes trail down her neck and to the sweetheart neckline of her dress of their own accord. Her ample breasts are mostly covered, but her creamy skin is begging for my touch. Okay, I'm the one begging to touch. My cock stirs and I'm glad I have an apron covering me as well as my jeans. *Jesus, get a grip, Trey!*

Looking back up to her eyes, I see a flicker of something I can't name, but then it's gone.

I move closer, my feet moving of their own accord. When I'm standing in front of her, I inhale her sweet scent. She does things to me that no woman ever has. She gives my heart a reason to beat.

I've never been able to give a woman my all. It's not who I am. It doesn't mean I've never thought about settling down, but with the upbringing I had, I had no intention of staying in one place too long.

But now I'm in one place in my life, a good place. I have a nice home and a great job—hard, but extremely gratifying when I put people who deserve it behind bars. Scum like Greg Peterson go to jail for a very long time. Attempted murder will do that to you. And again, I wonder how she knows him. It wasn't me that put him behind bars personally, but it was my firm.

I lean against the counter behind me, crossing my legs and bracing myself with both arms on the countertop.

"There's something you should know about me before this"—I gesture between the two of us—"if there is even a *this*, goes any further. I don't date. I've probably—no make that *definitely*—never had a serious relationship. That might not make much sense, but one day, I'll tell you why. I can't … *yet.*" My voice breaks as I continue. "But I will tell you one day. I figured you ought to know that a relationship is a completely new concept to me. I've never found that one special person that made me want to settle down. But with that being said, Evie, I want to date.

Specifically, I want to date *you*. If you're open to the idea."

I take a deep breath. I don't lay myself bare, not for anyone. But maybe it's time I learned how.

The lyrics of a song I'm not familiar with wash over me, talking about just a kiss and not wanting to push things too far.

It's in that moment that I lean forward to wipe a smudge of flour from Evie's cheek, brushing my thumb delicately over her skin.

Unable to deny the chemistry I feel crackling between us every time we're in the same room, I take advantage of the fact that we're alone and do the one thing I've wanted to since I first saw her; I lean in and softly claim her soft, full lips with my own. Just a tender kiss, no pushing it further than she's willing to let it go. I pull back and look at her, seeing emotion swirling in those grey orbs. Did I do the wrong thing?

Chapter Nine

Evie

Am I breathing? I'm not sure. After his words about not dating, but then kissing me, he sure does give me mixed emotions. But I know one thing—I want another; I want to feel his soft lips upon mine once more.

I lean towards him, first giving him a sweet kiss, but just as I try to deepen the kiss, I feel him pull back slightly.

"Why'd you stop?" I ask, a little hurt by his reticence.

As I look into his captivating eyes, I try not to let the hurt of being rejected show on my face. He gives me a small smile and takes a deep breath before replying.

"I don't want you to feel under pressure," he says, cradling my cheek in one of his large palms. "I understand why you have your guard up, and I don't want to force you into anything that you wouldn't feel comfortable in doing."

I feel butterflies swirl in the pit of my stomach at how kind he is, but I know what I need—that's to feel his lips on mine. Deciding to show him instead of telling him, I sidle closer to him and trail my hands down his chest.

Before he can move away, I thread my fingers through his belt loops, and I pull him closer to me. Standing on my tiptoes, I press my lips against his in a soul-crushing kiss. Opening my mouth, I lick the seam of his lips, silently begging for entrance.

He tentatively opens his mouth and slips his arms around my waist as he pulls me closer to him. His tongue dances with mine as we continue exploring each other's mouths. His kiss is so fierce, so passionate, that I'm surprised I don't spontaneously combust on the spot. I feel heat pool between my legs as I move closer, trying to press my entire body to his; we fit so perfectly it's like we were made to be joining puzzle pieces. I feel his budding erection against my stomach.

Slowly he stops the kiss, breathing heavily. I look up and see his pupils are dilated. A slow feeling of satisfaction ripples through me, knowing that I affect him just as much as he affects me. He gazes into my eyes with such ferocity swirling in them, I feel protected—*safe* even. I know that he would do *anything* to protect me. And with this one look, I have the confidence to finally voice what I think about him—what I think about *us*.

"I don't do the dating thing either. I haven't done the dating scene for a while. I won't push you, but when you're ready to talk, I'm here to listen. I know that I like you; I can feel that there's *something* here—between us. And whatever it is, I want to explore it. I want to get to know you, and you can't understand how happy it makes me that you seem to want the same thing as I do."

I take a deep breath as I try and tell him how I feel, without letting anything about *why* I haven't dated in a while slip. I see him visibly relax and smile at my comment.

"You don't understand how relieved I am. I'm glad that we feel the same."

I lean into him, resting my head on his chest. His arms sweep around me, and he holds me in his embrace. The smell of his aftershave sweeps over me, encasing me in a cocoon of warmth and comfort.

"I really don't want to move. However, we need to add the fruit and put this tart in the fridge. Otherwise you won't be able to taste your creations before we have to leave."

He chuckles and lets his arms drop from around me. Begrudgingly, I move away from his warm body.

"What fruit do we put on it then?" he asks as he looks at me hesitantly.

I try not to laugh at his obvious uncertainty when it comes to baking.

"Whatever you want. It's your creation."

"Would strawberry and kiwi work?"

"Oh my god, that would taste awesome. You cut the fruit and I'll get to cleaning up."

Before he has a chance to reply, I hand him a punnet of strawberries and a kiwi to slice before busying myself by grabbing all the utensils that we have used and washing them up.

When I turn around, I see Trey leaning against the counter, his eyes glued to what I can only assume is my ass. When I chuckle, his eyes shoot up to mine and he gives me an unapologetic grin.

"Caught red-handed. What can I say?"

His smile is salacious as he watches me wiggle my ass on purpose.

I shake my head from side to side and start to put all the utensils away. Then I make my way towards the counter and help Trey place all the fruit he's expertly sliced onto the tart.

Once we've finished, I grab the cheesecake out of the fridge, as we still haven't decorated that either. I decide to add a chocolate ganache to finish off the cheesecake, so I grab some chocolate and a bowl to melt it in. Once I'm done, I wash up as I wait for it to set.

When we're finished, I grab a knife and plates out of the drawer and nod my head for him to cut into the desserts. Sitting on stools next to each other, I watch him as he takes his first bite of each one. I see his eyes widen in delight.

"Man, this tastes great. How does something so simple taste so good?"

"It's not that hard. Plus, you chose the flavours, so I'm glad you like them." I smile up at him.

He shakes his head at me.

"No, this was all *you*. You're an *amazing* baker."

I shift on my stool as he holds up a forkful of tart for me to eat. He's so thoughtful, and I like that about him.

"You don't like compliments, do you?" he asks in a whisper.

Shock flows through me at how observant he is. The only person to ever give me compliments, aside from my parents, is Ry. I've never been used to being complimented. It makes me feel slightly uncomfortable, due to Greg only ever degrading me and making me feel worthless.

"It's not that I don't like them." I rack my brain for an easy excuse. "I'm just not used to them is all."

"Hmm." He looks at me thoughtfully. "Well, you better get used to them then."

I chuckle and nod my head at him.

How can somebody I've only just met make me feel so comfortable? He doesn't act cocky; he doesn't act as though he's used to getting what he wants. He isn't arrogant in the slightest. He's the complete opposite, very sweet and thoughtful. So different to how Greg was.

Greg was cruel and knew he could get away with what he wanted. He knew I wouldn't leave him—knew I was trapped. But yet here Trey is, proving that not all men are like that.

What he did earlier was nothing short of heroic, and I have been trying my damned hardest not to show openly how it has affected me. I've felt a slight sense of terror since then, and I know if I let it show, Trey would want answers. Answers I'm not willing to give.

"I think this may have to be added to the specials board," I say with a smile.

"Really?" He looks at me in disbelief. "Are you serious?"

"I wouldn't say it if I wasn't. I always go crazy with new recipes, and I sometimes forget how amazing something so simple can taste."

"You know you need to name it after me, right?"

I pretend to think about it. "Well, it is mandatory."

Chuckling, he places the empty plate in the sink before turning on the water and washing it.

We make our way through the shop, closing things down as we go. Just as I've pressed the button for the shutters to go down, he finally breaks the silence.

"I really enjoyed tonight. Thank you for teaching me how to do the basics."

I turn around and face him, finally noticing how close he is to me.

"It was fine. You're very good. Tonight was amazing; thank you for asking me out."

I sidle closer and smile up at him. Leaning down, he presses his soft lips against mine in a sweet kiss. Then he walks me to my car, but just as I go to get in, I turn.

"Umm, would you—if you're not busy that is—like to come to the Easter fair with me, Ry and Maya on Monday?"

I suddenly get really nervous and feel my hands turn clammy. He smiles down at me.

"I'd love to. I'll see you Monday."

***

"So how was it? Was it great? Amazing? Did you get some one-on-one action?"

I jump at the sound of Ry's amused voice coming from the sofa.

"Why are you sitting in the dark, Ry?"

I squint as I turn on the standing lamp in the corner of the room.

"You won't get out of my questioning easily, love. How was the date?"

Smiling, I fall onto the sofa and place my feet in Ryan's lap.

"It was like you said it would be. Amazing. It was fun; he was so sweet. It wasn't forced at all ..."

"But ..."

I look at Ryan confused.

"What do you mean by *but?*"

"There's something on your mind. You're keeping something from me. I'm not stupid; I can see the cogs turning in your head. What happened?"

I huff and grab the glass of wine from his hands, swigging the remainder down, readying myself to tell him. Ry watches me with his eyebrows raised, waiting for me to get what I need off my chest.

"It isn't anything that Trey did. He was amazing; I could really see a future with him. But sadly, I don't see that happening now."

"And *why* is that?"

I proceed to fill him in on the events that happened before Trey had appeared, trying to stay calm. When I'm finished, Ry just sits there, gaping at me. Suddenly, it's like a switch flicks in his head, and he turns to me with an angry expression on his face.

"You want to leave now, don't you? You're going to try and run away from your problems, aren't you?"

I stare intently at the fireplace. Is it really that bad that I want to leave? After suffering abuse at the hands of Greg for all those years and then finally managing to free myself of his hold over me and leave, I believed that he would never find me. That was a foolish mistake. I knew someday that he would figure it out, especially as he always said he was well connected. I just hoped that I would be able to stay here a little longer, be able to get to know Trey more, and to have a life for Maya.

Anger bubbles inside of me at the thought that Ry would think I'm running away from my problems. I'm not running away—I want to protect Maya, protect *him*, and everyone that I have become close to. I don't want anybody in harm's way because of something that I have done, something I have endured.

"I didn't count on him finding me. I thought I was safe! It isn't my fault that he knows people. Is it selfish of me wanting to leave? No! It isn't selfish that I want to protect my daughter, want to protect my family. I'm *not* running away from my problems, I'm *making* them go away. I'm preventing anything else from happening to the people I love.

I'm protecting you. Why can't you see that?" My tone comes across harsher than I intended.

Ry looks over at me and wipes away the few tears that have managed to escape.

"I didn't mean it like that, love. I just want you to see that you don't have to run away at the first sight of danger, that what happened doesn't mean you aren't safe. Just look at what Trey did. He *protected* you, and I know for damn sure that he would do it again in a heartbeat. He cares about you. A blind man could see that. You need to try and let go. Greg is in prison, and I'm sure that he won't send anybody else after you after what happened today. You will *never* be able to fully run away from him, it's impossible. But what you *can* do is show him how much better your life is. If he sees just how much you're still affected and scared by him to this day, he has won. You need to be the strong woman that I have come to know over the past six years."

"I don't know, Ry. Everything is telling me that I need to leave. I want to do what I know will keep Maya safe, what will keep you safe. I can't go putting people in danger, and I don't want to paint a target on people's backs."

Ryan huffs and a worried look spreads across his face at my revelation, knowing that I've made my mind up.

"Stay until after Easter, give yourself a couple of days to think about it. Look before you leap. You need to see that you have options here. You don't just have to turn tail and run away. Please think things over, for me?"

I nod my head. I know that I won't change my mind. I have already made my decision. I *am* going to leave, and I know nothing can change that. But I'll agree with Ry for now to save an argument. My family are the most important thing to me, and I can't let anything happen to them. I *won't* let anything happen.

***

The incessant knocking at the door confuses me. Nobody I know is coming over, not until we go to meet Trey at the fair later on. Ry managed to talk me into staying for now, saying that it was good for Maya to spend the rest of the week here. I backed down, knowing that she was excited for the fair. I don't want to take that from her. Ry has been staying with us since Friday, probably to make sure that I don't start packing, or do anything drastic, and he won't leave my side.

Thankfully, Maya bought my lie about being ill. It didn't take much, seeing that I look like crap thanks to dark circles under my eyes from lack of sleep.

Ry bouncing up and opening the door grabs my attention.

Just as I go to stand up from where I'm sitting with Maya on the floor, playing with her dolls, I freeze as I hear a familiar voice.

I slowly turn around, and before I get a chance to get a word in, Maya jumps to her feet screaming.

"Nanna! Grandpa!"

She flings herself into my father's waiting arms, and he plasters on a smile and listens to her as she tells him what she's been doing.

Since walking through the door, my mother's attention has been trained on me. I try to hold back tears as I see her face, so similar to my own, and the sorrow that's barely disguised there.

"Mum? W-what are you doing here?"

I see Ry standing in the hallway, looking smug. That's when it hits me. The sneaky ass called my parents.

"Well," my mother replies as she comes to sit beside me so she isn't overheard by a certain young lady who is currently being entertained by my dad, "your father and I got quite an interesting call from Ryan the other day, saying that you are hell-bent on moving away again. He said he was worried and that he couldn't convince you otherwise. So we left and made our way over as soon as possible. Want to let me know what all this is about?"

I glare at Ryan. I thought he was satisfied enough with me staying until the end of the week. That was the deal, not him calling my parents because he was worried. He knows that getting my parents involved would give me no choice but to stay—my mother and father are the most stubborn people on the planet. Wonder where I get it from?

I look over at Maya, who's now sitting in my father's lap, content. It's nice to see, as we only get to see them a couple of times a year. My dad turns and addresses Ry.

"Son, would you mind taking Maya upstairs or something so I can speak to Evelyn please?"

Ryan instantly coaxes Maya upstairs with the promise of them having a makeover.

I wince at the use of my full name, knowing it's because he's annoyed. He's only ever called me Evelyn a handful of times in my life. He was the first person to call me Evie and would only use my proper name when he was angry at me.

"Sit."

He nods his head to the armchair across from him, while my mother sits beside him. The last time we sat like this was when he decided to give me "the talk" and scarred me for life in the process.

"Why is it that because a couple of goons appear at your shop you've suddenly decided to leave? Worrying Ry to the point that he's called us and asked us if we can try and knock some sense into you?"

I sigh, shifting uncomfortably at his disappointed tone. I keep quiet, knowing that he hasn't finished.

"And why is it that you've *finally* found a guy?"

I open my mouth in protest, but my father speaks over me.

"We know all about it. Ry has filled us in. I would like to meet this guy. Anyway, back to the point. You're suddenly all for moving away, because of some asshole that has been put in prison. He can't hurt you; you need to understand that. I know you're scared, but you cannot act like this at the smallest thing that has got to do with *him*."

"I know he can't hurt me; it isn't *me* that I'm bothered about. I've got Maya to care for. He doesn't know about her, and I want to keep it that way. Everyone is just going about and assuming that it's because of me that I'm doing this, but it isn't. I know he's in prison, I know he can't get to me. But last night was just an insight into *who* he has on his side, and *who* he can get involved to make my life hell. Especially since he now knows what town I'm living in. What am I meant to do? Just stay here and wait for him to inevitably send more people? Leaving is the safest option; it protects Maya."

I take deep breaths, trying to calm myself, not wanting to shout and cause Maya to panic. For all she knows my parents have come to surprise her for Easter.

"You won't be doing anything." My mother's harsh tone cuts through the air. "You're comfortable here, Maya is comfortable. You aren't uprooting your life for some lowlife."

I can see why they don't want me to move, but it feels like they just don't understand. I need to be able to feel protected, feel safe in letting Maya grow up in an environment where she doesn't have to be worried that something could happen to her. Why can't they see that I'm doing it for *her* sake, not mine?

"You have no option in this. Your father and I are staying for a couple of days. We don't know how long yet. We just need to make sure that you get this nonsensical idea of moving out of your head and see that you don't make any drastic decisions. We want to spend time with you and Maya, but you will *not* be leaving—*end of.*"

"You won't even let me have a choice in this matter? This is *my* life."

My mother gives me a disproving stare, letting me know that this conversation is over. People always think my mother is the soft one and that my father is the stern one. But in reality, it's quite the opposite; my father would let me get away with murder as a child, and it would be my mum that would discipline me. I know when she gives me *that* look she means business.

I may be nearly thirty, but there are some battles that I know I need to fight at a later time.

The sound of feet pounding down the stairs and Maya squealing causes us all to relax, and a large smile spreads over my parents' faces.

"Stop, Ry! Nanna, Uncle Ry keeps chasing me."

Maya looks up at my mother and sticks her bottom lip out in a pout.

Mum laughs as she sees Ryan standing there with children's makeup on his face.

"Is that lipstick on your eyes, Ry?" she says as she squints at him.

"Yes, Mrs Smith, Maya said that that's what it was for, and I won't disagree with the professional over there."

"What have I said about calling me that? It makes me feel old. Call me Louise."

"Sorry, Mrs—Louise." Ry gives her a sheepish grin then turns towards me. "You really need to get ready; the fair starts in an hour."

I turn to look at the time and groan.

"Okay, I'll run up and get ready. Ry, can you make sure the cupcakes are in the box for Mrs. Carter's stand, please?"

Before he has a chance to reply, I'm running up the stairs to get changed.

***

Trailing behind my parents who are on either side of Maya I hear my phone chime. It's a text from Trey.

>I'm standing by the candyfloss stand.

>Ok, I'm not far.

Just as I put my phone away, we round the corner to the candyfloss stand. Before I have a chance to warn my parents, Maya screams his name and makes a run for him. Just as she reaches him, he crouches down and swoops her up in his arms while chuckling.

"Why, hello little lady."

As soon as I hear his voice, I make my way around my parents.

The sight of him takes my breath away. With his dark blue jeans and a grey short-sleeved t-shirt on, he looks extremely handsome. I find myself subconsciously walking faster to get closer to him, but then I suddenly realise that I don't know how to approach him after our date. Do I stay a pleasant distance away? Walk up and kiss him? Or do I just act like nothing happened?

Without giving me a chance to make my mind up, he loops his free arm around my waist and gives me a quick peck on the lips.

I feel butterflies swirl in my stomach at the innocence of it.

I've never been for public displays of affection, I've always found them to be quite tacky, but yet there's a sweetness to what he just did.

I hear Maya giggle and watch as she scrunches up her nose.

My father obnoxiously clearing his throat brings me back to reality, reminding why they're here. I try and keep the sorrow that I feel off my face.

I turn and see a large smile on my mum's face, while Ry is whispering god knows what in her ear. My dad on the other hand is looking at Trey with a look on his face that I can't just place. He doesn't look concerned, more thoughtful.

Before I can make the introductions, Maya speaks up.

"Nanna, Grandpa, this is Trey. He's really nice and plays colouring with me, he's also took Mummy out."

"Does he play with you, sweet pea? That sounds fun."

My mum steps in, looking at my father's face as she does so, knowing that he wants to say something. Smiling, I step into Trey a little, relishing in the heat that is radiating from his body. I feel my body instantly relax from the events that have happened today. For the first time since our date, I feel content.

Chapter Ten

Trey

I wasn't expecting to meet Evie's parents when she invited me to the fair, but I try to keep the shock from registering outwardly.

Her father shakes my hand and introduces himself as Robert, before introducing me to his wife, Louise. He seems friendly, if a little over-protective.

Her mother smiles widely at me as she shakes my hand. I can see where Evie gets her looks from. Her mother was probably quite a striking looking woman in her heyday. She's still striking enough now, for an older woman. She and Robert make quite the handsome couple, and it makes my heart pang in my chest as I think of what my own parents might have been like.

I don't even have any family photos, nor do I know why Leah and I ended up growing up in care. I don't have any possessions from that time in my life except for Rabbit, Leah's childhood best furry friend, who now resides in my study with an eye missing and his stuffing a little flat.

Ryan greets me with a clap on the back and a "Hey, gorgeous." He's got such a cheeky side to him. It's why I think he and Joe would make quite the couple.

Speak of the devil. Joe walks around the candyfloss stand just as Maya is putting her first handful of pink sugariness in her mouth.

I didn't tell Evie that I was bringing Joe in case she told Ryan. I know this was meant to be a date, but that he'd be coming along to keep Maya occupied on the rides. Evie told me she isn't really one for the waltzers, whereas Ryan would go on them multiple times in a row. And it would seem Maya is exactly the same.

"What's up?" Joe greets as he comes to join our group.

"Hey, man," I reply and make quick introductions to everyone.

Joe's eyes seem to twinkle as he looks at Ryan and his body language subtly changes. I look between the two of them and am sure the sparks of electricity between the two are visible. I can only imagine that if they touched, they'd set each other on fire.

"Mummy, can I go on the waltzers with Uncle Ry now, please? You said I could if I was good. And I've been good, haven't I?"

The sweet little girl eating candyfloss in my arms looks to her mum for confirmation.

"Yes, you've been good, sweetie. But it's up to Uncle Ry. I'm sure if you ask him really nicely, he'll take you."

Maya's head swivels in Ryan's direction and he beams a grin at her, which in turn makes Joe smile.

"Pleeeease, Uncle Ry," she asks, drawing the word out.

"Umm … lemme think about that one …" he tries to give her a serious face but fails.

"Come on then, darlin', let's go. One time though, okay? Maybe we can go on them again later."

Maya squeals as I put her on the floor, and she shoves her leftover candyfloss at Evie as she runs to be scooped up by her pseudo-uncle.

"Umm, manners, little miss," Evie says as she tries to give Maya a stern look of her own.

"Sowwy, Mummy. Please can you hold it for me?"

Her toothy grin makes Evie chuckle as she nods her head, just before Ryan turns to take her on the one ride that makes my stomach churn.

"Hey, Joe, why don't you go with them?" I suggest as I look at my best friend, catching him staring at Ryan's ass, the way he's half turned away.

"Would that be okay with you, Maya?" Joe asks.

She gives him a nod and Ryan smiles a smug kind of smile at Joe.

The three of them head towards the ride, which leaves me with Evie and her parents. I could cut the tension rolling off her father with a knife. His face says he's relaxed, but he must be a master of the poker face because his body language suggests otherwise.

"Shall we go and get hotdogs or wait until they come back?" Evie asks, oblivious to her father.

"I actually think I'd like a beer. How about you, Trey? Shall we go and grab drinks while the girls grab the food?" Robert asks in a friendly enough tone, but I understand the unspoken and know I have no say in the matter.

"Sure. I'll take a chilli dog with cheese, if you don't mind?" I ask as I hand Evie some cash.

"No problem. I'll take a white wine spritzer and so will my mum."

I nod as I turn to walk away with Robert. He's already a few strides ahead of me and I'm sure glad they serve alcohol here. It's going to take a cold bottle of beer to swallow whatever it is Robert needs to get off his chest.

"So," he says, pausing ominously, "I hope you don't mind, Trey, but I'd like a talk with you about my daughter."

I hate it when people say "I hope you don't mind," because it means they're going to say or do something whether you mind or not.

"I don't mind, Mr Smith."

"Good, then let's talk."

We walk towards the beer tent, keeping stride with each other, trying to blend in with all the other fairgoers here.

"I am known to be pretty blunt, Trey, so I'll get right to the point."

I know what's coming next. I may not have had many real relationships, if any, but I know enough to make an educated guess he wants to talk about the nature of our relationship.

"Of course, Mr Smith."

I feel like an errant schoolboy who daren't use an adult's first name.

"Please, call me Robert. Mr Smith makes me feel so old," he says with a small smile. "I wanted to talk to you about your relationship with my daughter. I hope you'll understand that I appreciate honesty above all else and can sniff out a lie from a mile away."

"I wouldn't dream of lying, Robert. What exactly is it you'd like to know?"

"Everything there is *to* know."

I scrub a hand over my face as I sigh a little. I hadn't expected to be ambushed by Evie's dad today. I mean, it's not every day that you take a girl on one date—even though I didn't really take her further than her own bakery—and then meet their parents.

"Evie and I have only been on one date, Mr Smith." I pause as he gives me an awkward smile over accidentally making him feel old. "Sorry, Robert. Umm … I met Evie quite recently and we are just getting to know each other."

"But you know each other well enough to be on friendly terms with her best friend," he interjects.

"Yes. I met Ryan first, actually. It's him I have to thank for making introductions to your daughter. I'm known for my sweet tooth and first met the pair of them at *Queen of Tarts*. I have a lot of respect for Evie. She's a real sweetheart, and I know people can take advantage of a woman of such a disposition—" I gulp, feeling my mouth dry out. "I would never dream of doing that, I swear."

"Good to hear," he replies as we get to the beer tent and order our drinks.

After paying for our drinks, we start to walk towards a small picnic bench. Taking a seat opposite him, I look him square in the eye so he can see and feel the truth of my words.

"Okay, here goes. Umm … I don't normally date. I don't have much spare time. My work takes up a lot of my time," I say, glossing over my own past and reasons for not dating. He wanted honesty and he'll get it, but not about my past. Even Evie doesn't know anything like that yet, and I am damn sure her father won't be the person she hears it from.

"I am a solicitor and my cases can be pretty time-consuming. But meeting Evie has opened me up to the idea of dating. She's beautiful, funny, intelligent … but you know that already, of course."

"And what are your intentions going forward, may I ask?"

"Well, I'll be honest, I don't really know. Like I say, we've only had one date. But if I try and look to the future, I can picture Evie and Maya in it. I understand you may see it as unconventional to have met her daughter so early on, but actually I met Maya before I met her mum. She was hanging around with Ryan at the bakery over her Easter half-term and she asked me lots of questions and if I would sit and colour with her."

I pause and take a much-needed swig of my beer. At this rate, I'll need another in my hand before we head back.

"I don't really know where the future is headed, Robert. I'm not the kind of guy who usually plans these things out. I play it by ear and see if someone is really interested before settling down. I've never been married, and I don't have children of my own. I own my own home and am partner at my law firm." Goodness knows why I'm telling him all this, but I am. "I really like Evie. And Maya is such a sweetheart. I care about them both, even though I've only known them for a relatively short amount of time."

"Do you want to get married? To have children of your own?"

"Honestly, Robert, I don't know. I've never really thought about it much. I have only thought as far as that, if I met the right woman, then yes, I would marry her and would like to have children. I didn't have an easy childhood; I grew up in care. So I made a promise to my only real family, my little sister, Leah, that I wouldn't have children unless I was completely committed to someone. I wouldn't ever allow a child of mine to be in the same position I was."

Shit! I scrub a hand over my face and mentally chastise myself for letting that much information out. I only hope I can tell Evie about it before Robert does it for me.

"I'm sorry to hear that, Trey. No child deserves to bounce around in the care system. There are too many people that slip through the cracks. But you seem like you have a handle on life now. You're a solicitor; you have your head screwed on straight. And you're a straight shooter, much like me, so I appreciate the honesty."

"I care about Evie, Robert. I do. When I picture what the next few months or the next year might look like, Evie is in every picture. She's the one truly good thing in my life."

"That's good to hear, son," he says as he claps a hand on my shoulder and stands.

As we make our way back to the others, I have to ask something.

"Robert, I hope you don't mind, but I need to ask a small personal favour."

He stops walking and turns to look at me.

"I haven't told Evie about my past. It's something that hasn't come up yet. She's not asked about my family, and volunteering the information doesn't come naturally to me. I told you because you asked a question to which I promised to tell no lies. I'm not saying I'm lying to Evie," I hasten to add, "I just haven't been able to pluck up the courage to rake over a past that's as ugly as mine."

"I get that son, and I promise you, she won't hear it from me. You be good to my little girl, and you and I won't have any problems. I understand that you'll talk about these things with Evie in your own time; it isn't up to me to rush you. I'll be honest with you, son, she's had a tough past herself. It isn't my story to tell, but I'll say this; a man laid hands on my baby girl and I wish I'd cut every *fucking* finger off his *filthy* hands … one by one, very *fucking* slowly."

It takes a moment to digest what he said, and that he seems the type to not like foul language, yet he spat that word with such venom.

The fact that a man would raise his hands to a woman is something I find abhorrent. The hairs on the nape of my neck stand on end, and my blood simmers in my veins, as I think of some piece of shit laying a hand on Evie.

She's so precious. She's light to my dark. Soft to my hard. Loving to my … well, not unloving, but unwillingness to *show* love. My past is poisonous, and I'm scared that it'll leach into Evie's life and poison her view of the world. But by the sounds of it, she already knows a little poison of her own.

It cuts me to my soul to know a man abused such a wonderful woman as Evie. What did she ever do to deserve that kind of lowlife in her life? Absolutely nothing. No woman *deserves* such treatment, but Evie deserves it less than anyone I've ever known.

I can see why Evie hasn't told me anything herself yet, I'm not exactly her boyfriend, nor am I her confidant, and I know it's hard for people to open up about this kind of thing. I deal with it enough at work, and the ramifications of it, to know that it's so hard to trust. Trust is earned, not given. And I find myself wanting to earn Evie's trust even more now. I want her to know I would never, ever raise a hand to her.

What shocks me is, of all the women I've seen that have been abused, they all had this haunted look about them. But Evie doesn't. She doesn't look like a victim—god I hate that word—or a survivor. Right now, as I look at her in the distance, I see her through fresh eyes. She's a warrior. She hasn't let anyone bring her down.

Whoever this guy is, he'd better hope we never cross paths because I will do what her father didn't; I'll tear him limb from limb after removing his finger and toenails with rusty tweezers, then chopping off his fingers and toes slowly and individually. I'll chemically castrate him and feed him his own testicles. Shit, my thoughts got dark.

I look at Robert and see a silent understanding. He knows where my mind went to and why I've been standing here quietly seething.

Taking a couple of deep breaths, I steady my resolve. Shoulders back and head up, I look at Robert and see him smile in gratitude.

As I live and breathe, I swear that no harm will ever come to Evie at my hands or those of any other man. I would take a bullet for her. My heart knows that to be true.

***

Maya and the boys went on the waltzers three times in a row, even though Evie had said only once.

Joe and Ryan walk back to us with stupid grins plastered on their faces as they both hold hands with the little girl who's stolen a piece of my heart. They swing her to and fro between them, singing some silly song.

The smile on Evie's face as she watches them is beautiful, mesmerising. She's one proud mummy bear as she watches her gorgeous little girl. Their bond is really quite something to behold.

I didn't imagine dating anyone, much less a single mother. Not because there's anything wrong with *them*— it's *me*. I'm scared of poisoning the innocence of a child. My past haunts me, and I'm afraid of it rearing its ugly head.

But meeting Evie changed my mind somewhere along the way. I decided to risk my heart on something uncertain. It wasn't a conscious choice, the two girls just made their way under my skin and buried themselves deep.

Knowing what little I know about Evie's past, my heart aches for her. Her pure beauty on the inside was touched by something so ugly, but it hasn't made her go off the rails—something I've seen happen far too often in my line of work. She's a fighter. A mother. A warrior that touched the darkness and came out alive. If I wasn't already in awe of her, I damn well am now.

"Hey, little miss," I say as Maya runs over to where I'm standing with my arm around Evie's waist. "How was the ride?"

"Awesome. Uncle Ry and Joe squeezed me in the middle of them cos I'm so little."

"And you went on more than once," Evie chides in a gentle way, letting me know she's teasing.

"Sowwy, Mummy."

"Don't be sorry, sweetie. I'm glad you had fun."

"Are you ready for some food?" I ask as I lean down to scoop her up.

"Can I get a big hotdog?"

"Ooh, that depends … is your belly big enough to hold a big hotdog?"

I tickle her ribs and she laughs at me.

"Yes."

She nods emphatically, so we walk over to grab some food. My own chilli dog was gone the minute I got back to Evie, and honestly, I could probably eat three more.

I watch Ryan as he orders for him and Joe. They exchange heated glances as their hands brush against each other. Honestly, I like the idea of Ryan and Joe being together much more than the idea of him and his bunny-boiling ex-girlfriend. She was an apathetic, amoral sociopath. Okay, I'm no doctor, but that's my unofficial diagnosis.

Ryan is a much more easy-going, funny, kind, gentle guy. His nature is the polar opposite of Natalie.

Watching the pair of them sit at a picnic table, eating and undoubtedly flirting—I can't hear their words but I'm good at reading body language—I feel like the two of them could very much become a thing. I hope they do, because my best friend deserves the best man or woman to enter his world and sweep him off his feet.

Joe is kind, fun-loving, gentle and very loving. He's taught me so much over the years, even when he hasn't been trying. I don't know what I did to deserve such a friend, but I'm glad to have his friendship. It's the most solid bond in my life—or it was until I met a woman who refuses to be ignored, simply by being herself.

As we walk round the fair, letting the boys take Maya on a good many rides, the air is full of laughter. It's easy to see how much Mr and Mrs Smith love their daughter and granddaughter. A prime example would be Robert going on a ride with the two girls and then coming off looking green around the gills, but still smiling his way through it.

I've never had a day like this in my life. One with family, friends and strong bonds. It's something a lot of people take for granted, but not me. As I walk around, holding hands with Evie or slipping my arm around her slender waist, I take it all in. I breathe in the love and rich laughter floating around me. It's hard not to want it all. Love, family, happiness. Three things I never thought I'd find, but which seem to be finding me and filling the cracks in my paper heart.

***

Our day at the fair drew to a close with me winning a gigantic rainbow-coloured unicorn on the tin-can alley stall. Of course, I gave it to Maya and delighted in the bone-crushing hug she gave me as she peppered my face with kisses of thanks.

Once we got the girls back home, I asked Evie for a moment alone after she'd settled Maya in bed. I didn't get it until I'd read Maya a bedtime story. Evie had come downstairs with a book in her hands and a shy look on her face as she walked into the lounge and told me what Maya had asked for.

I read *Green Eggs and Ham* to Maya and she joined in on several of the lines, knowing them word for word. She giggled as I used my silly story-telling voice—something I didn't even know I possessed.

Then her sweet giggles finally changed to a soft snore as she lay under her Disney princess covers. If I'm right this time, it's Cinderella. I didn't ask because Maya wouldn't let me live it down if I got it wrong.

As I pad downstairs and into the living room, I see Evie curled up on the couch. Her eyes are closed, but they open the moment she hears my footsteps.

"Thank you."

"What for?"

"For reading to Maya. I tried, but she begged for you."

"I really don't mind. She's a great kid. That unicorn is a bit big for the bed though."

"Trust me, she'll sleep *on* it rather than next to it with the way she wriggles."

The sound of her laughter makes my heart beat faster.

"Would you like a coffee?" she asks almost shyly.

"I can't." I hate the look on her face as I decline, but I have a morning run with Joe planned and I am shattered. "I hate to say no, and normally I wouldn't, but Joe is a drill sergeant when it comes to our morning runs."

I stand toe to toe with Evie and slip my arms around her waist. She snuggles into me and I feel a smile take residence on my face, something that is happening far more often since meeting her.

"I would like to take you out tomorrow night though, if you'll let me."

"Really? That would be lovely. What did you have in mind?"

"Well, I've already kind of booked a table somewhere. I wasn't assuming," I rush to add. "More like hoping. So, dress as you wish, but they have a no trainer policy."

Looking down at her worn-in Converse, I smile. Evie looks up and her grey eyes mesmerise me. I lean down and kiss her gently. I go to pull away, but her arms wrap around the back of my neck and her tongue seeks entry to my mouth. Allowing her to deepen the kiss, I feel my cock begin to stir. She casts a spell on me that keeps me from doing anything except breathing her in, kissing her as if there isn't a tomorrow.

"Wow," I say as we part, both of us breathless.

The blush spreads across her skin and makes her look even more beautiful.

I once thought that too-much-makeup and airbrushed-model looking women were the most attractive. How wrong was I? The real beauty lies in the pure of heart, like Evie. She's incredibly beautiful inside and out. Her grey eyes look like beautiful grey diamonds. I've not seen many of those, but the ones I have are an exact replica of Evie's stunning gaze.

Her slender figure isn't stick thin, but there's nothing more attractive than a curvaceous woman. Creamy skin that smells of something uniquely Evie, an ample cleavage, an endearing shyness, these are all things I didn't know existed. But now I do, I know I don't want to let them go.

Unable to help myself, I lean in to steal one more breathtaking kiss.

"I really should get going. If I don't, I won't want to leave at all."

Chapter Eleven

Evie

I know I need to let him go, but the feel of his arms around me brings me a sense of comfort. We make our way through the house towards the front door, and he stops and turns to me before he walks out. I stand there and hold my breath, seeing the unasked question in his gaze.

"I don't know if you might feel this is too soon, Evie, so please just tell me if it is. I know we've only been on a couple of dates, but I feel there's a connection between us. And because of that, I want to make us exclusive. We don't have to put labels on it. We don't have to do anything you don't *want* to do. The last thing I want is to put pressure on you. But there's nobody else for me, Evie. I told you I don't date. That much is true, or should I say *was* true, until I met you. I want to do this, but only with *you*."

I feel my heart speed up at his question, at what he's saying. Some may say it's too soon, but I know what I want, and that's him. I answer as quickly as I can, not wanting to keep him waiting like I did for our date.

"Honestly? It may sound weird to others, but I don't think it's too soon." I take a deep breath, trying to calm the pounding in my chest. "I'd be happy to put a label on it, to acknowledge that I'm yours and you are mine. There is no pressure in this. I want the same as you—I want *you*."

I feel a huge weight being lifted off my shoulders as I finally voice what has been spinning through my head throughout today. The fair was a true eye-opener—the way he acted with my parents, and the way he acted with Maya, really brought forward my feelings for him. People say that a single mother always looks for a man to be the father for her child. But that's not the way *I* work. I would rather raise my daughter alone than get with a man just so she has a father in her life.

But just the way that Trey acts with Maya, when she isn't even his daughter, really shows me how much she needs a father figure in her life. Somebody to be there to protect her when I can't, or to be there for her in a way that a father can. Will that be Trey? Time will tell. But I know I'd like it to be. What I feel for him is something I haven't felt in a long time. Maybe ever.

"I need to get going," he says. "I'll see you tomorrow for our date."

I stand on my tiptoes and give him a soft, yet sensual, kiss that sends tingles through my body.

"Goodnight. Get home safely."

As I close the door behind him, I hear him pause. Only after I've locked the door do I hear him retreat to his car. Just that small gesture makes heart melt slightly.

I go through the house, turning lights off as I go, and quietly make my way up the stairs. I try to tiptoe past the room my parents are asleep in, knowing that there's a particular floorboard that creaks just outside their door. I peek through the crack in the door of Maya's room, and I try to contain a laugh as I see her sprawled all over the unicorn that Trey gave her. After making sure that she's okay and placing the blanket back over her, I finally make my way into my room.

I plonk myself onto the bed and go over today's events in my head. It's been an emotional rollercoaster, with my parents appearing and then Trey asking to be exclusive. I realise I've fallen in love with this dysfunctional family of mine, and I really need to think about what I want to do about Greg. I don't want to make a snap decision too quickly. I make a mental note to speak to Ry about it all tomorrow before drifting into the most blissful sleep I've had in months.

***

I'm scrubbing the kitchen floor when the sound of Ry walking through the door startles me. I look up just in time to see him walk into the kitchen, arms laden with bags as usual.

"I brought the extra cleaning supplies that you needed, but I also brought snacks."

"Do you mind? Take your shoes off and get your mucky feet off my clean floor," I say with a teasing smile.

He has an evil grin as he pulls out an assortment of chocolate and crisps. I chuckle at his constant need for sweet things. If I'm not baking, he's always buying sweet stuff from the shops—his cupboards are quite impressive. He eats healthily and limits himself to how many sweets he can have, but he finds a way to sneak extra in.

Taking advantage of my parents taking Maya out for the day—they wanted to go the cinema and out for a meal as they haven't seen her in a couple of months—I've deep cleaned both of our rooms, placing a lot of Maya's unused toys in a charity bag in the process. I've cleaned the living room, and now I'm onto the kitchen.

I was unprepared, to say the least, so I asked Ryan to get some more cleaning supplies for me. Thankfully, he was coming over anyway. However, let's just say I'm not looking forward to the real reason why he's here. I know he wants to talk to me about my meltdown the other day, but to be honest, I've just pushed it to the back of my mind, trying my damned hardest to forget about it.

"Where'd you go, gorgeous?"

I blink back the haze that has taken over my thoughts and look over at Ry, who has a concerned look on his face.

"Honestly?" I wait for his nod. "I've just been thinking about the events that have occurred over the last few days."

"I know it's been hard, but keeping it to yourself is not going to solve any problems. You need to talk about it, voice what's been going on in that pretty little head of yours. I'm here for you to scream, cry, rant. I don't care *how* you need to voice it, I'm here for you through all of it—the good, the bad and the dirty."

I chuckle at his small reference to one of his favourite bands, Panic! At the Disco. He listens to them so much that he often says part of their songs during a sentence and doesn't realise.

I sit there silently for a couple of seconds, trying to sort through the mush that has become my brain over the last couple of days. I'm usually able to keep my thoughts pretty controlled; I'd like to think that they're in neat little folders with little tabs labelling each one, like in a filing cabinet. But lately they've just scrambled all into one, and I haven't been able to distinguish one thought from another.

"I just … umm … it's hard, you know? Like, Trey asked me last night if we could become exclusive and—"

"Hold up! Back up right there. Trey asked you what?"

I look up and giggle at the over-enthusiastic expression on his face. It reminds me slightly of Maya when she was on a sugar high from eating all that candyfloss at the fair yesterday.

"Yeah … He asked me after he read Maya *Green Eggs and Ham*. It was sweet. He told me that he doesn't do things like this, but he wants it to do with me. I obviously said yes. He's the first person I've wanted to take interest in since Greg, and above all, he makes me feel something." I look up and see Ry grinning wider than I thought was possible. "Oh my god, I bet I sound like a blushing school girl." I groan and shake my head.

"You sound like you've finally found somebody who is worth your time; you've finally got an interest in somebody. So you need to take it by the balls, both metaphorically and realistically." He waggles his eyebrows. "You should feel special. It's a huge moment and a step forward in your life. And *excuse me?* Maya asked for *Trey* to read *Green Eggs and Ham*? That's *our* bedtime story. I'm going to have to have words."

He pulls a fake mean face, and I giggle, knowing he's joking. I can see how happy he is that Maya has managed to come out of her shell, and how he's pulled me out of mine also.

"She wouldn't let me read it to her. It was weird letting somebody other than you do it. It was a happy weird, but weird, nonetheless. I just sat on the sofa and nearly fell asleep. It was nice, just getting to relax and let somebody else do something for a change."

I get up off the floor, having finished cleaning the spot I was on, and move to sit at the table opposite Ryan.

"See, you're taking baby steps," he says. "No offence, but you can be very controlling. It's not a bad thing, you'd be one hell of an organiser, but you're taking the steps forward to let yourself be open to change, and that's pretty damn amazing. You've closed yourself off for so long that it will be hard to let things like this happen; you just need to be open to it. Does this mean that you'll definitely be staying?"

I inwardly groan at the question. I knew it was going to be brought up sooner or later. Most would prefer it to be addressed sooner, but I'm happy with ignoring it for as long as humanly possible.

"I don't know. I've been trying to think about it. But it's hard. I can't exactly just pack up and leave, now, can I? I don't really think I thought it through fully." I think aloud. "What am I going to do? How could this work? I'm going to have to try and …"

I try and catch a breath as I feel the building anxiety travel throughout my body. I feel my chest constrict as I try and focus on the problems that have suddenly entered my mind. The pressure of Ry's hands that suddenly encase mine slowly makes my brain focus.

"You need to calm down, take a deep breath, and focus on one thing. Stop trying to come up with solutions to everything going through your brain at once. You need to try and solve the problems one at a time. So, tell me what comes to mind first. I want to help."

"I just—what do I do?" My voice cracks and I feel unshed tears brimming in my eyes.

"You need to follow your heart. Do you like Trey?"

I nod my head, too upset to talk.

"Then there's your answer. Why should you have to put *your* happiness last? Why do you put so much emphasis on what Greg *may* do? You've left that part of your life behind—you need to be able to move on, make a life for yourself. You can't continue living in the shadows of your past; you—like everyone—deserve to be loved and cherished. You can't continue your life like something bad is always going to happen.

You need to reflect in a positive state of mind. Thinking that your past is going to catch up to you isn't going to help you. Greg. Is. In. Prison," he says, punctuating each word individually. "How many times do we have to repeat that? He can't get to you. You are *safe*. What good is running away going to do? *Nothing*. Take it from me, I ran away and, yeah, it was under different circumstances, but it's relatively still in the same boat. You've found a place that you love, that you're comfortable in, and you've *finally* found somebody that you like. So, take it and go with it. Don't try and sabotage yourself."

Just the way that he explains it makes it seem so simple, so why do I think it's so complicated?

I sit and stew for a couple of minutes, trying to wrap my head around how I'm feeling and what's going through my brain. By the time I feel like I've got a check on my emotions and how I feel, I look up, and Ry is still sitting there patiently, occasionally sweeping his thumb over my hand.

"I feel like I don't deserve to be happy, to be *loved*. It's hard to come to terms with what happened, even all these years later. It was a traumatising experience, so why would I want to place that onto somebody else? I'm scared of being left behind because people don't want to deal with somebody who is as damaged as I am."

I watch Ry's eyes widen while he takes a deep breath.

"You are worthy of love, and you need to be open to it. You will *never* come to terms with what happened! It was horrific, and I'm disgusted that he's only in prison. He should be castrated, or worse. How could you be placing it onto somebody else? If that person loves you, it isn't a burden. They would be able to help you get through the dark times that you go through. You are *not* damaged. *Nobody* is perfect, but you're the closest thing to perfect of basically anyone I know. I just wish you would open your eyes and see that for yourself."

"I don't know what to do. I don't want to leave, that's why I'm so confused. But I *feel* like leaving is the best option. If Greg has managed to find out what town I'm living in, then what else can he do? How can I protect my family? That's why I feel like I need to leave. I want to protect the people that mean the most to me. So, to me, leaving is the best option, because, let's be honest, what else can I do?"

I feel a huge weight being lifted off my shoulders as I'm finally able to put into words how I've been feeling, what I've been thinking.

"Isn't there some form of restraining order you can take out against him? Do you already have one? I'm not big on legal things, but surely your dad, or even Trey would be able to help you with doing something like this? You need to be able to come to some conclusion where you don't have to leave. What would you do with this house? With *Queen of Tarts*? What did you expect to be able to do with it?"

"I never got a restraining order on him because he was practically placed straight into prison after the court case, so I didn't see the point in getting one. Stupid I know, but it never crossed my mind really. I should get one though, if that's what it takes to take the extra necessary steps to make sure that *I'm* safe, that *Maya* is safe. I would give everything to you. You're an amazing employee, so I would put *Queen of Tarts* in your name. It would become yours. I would sell this house or give it to you. I have it all thought out. I know roughly what I want—*wanted* to do with everything."

Ry instantly pulls back in shock at the thought of me giving him the bakery and the house. I don't think he's realised how much he means to me or what I would do for him after everything he's done for me.

"You have it *all* thought out, do you? That isn't thought out. You can't just give me *Queen of Tarts*. I have *no* idea about baking, about what to do in that aspect of the bakery. And—*news flash*—you need to be able to *bake* to be able to run a *bakery*. You obviously don't have *everything* thought out."

"I have what I *needed* to have thought out, thought out. Obviously moving isn't really the best option. I need to stay and think things through, talk about what's happened, along with the necessary steps that I can use to prevent him from getting near us. I hadn't thought about the baking aspect all that much, it was just an immediate instinct to leave. I'm sorry if I upset you with that; you didn't deserve to have to go through that with me."

Before I can prevent them, tears stream down my face at the thought of putting somebody who I view as family through that. In my selfish need to leave, I hadn't thought about how it would affect Ryan and what it would put him through.

At the sight of my tears, he stands up and moves to sit on the chair next to me. Pulling my body into his side, he squeezes me.

"There is no need to be sorry. You thought you had managed to get away from all of that, get away from Greg. You didn't expect somebody close to him to find you and rag you around like that. There is *no* need for *you* to feel sorry about how *I* feel. I understand the reason why; it was something that you couldn't wrap your head around, and your fight-or-flight instincts kicked into overdrive. You chose flight rather than staying to fight. You're scared, and you're trying to make sense of what has happened. I'll be here for you every step of the way. If you feel the need to leave, I will support that. I just want you to know that there are other options."

"Thank you, I can't tell you how much your support means to me. I *promise* that I won't do anything drastic. I'll think it all through before I make a decision. I'll speak to Dad about it and see what he says, okay?"

Ry nods his head, obviously happy with what I've said. He thinks I've turned a corner, and who knows? Maybe I have.

"How about we do something to cheer us up? Want to eat our weight in junk food and watch a movie while we wait for everyone to get back?"

A smile stretches over my face.

"You know just what I need to cheer me up when I'm down. What are we watching?"

***

The front door opens just as the credits for *The Conjuring* appear on the screen. In my opinion, modern horror films have become a joke. They literally think that having somebody walk around with a bloody face is scary. Ry and I find it hilarious, and we find ourselves watching bad horror films just to laugh at them. Thankfully, *The Conjuring* is the one horror film that I can watch over and over again. It isn't scary per se, but it's one of the best modern horror films that has been made.

Maya runs into the living room before my parents have made it through the hallway. My mum laughs at the empty wrappers spread all over the coffee table, and even the floor. When Ry said we should eat our body weight in junk food, he wasn't joking. Thankfully I had managed some restraint as I'm going on a date with Trey later.

"How was the movie, sweetheart? Did you enjoy it?"

Maya instantly jumps up and down on the balls of her feet in excitement.

"Oh! It was amazing, Mummy! Nanna and Grandpa even broughted me popcorn!"

Ry and I share a wide-eyed stare, acting up how excited we are for her.

"Wow! That's amazing, sweetheart! I'm glad you had fun."

She comes and gives me a hug before jumping on the sofa next to Ry to tell him in great detail what happened in the movie, asking my mum to chime in on occasion. I chuckle and grab all the wrappers to put them in the bin. As I get into the kitchen, I see my dad standing there with a cup of coffee in his hands and holding out another one for me.

"Thank you."

He stares at me for a second, his keen eyes taking in everything that I'm doing and how I'm acting.

"What's happened today? You seem less on edge, calmer than you were earlier. It's good, don't get me wrong, but you never get over something this quickly."

I take a deep breath and quickly fill him in on everything, taking more time to ask him about the restraining order. He didn't go into the police force, as he said he didn't want to follow in his father's footsteps, he wanted to make a life for himself in a different department. But my uncle has, and with my dad growing up in that environment, he knows quite a lot about the law.

"It would easily be a possibility, and it wouldn't take much as your case is already on file. So they wouldn't have any trouble figuring out how long the restraining order would be for, especially if you tell them about the recent events. You have a camera outside your shop, don't you?"

"Yeah, I installed it after you bugged me about it for a month."

Not long after I had bought the plot that is now *Queen of Tarts*, my dad spent an entire month sending me links to proper security measures to make sure I felt safe while working. After he'd bugged me about it for so long, I finally relented and ended up buying CCTV cameras that spanned around the entire store. I'm glad I did now. Just goes to show, it pays to listen to my father.

"Don't get mad at me, but I kind of did some digging," he says as he looks at me thoughtfully. "There's a local law firm that has a great reputation: McDonough, Kinsella and Lloyd. I think you should make an appointment with them and take it from there." He winces as he looks at me to gauge my reaction to his snooping. "I'm glad you decided to change your mind. It's for the best."

I smile at him, noticing how much more relaxed he seems since he found out about me not wanting to leave immediately. I know it will be hard not listening to my instincts, but somewhere, deep down, I knew it wouldn't be for the best.

Chapter Twelve

Trey

Showered and dressed ready for our date, I splash on some of my favourite aftershave and grab my car keys from the bowl by the front door.

I take a look in the hallway mirror and run my fingers through my hair. Kitted out in a pair of black suit trousers, my favourite dark grey shirt and black tie, I hope I look as good as I feel.

I have butterflies in my stomach—an unusual feeling for me—and my palms are a little clammy. It's okay to admit I'm nervous, I guess.

I told Evie I don't date. I really don't have much experience when it comes to relationships. Bobby was the last woman I was seeing, and that was a no-strings arrangement between two consenting adults—although I get the feeling Bobby would have liked it to have been more, judging by her turning up at my office and the subsequent phone calls and texts that I've kept ignoring. Or maybe she's still mad that I called out Evie's name during sex. She said she wasn't, but what women say and what they *mean* aren't always the same thing. I've learned that the hard way.

But with Evie, there's this easiness. She makes me want to be a better man, a man worthy of her trust, and maybe one day her love. *Love? Where did that come from?*

Evie is easy to get along with, down-to-earth, genuine … she's also a little sassy—which I rather like—and I can't quite explain why I'm so drawn to her.

Before Evie, I would never have considered dating, never mind dating a single mum. It's not about her being a single mum, it's about the fact that I'm not exactly Father of the Year material. But Evie isn't asking that of me. She isn't even asking me to try. She's not asking anything.

It's me. I'm asking her for commitment. I'm asking her to give this a try.

As I get in the car, I turn on some music. "Home" by Depeche Mode comes on, and I find myself singing along. It's rumoured to be a song about addiction, when Dave Gahan got sick and nearly broke the band apart. Something I can relate to on some level because of my sister Leah. She was an addict and she tore my world apart forever. She had so much left to live for. Why couldn't she see that?

I'll always punish myself for not seeing the signs sooner, for not helping her get clean, for not being there when she died. Maybe if I'd been there that day, I could have saved her.

***

"Leah, Leah, wake up! It's me, Trey. Can you hear me?"

I look at my sister's prone body. As I shake her, I notice the needle still piercing her skin. Fuck! Slipping my phone from my pocket, I shakily dial 999.

As I hang up, I try mouth-to-mouth and chest compressions. I can't feel a pulse, but it might be because I'm not doing it right. I don't know what I'm meant to do. I'm nineteen. Leah just turned eighteen. I've seen evidence of her drug use before, but I've never had to try and revive her.

I call her name repeatedly, as if that'll bring her back to me. But I know in my heart she's beyond saving. She's gone. She was probably dead for a while before I got here.

Her skin feels cold and her lips look cyanosed. My efforts are in vain.

The ambulance arrives, and I ask them to give her something. Maybe naloxone will bring her back, I think to myself.

When the paramedic tells me it's no use, I sit and sob. I cry for myself, for the loss of my beautiful sister, my only remaining family. But mostly I cry for her. For everything she could have had but will never get the chance now.

Was this my fault? Did I work too hard at school to pay attention to Leah? Was I blind to her struggle? I must have been.

I knew she took drugs. She knew I didn't like it. Knew I wanted her to get clean. But she said it helped her cope with the shitstorm that was her life. No matter how many times we talked about it, she would always make promises, only to break them a couple of hours later.

She was just a helpless kid, broken by the people who should have protected her. I took beatings for her, anything to make her abusers take less notice of her. I'd do stupid things to get into trouble, so they'd leave her alone, even if only for a little while.

But then, when I was old enough, I aged out of foster care and was studying law. I wanted to be able to lock monsters like them away. I would give anything to protect my sister, but now she's gone, and I only have myself to blame. I was too busy studying and busting my balls to get the qualifications I so desperately needed, that I didn't see my sister's pain.

She aged out of foster care the year after I did, and I wanted her to make something of her life now that she was free. I wanted her to do something with her life, make something of herself. But the siren song of cocaine and eventually heroin was too strong for her to resist. Promises of getting clean were swept away by her next hit.

The paramedics tell me that a doctor has to provide a death certificate. I guess it's up to me to arrange her funeral. Something I hoped I'd never have to do, but something I knew was inevitable.

There's nobody else to help me. We have no family. I guess the money for the funeral will come from the inheritance our grandparents left us when they passed away, but I couldn't give a fuck about the money. All I want is my sister back. I hate myself in this moment for breathing without her. I want to lie cold in the ground with her, so she isn't alone.

I drive myself slowly insane wondering whether she meant to die or was just after her next fix. Did she do this on purpose, or was it an unfortunate accident? She was the product of her circumstances, and I can't help but grieve for the life she lost. Maybe she's better off wherever she is now.

I don't believe in God, or Heaven, but I'd like to think she's somewhere, pain-free and happy at long last. Her body might be here, but her soul is elsewhere.

***

I don't notice the tears until I realise my cheeks are soaking wet. Leah was my responsibility, and I couldn't see a way of helping her. She couldn't see a light at the end of the tunnel, and whether the overdose that took her from this world was accidental or on purpose, I'll never know.

Shaking away the vivid memories of Leah, lost, alone and gone from this world, I pull myself back to the present. There's no point living in the past; my counsellor told me that.

After Leah died, and I'd arranged the small funeral, I sought the advice of a counsellor, Angela Davenport, and she told me that having one foot in the past and one in the present was no way to live. She said I had to let go of my guilt, that it wasn't my fault that Leah was trapped in an endless cycle that she couldn't break even if she said she wanted to.

Taking in a few deep breaths, I steady myself. My knuckles are white on the steering wheel, so I relax my grip slightly. This isn't the side of me I want to show Evie on a date.

I open the window for some fresh air and change my playlist for something more upbeat. "Say Amen" by Panic! At the Disco plays, and I can't help but sing along. It's a catchy tune.

Pulling up outside Evie's house, I turn off the music, so her neighbours don't make a noise complaint—I like my music loud—and grab the bouquet lying on the passenger seat. Making sure to grab the brand-new Harry Potter colouring book too, I get out of the car and walk towards the front door.

I see Maya peeking out of the window, the net curtain pulled aside so she can see me more clearly. Waving at her, I beam her a grin as she runs from the window, opens the front door and launches herself at me.

Careful not to crush her or the flowers, I hug her to me.

"Hey, little lady, how's my favourite girl today?"

"Mummy said I could stay up to say hello, but then I have to be a good girl and go to bed. Nanna and Grandpa are here. They look after me so you and Mummy can go out."

"Well, I'm glad I get to see you before you go to bed."

"Can you read my bedtime story?"

She looks up at me with pleading eyes, and I don't have the heart to say no.

"No, baby, he can't. Not tonight. We have to be somewhere," Evie says as she greets us at the door.

"Awww." Maya pouts at Evie and then at me.

"Sorry, sweetie, but we have to do what Mummy says. But I've got a present for you."

Her eyes light up as she looks at me with a huge grin.

"It's the new one, Mummy. The one I asked you for," Maya says as she takes the colouring book from me.

"Wow. Isn't that nice of Trey? What do we say?"

"Thank you, Trey."

"You're welcome, sweetie."

She hugs me hard before running to the lounge to show her new book to her grandparents.

"And these are for you," I add as I hand Evie the flowers.

"Oh Trey, they're beautiful. Thank you."

"You're most welcome." I slip an arm around her waist and drop a kiss on her head.

"They smell amazing, are they from Forget-Me-Not?"

"How did you know that?"

"Georgia just has this amazing way with flowers. I love looking at her window displays. I've never had anyone buy me flowers before, well, except my parents that is."

"Well, I thought a beautiful lady deserved beautiful flowers."

"You're so thoughtful," she observes, as she stands on tiptoe and slants her lips over mine.

I wrap my other arm around her, trying my hardest not to crush the flowers as I crush my lips to hers in a dizzying kiss. I lick the seam of her lips, silently pleading for entry to her mouth. She opens to me and lets me explore her mouth with my tongue. She tastes like strawberries with a hint of balsamic vinegar. She must have been testing flavours this afternoon.

My blood sings in my veins as she takes control of the kiss. Normally, I like to be in control, but I'll happily relinquish the reins if it gets me hard the way she's starting to now.

Breaking the kiss, I look into her eyes and see a haze of lust. My pulse slowly returns to normal before I speak.

"If we don't stop doing this, it'll be *hard* for me to do anything." I emphasise the word, so she knows what I mean.

Evie giggles, and damn if my heart doesn't soar at the sound of her melodic laughter. She slips her hand into mine and pulls me into the house.

"I'll just put these in water, and we can get going. Are you ready to tell me what we're doing?"

"I'll take those for you, darling," Louise interjects before I can answer. She takes the flowers from Evie and heads for the kitchen.

In the light of the hallway, I get to fully admire the way she's dressed tonight. She looks divine in a black lace, off-the-shoulder dress. It has a sweetheart neckline but is modest so her perky breasts are mostly covered. The dress has a nude-coloured layer underneath—I don't know enough about women's fashion to know what the word for it is—and the black lace makes up a floral type pattern.

She's paired it with a pair of red heels that lace up around her slender calves. So help me if the sight of her like this doesn't make my cock twitch almost as much as the kiss did.

"We'd better get going; we don't want to miss our reservation," I say when she catches me staring.

We say goodnight to her parents and Maya before walking to my car. I open her door and wait until she's settled to close it.

Her legs look like they go on for miles, and I can't help but wonder what they'd feel like wrapped around me. They look like they'd be silky smooth to the touch.

God help me, I want to bury myself between them, just to feel them wrapped around me. Tonight is going to be difficult if I can't get sex off the brain. But she does something to me that I haven't felt in a long time.

I didn't feel this for Bobby. She was just pure sex and nothing else. I didn't mean to use her, but she used me back just as much. Didn't she?

But the way I feel about Evie is undeniable. There's an electrical current passing through the air around me as I get in the car beside her. I can't breathe. The current is palpable. It's crushing my lungs, making it impossible to take a deep breath.

I open the window slightly to get some oxygen flowing around me. My cock is hard, and I need to think of something, *anything*, to get my mind out of the gutter. Sex with Evie wouldn't be just sex. It would be something otherworldly. I know that without even having experienced it.

We pull up outside the restaurant without me even knowing how we got here. I was so lost in thought that I don't remember even starting the engine.

"Le Petit Château?" Evie asks in surprise. "I've been dying to come here since it opened, but Ry won't eat French food. Thinks it's all frog's legs and snails."

We enjoy a delicious meal consisting of Coquille Saint Jacques, followed by Blanquette de Veau and finished off with a coffee and chocolate flavoured Religieuse, each course paired with a wine that goes best.

"Mmm … that makes me want to create my own rendition of a Religieuse," Evie says as she puts her cutlery down and dabs at her lips with her napkin.

"Do it! You could infuse all manner of flavours."

"I might, you know. But if I do, it won't beat that one, that's for sure. If you'll excuse me, I'm just going to nip to the ladies' room."

She stands, and I can't help but watch her ass sway as she walks.

Those legs really do go on for miles.

I pay our bill while she's gone and get them to box another Religieuse to take away.

When she comes back, her red lipstick looks refreshed and her pearly white smile is dazzling as I hand her the delicate box. She inhales the delicious aroma and links her arm through mine as we step out into the cool night air.

"Thank you for tonight, Trey."

"It was my pleasure. I must confess, it was Ryan that suggested this place. He said he couldn't handle escargot or frog's legs. I told him that's not all French cuisine is, but he wouldn't listen."

"Well, I'm glad we came. I've been dying to dine here since they opened last year."

"I'm glad I got to bring you here for the first time."

"The food was amazing. So was the wine. I know you didn't drink much of it, but trust me, it was fabulous."

I didn't drink much, knowing I was driving. But I loved the look on Evie's face as her taste buds experienced the flavour combinations in the wine. I must admit, the robust red served with our main meal was delicious.

Wrapping my arm around her as we walk to my car, I draw her in close.

As we get to the car and I open her door, she stops before getting in. Leaning up slightly, she claims my lips in a tender kiss. I don't have to beg for her to open her mouth; she does it on reflex. I taste hints of chocolate, coffee and wine, a delicious combination and a dangerous mix for my libido.

Our tongues dance together in a steady rhythm. Evie's whimpers are swallowed by me as I hungrily take all she has to give.

My cock twitches, and I can't help but moan. I push her against the car and press myself flush to her so she can feel what she does to me. Her breathy moan only spurs me on more as I grind my budding erection against her.

Evie's arms wrap around my neck, pulling me closer to her. I deepen the kiss as a groan reverberates through my chest. What is this woman doing to me? Whatever it is, I can't get enough!

Pulling away, I take in a deep breath in an effort to steady myself.

"Did I tell you look stunning tonight? I don't think I did."

The blush that colours her skin is visible under the light from the nearby lamppost.

"I think I got lost in my thoughts and didn't voice them," I add.

"Thank you. Ry helped me choose this dress on a recent shopping trip. He has a good eye for these things."

"He sure does. Remind me to thank him."

I hold the door open as she gets in and then closes it behind her. Walking around the back of the car, I discreetly try to make my erection less visible. I hope she doesn't catch me in the rear-view mirror.

I start the engine, but I don't pull out of the car park straightaway. I look at Evie. She looks demure, every inch the classy woman. Her legs distract me as I once again long for them to be wrapped around me.

"Can I be honest?" she asks quietly.

"Of course."

"I don't think I'm ready for this night to end yet. It feels good to be wrapped in our own little bubble."

"I was just thinking the same thing. But where can we go? Your house is out of bounds due to your parents and Maya—not that I don't think they're wonderful," I hasten to add before she can say anything. "I do think they're great. But I like having you to myself."

"I like it too." She pauses and her tongue darts out to wet her lips. "More than I thought possible," she confesses in a barely audible whisper.

"My place is empty …"

The suggestion hangs in the air for a moment, and it feels as if we're suspended in time before she answers.

"Take me there," she replies with a dark look in her eyes. Her pupils are dilated as she looks me up and down.

We both know what's on the table. We don't *have* to go there, but it's a possibility.

I pull out of the car park and make my way towards my house slowly, giving her a chance to change her mind.

When we pull up on my driveway, Evie looks up at my house, cloaked in darkness except for the security light.

"It's more impressive in the light of day," I say.

"I believe you. It's beautiful."

"Well, it's perfect for me, that's for sure. If a little empty feeling sometimes. It has a great size back garden and three bedrooms. The master has an en suite, but there's also a roomy bathroom with a claw foot tub and a shower in the corner." My mouth rambles on as my brain searches for something to shut me up.

I look at Evie, and she smiles a shy smile up at me.

"Sorry, I'm rambling. I don't normally prattle on so much."

"Don't worry. I think it's cute."

"Cute? Cute is for babies," I tease.

"Well, I can't exactly say your rambling is handsome, can I? But *you* certainly are."

I lean in and ghost a kiss across her lips, pulling back before she can respond.

I get out of the car, walk round and open Evie's door. I offer her my hand as she steps out and pull her against me as I shut the door and lock the car.

The scent of her perfume is intoxicating, and I admit I like being wrapped in this bubble as much as she does. With an arm around her waist, I guide her to the front door, where I end up fumbling with my key as I try to get it in the lock. My hand shakes as I feel a sudden pang of nerves.

Is what I want the same thing Evie wants? I don't want to pressure her, I already told her that, but I can't deny how attracted to her I am. And it runs deeper than attraction, or lust … it's something I daren't name for fear of rejection. My heart couldn't take it if Evie didn't feel the same way.

We're connected on some other level. It's not just physical. We haven't been intimate yet, so it can't be about that. I've done something with her I've never done before. I've connected with her based on emotions and real feelings, something I didn't know I possessed.

I open the door and flick the light switch, illuminating the hallway. Evie's eyes dart to the ornate mirror and then to the artwork on the opposite wall.

"Is that a SWAK original?" she asks, surprising me.

I didn't think many people knew the local artist. It's not like they ever appear in public. The artist could be a man or a woman. Nobody knows.

"You know the artist?"

"Yes. Well, I don't own any of the artwork; it's a bit pricey for me. But I'm an admirer. Ry took me to the pop-up gallery a few months back, held in a disused building."

"Really? How did I not see you there?"

"You were there?"

"Yes. I've been a long-time admirer of their work. Sealed with A Kiss—it's quite a sweet acronym if you think about it. And there's something in each picture that boasts of love. It's like the artist has cut open their veins and bled onto each canvas. It encompasses an abundance of love, joy, elation."

"You're a secret romantic."

"Not really. I've never really been in love. But you can't help but be drawn in by the emotions in the exquisite paintings."

"That's a shame," Evie says as she gives me a tender look.

"They say you can't miss what you never had," I reply simply.

"I thought I was in love once. Until it went horribly wrong."

I pull her to my chest and wrap my arms around her, not wanting to give her time to reflect on things in the past. Inhaling her sweet scent, I plant a kiss on her head before offering her a coffee or a glass of wine.

I pull a stemless wine glass from the kitchen cabinet, put it on the island and take a bottle of white wine out of the fridge.

"Is white okay? I don't seem to have any red in the house."

Evie nods, so I pour her a glass and grab a bottle of water for myself. Setting them down on the island, I pull a stool out for Evie to take a seat.

Pulling the stool out next to her, I sit and open my water. I don't know what to do with myself now we're here. I know what I *want* to do, but I suddenly feel nervous. Excess adrenaline pumps through my veins as I sit and watch Evie.

"This kitchen is gorgeous."

"Thanks. I like clean lines and feel the black, white and chrome go well together."

"They do."

Evie nervous entwines her hands in her lap as she looks at me. She bites her bottom lip into her mouth, and I can't help but want to bite it myself. Her glossy red lips and her stormy grey eyes are a dangerous combination.

Closing my eyes, I picture her lips wrapped around my cock. Her head bobs up and down as she sucks me hard and fast, soft and slow.

A groan escapes me before I can stop it.

"What's on your mind, Trey? Tell me what you're thinking."

"I—"

I look at her and take a deep breath, deciding to just be honest.

"I was thinking how much I want you."

"And what would you do with me?"

Her hooded gaze mesmerises me, and the words just come right out.

"I'd taste that wine on your lips. Delving my tongue inside your mouth, I would kiss you so thoroughly you wouldn't know which way is up."

I watch her squirm on her seat as the words tumble out.

"I'd unzip the back of that dress and let it pool to the floor. Then I'd step back and take in the glorious sight before me—you in just your underwear. I'd kiss a trail from your lips to your ear, then to your shoulder and the hollow of your throat … then I'd unclasp your bra and lick circles around your nipple before gently biting it and tugging on it as your hands grasp my hair and pull me closer."

There's a flush across her skin as she absorbs my words.

"I'd place gentle kisses between the valley of your breasts and down to your navel."

"Trey," she says breathily. "Stop."

I stop talking and wish my erection would go away. She told me to stop; she doesn't want what I want. *Fuck!* I know I'll be having visions of all those things and more later.

Evie's hands come up to cup my face and she leans in to kiss me tenderly.

"I meant stop talking. I didn't mean you couldn't show me what you want. All of those things you said and more."

Her voice is husky, turned on. I read the signals wrong. I don't need any more encouragement when she reaches her hand out and strokes my cock over my trousers.

My cock throbs, begging to be buried inside her.

Standing, I pull Evie to her feet and reach around her to unzip her dress. It pools to the kitchen tiles and I smile as I look from her feet, up her long, lean legs, to her perfect hips and curves in all the right places.

She's wearing black lace panties and a strapless matching bra. Fuck, if I thought I was turned on before, that didn't have anything on what I'm feeling now.

I lean in and claim her lips in a sweet kiss. She opens her mouth to me, inviting me to taste her the way she knows I need to.

Grabbing a handful of her long, dark hair, I pull it gently, exposing her neck to me. I kiss my way down the side of her neck and to the hollow of her throat. I feel the vibration of her low moan.

I take a step away from her and look at her as she stands before me in her underwear. She's beauty personified. A raw beauty that should be carved out of marble for all to admire. But no, she's mine. Nobody else gets to see this body but me.

Unclasping her bra, I discard it on the floor and lean down to gently circle her nipple with my tongue. My soft touch elicits another moan. The air is filled with electricity, like when you're caught in the middle of a thunderstorm. You can feel it pressing heavily on you. It makes me want to capture this moment forever.

I trail my hand down between her breasts and stop at the top of her panties as her breathing hitches. Biting down on her nipple, I pull it taut before moving to do the same to the other one. Then I dip my hand underneath the material of her panties, and I find her clit with my thumb, exerting a gentle pressure in a circular motion as Evie's back arches and she grabs my hair with both hands.

Sliding one finger between her folds, I wait for her to signal for me to stop, but she doesn't. I gently push one finger inside her and feel her clench around me.

Her breathy moans as I hook my finger to hit her G-spot spur me on. I move in and out of her in a steady rhythm.

"Trey," she moans as the air crackles around us.

I look up at her; she has her eyes closed and her head thrown back.

She whimpers at the loss of my touch as I move to pull her panties down. She steps out of them and stands before me in just those *fuck me* heels.

Squealing as I wrap my arms around her and lift her up, she giggles as I place her on the cool marble kitchen island. I stand between her legs, and she wraps them around me as she draws me closer for a kiss.

I kiss down the side of her neck and feel her skin break out in goosebumps in the wake of my lips. I make my way to the hollow of her throat and place a tender kiss there. Soft whimpers leave Evie's lips as I kiss between the valley of her breasts. Her breaths come more quickly as I make my way lower.

I tease her clit with my finger, making her whole body shudder. I need to be buried inside her; I groan at the mere thought of what she'd feel like wrapped around me.

Moving up her body, I take one taut nipple in my mouth as I gently slide my finger back inside her. Her back arches and her head drops back as I speed up my movements.

So many times, since meeting her, I've thought of doing this. But it's better in reality than any of my dreams. She's here, naked, wanting this just as much as me.

I slide another finger inside her and increase my tempo. Hitting her G-spot makes her moan long and loud into the night.

Fumbling, I manage to undo my trousers and try to push them down but fail spectacularly. Thankfully, Evie comes to the rescue and slides my trousers and boxers down, allowing my cock to spring free.

"Shit!" I curse as I realise I didn't prepare for this, and my only condoms are upstairs.

"What is it?" Evie asks breathlessly.

"The only condoms I have are upstairs."

"Then lead the way."

I don't want to move from where I am, but at the same time, I think of our first time being on the cold marble of the island. Not happening.

I move from between her legs and she hops off the island, taking my hand in hers.

As I lead the way to my room, neither one of us speaks. It's almost like we'll burst the bubble that envelops us.

As I push the door open, I'm suddenly glad I made the bed this morning. Not that she'll be looking at the state of my room, but still.

Evie sits on my bed as I grab the box from my bedside drawer. I pull out one foil wrapper and place it on the bed beside her. Leaning in to kiss her, I push her back slowly so that she's lying on my bed. I push her legs apart and position myself between them.

Kissing a trail up the inside of her thigh, I take my time in case she changes her mind.

"Trey, please … I-I need y-you," she pleads.

Without any more hesitation, I give her what she needs, my tongue buried inside her. Her back arches off my bed and her hands grasp at my hair.

"Oh, Trey … Oh god …"

I move my tongue up to her clit and suck it as she moans my name loudly. I slip my finger back inside her and she clenches around me once more.

Writhing under my touch, she lets go of my hair and grasps at the sheet beneath her. Pushing another finger inside her, I increase my pace.

"Trey … I-I'm … I'm … Oh goooood," she moans as I hit her G-spot over and over until she comes around my fingers.

"Shit, baby, that was hot."

I crawl up over her body and kiss her passionately, the taste of her still on my tongue.

"Make love to me, Trey, please. I need you so much."

Wasting no more time, I tear into the condom wrapper and sheath myself in it. Aligning myself with her, I push inside her, slowly.

She wraps her arms around me as I lean down to kiss her, and I push further inside until there's nowhere left to fill. I'm buried as deep inside her as I can be, and my god, it feels so much better than I could have imagined.

***

As I drive Evie home, she rests her hand on my thigh and keeps glancing at me adoringly. She's so beautiful, and I still can't believe she's mine. She let me make love to her, a first for me because it's usually just sex, nothing more than gratification.

After taking a shower, she'd come out wrapped in my towel, and I swear my heart grew in size as I looked at her. So gorgeous, and all mine.

We pull up outside the house, but neither of us moves, that bubble still intact.

Leaning over, Evie places her palm on my cheek and draws me in for a kiss. I rest my hand on her thigh and she squirms. Her tongue dances with mine in a sensual kiss as I slide my hand higher until it's underneath her dress.

"Trey," she moans huskily.

"Yes?"

She doesn't respond, instead claiming my lips with hers once more.

My hand slips higher until it's at the edge of her panties.

"Trey, anybody could see," she says, breaking our kiss.

"It's too dark."

"What about my parents? They could look out of the window."

I dip my hand underneath the lacy material and feel she's already wet. Fuck. I wish she'd been able to stay the night. I pull her closer with my free hand, slanting my lips over hers and swallowing her moans as she does nothing more to stop me.

As I push my finger inside her, she clenches around me and squirms in her seat. My body aches deliciously from earlier, no doubt hers does too, but I want her again, so badly. But there's nothing I can do about that now.

Her hand dips below the jogging bottoms I threw on to drive her home. I'm not wearing any boxers, so her hand immediately comes into contact with my cock. It stiffens under her firm touch.

Moaning, I up my pace as I touch her intimately, here in the darkness of my car, where anybody could walk past and see. But I'm beyond caring when she pulls my cock from my boxers and begins to stroke up and down. Her grip is firm, and her hand moves in time with my finger.

I slide a second finger inside her, and she groans as I build the perfect rhythm. She matches my pace, and soon we are both moaning, our kisses less synchronised because neither of us can concentrate.

"Oh god, Trey … Ohhh fuck …"

"It's okay baby, let go. Come for me. Let yourself come undone."

I nibble at her collarbone as I hit her G-spot over and over. Her hand still works me over and I'm close to the edge. Too close.

"Evie … fuck, Evie … ohhh shit … fuuuuuck," I moan as I fall off the edge of the world.

Her hand comes to mine and increases the pressure. She's teetering on the edge, and I know what will take her over.

I lean down and push her dress down on one side with my free hand. I waste no time as I bite down gently on her nipple. I pull with my teeth, knowing the pleasure/pain theory isn't just a theory.

Evie's hand comes to the back of my head, encouraging me closer, so I bite her harder and rub her clit with my thumb. She pushes my hand away and plays with her own clit, so I use my fingers to fuck her as hard and as fast as my cock pumped in and out of her earlier.

"Ohhhh Trey, please, ohhhh," she moans.

I bite harder and add another finger as I pump in and out of her. Her legs tremble as the pace becomes too much for her to hold back any longer.

I quickly move up to kiss her and swallow her moans as she reaches her sweet climax. With the unmistakable scent of sex in the air, I kiss her harder. I bite her bottom lip like I promised before pulling my fingers up and sucking her essence from them.

Making love to her earlier had been sensational, but this euphoric feeling from the fact we could have been caught but weren't—that's a dangerously heady feeling.

***

Waking suddenly, I find my bed empty, but my mind is full. Full of images of what I wish had happened when I dropped Evie home.

In reality, I'd dropped her off, walked her to her door and bid her goodnight before retreating to the car and heading home.

I decide to quickly jump in the shower to wake myself up properly for a full day at the office.

Chapter Thirteen

Evie

I wake up in one of the best moods I've been in for a while. I jump out of bed and walk over to my wardrobe to choose my outfit for the day. Knowing I'll be going to the law firm later on, I choose something smart and business-like: a black knee-length pencil skirt paired with a bright red blouse, with matching strapless red heels. As an afterthought, I also quickly grab a black suit jacket. I'll just leave it in my car until I get to the firm. I want to be formal for my appointment later, but comfortable while I'm at the bakery. Maybe I should grab some flat shoes for work while I'm at it, so my feet aren't aching by the time I get to the end of the day.

I put on a thin layer of makeup, only using concealer, bronzer, blusher and mascara. I put what I've used into my bag along with some powder in case I need to touch up before going to the law firm that my father recommended. Thankfully, he'll be coming over before I leave. He said it's to make sure I go there and that, when I do, I'm prepared. But I know that he'll leave with at least a couple cupcakes and will sit and eat his favourites in the car, otherwise Maya will run off with them.

If I hadn't had an order in from family for my cousin's son's first birthday, I wouldn't have come in today. I usually don't do birthday cakes, otherwise I would be doing them left, right, and centre in this town, but I make the odd exception, especially for someone I view as family. He and his wife wanted a smash cake so they could take some photos of their son with it, along with a sheet cake for everyone else to eat as they didn't want people to have to eat a cake with their child's spit on it. I couldn't refuse, as it reminded me of Maya's first birthday when I had done a similar thing, and seeing that I'll be there, it would be rude not to.

Thankfully, I only need to do the actual baking and assembly portion today as the party isn't until the weekend, and with the amount of people that will be there, they want to be safe and have just requested a chocolate cake with ganache, so that's simple enough.

As I pull into the parking lot, I see Ry standing at the till serving customers. I manage to run into the back without getting cornered for every detail of our date last night. Since we started dating, Ry has decided to live vicariously through me date-wise, wanting to know every single detail he can squeeze out of me. I'm hoping that he won't need to anymore, especially since he went out with Joe last night. I've decided that I'm going to get a little bit of my own payback of sorts. I'm going to question him within an inch of his life about that date of his.

I pull on an apron and decide to get the baking portion out the way, as the cakes will need to cook and cool before I can assemble them and place them in the fridge until I can start the decorating process on Friday.

I make quick work of making the batter and placing them in the preheated oven. While I'm waiting for them to bake, I decide to try and make my rendition of the Religieuse we had at *Le Petit Château* last night. Since eating it, I've been wondering how I can make it into something different, but still pay homage to the original creation.

I decide to connect my iPhone to the speakers that are in the corner of the room. As I put my playlist on shuffle, Aerosmith's "Dream On" blares through the speakers. I'm glad that I had soundproofing put on the wall that is adjacent to the restaurant portion; I can blare my music as loud as I want, and it won't disrupt the customers.

I've never been one for keeping to one genre. I have an eclectic taste in music and will listen to anything from Lady Antebellum to AC/DC. I do, however, go through stages of what I want to listen to, and lately I've been stuck in eighties through early two-thousands, with the odd relevant or older song mixed throughout, "Dream On" being one of my favourite golden oldies.

My mother constantly heckles me about my music taste, as she can't understand how somebody can love anything and everything. But to me it isn't the genre of the song that makes me like it or not; if I can relate to it or I like it, I'll listen to it. That's the beauty of music and art; it's subjective, and there's something for everybody.

While I'm making the Crème Pâtissière, I get lost in the music and don't notice Ry coming into the back until the smell of coffee hits me.

Before I can turn around and look at him, he snakes his arms around my waist, picking me up and spinning me around. When he lets me down, I turn and see an ear-splitting grin etched onto his face. I laugh—his happiness is infectious.

"What's put you in such a good mood? Was it the great date last night, or more?"

I waggle my eyebrows at him, giggling as I swat his hand away from the mocha flavoured Crème Pâtissière.

"Well … we went on that date last night, and it was … it was just amazing. I can't explain it, darlin', it was just great. I'm in Trey's debt for introducing us."

As he's talking, he jumps onto a seat and gets a dreamy look in his eyes. It's cute on him, but I hope that isn't what I look like when I talk about Trey. I cringe at the thought.

However, seeing my best friend this happy makes my heart explode with joy. I know he's had a hard time finding somebody that he likes, and him finding somebody that won't judge him brings me immense happiness.

"I'm so happy for you, Ry! I'm glad that you've found somebody."

I beam up at him as I drink my coffee, my smile nearly matching his. He does a little happy dance and then his eyes go serious.

"So how was your date? Your mum said that you didn't get back until late last night and you seemed on cloud nine. Even today, there's something different about you." He thinks for a moment. "Not confidence, but like you feel more assured. What happened?"

A small smile stretches itself across my face. I want to tell Ry what happened, but I feel I shouldn't. I know he won't go around telling anybody, but I like something being kept between me and Trey.

"Something totally did happen, didn't it?! You little minx. How was it? And you can't deny it; your little smile totally gave you away."

I groan, knowing that he won't give up until I tell him what he wants, and he will persist for the rest of the day if he has to.

"I hate that you can read me so easily. Not much happened. I mean, we had sex—"

I'm cut off before I can finish my sentence.

"You what!"

I wince at how loud he shouts. I quickly turn and look through the window to see if anybody heard him. Thankfully, I don't believe anyone did. I turn and look over at him.

"Can you say that any louder? We've got customers, and I don't want the entire town knowing within a matter of minutes. It isn't *that* big of a deal anyway."

I shrug my shoulders, trying to act nonchalant about the entire thing, when inside, I know how much it means to me to take that leap in a relationship.

"I-it isn't that big of a deal, huh?" he sputters at me, open-mouthed. "It's been—what?—six, maybe seven years since you've done *anything* of that sort with *anybody*. He must mean a lot to you. So don't try and act like it was nothing. It was *everything* and you know it."

He shakes his head at me, easily seeing past the wall I tried to build up. I groan.

"Okay, it did mean *something*, okay? Does that make you happy?" He nods his head eagerly. "It made me feel something, like I was being wanted again. It made me feel like I was *worthy*. What I'm worthy of, I don't know yet. But it was like something was just set aflame inside of me. He brought something out of me with his touch, his kiss, his gentleness; he made me feel *alive*. I want to explore that. I want to try and discover what this is. I've never felt anything like this before, not with *anyone*."

The thought of that scares me, but I know that I need to welcome it. Because if I wasn't scared, I know that this wouldn't be worth delving into. Something good always comes out of being a little bit scared. It shows you that you're going out of your comfort zone, pushing past your self-imposed boundaries, testing the limits and finding you're capable of more than you think. This may be a leap out of my comfort zone, but I'm hoping—no, I *know*—that something good will come out of it in the end.

Ryan's voice pulls me out of my thoughts.

"It does make me happy. You want to know why? Because I can see that you're happy, and *that* is what is important to me. I have *never* seen you like this before. In all the years I have known you, you haven't given a man a second glance, let alone get into his bed. And no, I'm not saying that you need a man to make you happy. You're very independent, and I know it will be challenging for you to be able to fully open up to him about your past, for you to fully let him in. But it's the fact that you've found somebody who you deem worthy enough to actually let them into this little cocoon you've constructed around yourself."

I smile and sniffle, trying to ignore the sting of unshed tears. When I look up at him, I see Ry's once happy face start to drop. Not wanting today to be a day of contemplation, I decide to continue grilling him about his date. I want to keep that glow he had on him when he first walked through those doors.

Once Ry leaves to go and deal with customers, I continue my rendition of the Religieuse. As I'm making the choux pastry, I let my mind wander.

***

One moment, I'm looking at the flash cards that are meant to help me prepare for my culinary exam later today, and the next, I feel myself slam into a rock-hard chest. All the air expels out of my lungs and I land in a lump on the floor. I take long and slow deep breaths, trying to get as much air back into my lungs as possible.

"Oh, my god, I am so so so sorry. I should have totally been looking at where I was going."

I look up, locking eyes with the man I had accidentally slammed into. He gives me a tentative smile and lowers a hand down to help me up. I reach up and clasp my hand in his and instantly notice how much larger his calloused hand is compared to mine. His larger frame captivates me; everyone at the university is scrawny and not attractive in the slightest, but his dark brown eyes and dark brown hair makes him stand out from the crowd. He has a slight mysterious attraction going on, and it instantly captivates me.

"No, honestly, it's fine. I should have been looking also. I didn't mean to walk into a beautiful woman like you. I'm, umm, Greg, by the way"

His eyes pierce into mine as his thumb swipes over my hand. I glance down, finding his stare too intense.

"I'm Evelyn. Nice to meet you. That isn't the way I usually like to meet people though." I look at my watch and notice the time. "Well … umm … I need to get going. Got an exam and all that."

I awkwardly point behind him at the university building. He smiles at my obvious awkwardness.

"That's fine, on one condition. I know it's soon, but I just want to know if I have a chance. Will you go out on a date with me tonight?"

I immediately go to give him my normal answer, but the hope in his eyes makes me pause. I know I won't hear the last of it from my roommate if I say no, so I decide to do the one thing I never do. I say yes.

***

Tears stream down my face as I remember the first time I ever met Greg. If I had just been watching where I was walking, I wouldn't have felt bad for walking into him, then I wouldn't have agreed to that date. That spiral of actions was effectively the start of what ruined my life. Ryan argues that he purposefully walked into me to get what he wanted—*me*.

I try and control the sobs coursing through my body. I have tried to repress that memory for years now. It may not be the worst memory I have of him, in fact it's probably the tamest, but now it scares me the most.

Whenever it manages to creep back into my mind, it seems to remind me of every reason not to fall in love again. It reminds me that people aren't what they actually seem to be, that everyone carries a secret they don't want to be discovered. And I know I'm contradicting myself, because I have a secret that I'd like to be kept to as little people as possible, but I'm slowly starting to heal and acknowledge fully what happened.

I know I will never be able to fully come back from those dark times, that they may stay with me until I die—as the actions of our past can dictate those of the future—but I'm taking the steps I need to take to change how I view things, and I'm gaining the courage to change my life. Starting with what I have with Trey. I am done with letting somebody else who is in my past control my life when I am *happy*. I laugh to myself. I *am* happy, and I'm *not* letting some guy who is behind bars, eating disgusting meals and getting a tattoo from a psycho with an infected needle, ruin my life when I have finally found somebody who could be it to me.

I turn and go into the booth on the side of the decorating room. I splash some water on my face and look in the mirror. Thanking myself for only ever wearing waterproof mascara, I make sure my face looks presentable before going back into the decorating room.

I see my father sitting on one of the stools already, with a chocolate and honeycomb cupcake in his hands. He gives me a sheepish smile when I get closer, and I chuckle at him. Whenever he comes to visit, the first thing he usually does is eat as many cupcakes as he can.

"Hey, sweetheart. You okay?" he asks as he eyes me wearily.

This time I don't have to plaster a fake smile on my face like I usually do. My smile just comes naturally, and I see him visibly relax.

"Hi, Dad. Yeah, I'm good. You alright?"

He nods his head, not wanting to talk with his mouth full of cake. After he's finished, he starts asking me questions.

"Have you got everything you need for the law firm later? A statement from Trey when he was here? CCTV footage saved on a disc?"

"A disc? How old are you, sixty?" I stick my tongue out at him. "I've got it on a memory stick. I forgot to ask Trey for a statement, but I'll text him and ask him later."

I giggle at his old way of thinking and his lack of knowledge with today's ways. I make my way back to the choux pastry, checking that it's cooled so I can place it in the oven.

"Discs are more reliable. Nearly every time I've used a USB it's wiped itself." He shakes his head at me in disgust.

"Oh, sorry for upsetting your delicate feelings. Has Maya been good today? It's been weird not having her here with me."

Every holiday, I always have Maya in the bakery with me. It's only on rare occasions when my parents are here that she isn't. Unless she's sick, then we spend the day at home. He smirks at my obvious discomfort.

"She's been great, as usual. We took her to the shop and brought her some toys, and then Lou has been cooking, with Maya hanging onto every word, as usual."

He laughs, and as I look at him, I see the brightness in his eyes that I used to get as a child when he was proud of me. I remember it mainly from my childhood, not so much after that as he was always away at work, so I didn't see him very often, although I always knew that if I needed him, he would be there in a heartbeat, so I don't feel I was robbed of anything.

"That's good. She misses you when you're gone. *We* miss you."

I sigh, knowing that their stay is coming to an end as they're leaving tomorrow morning. I make my way over to where he is sitting and rest my head on his shoulder.

"I know, sweetheart. I know you can't exactly just leave because of the bakery, but we will start coming down more often. I promise. And we want to make sure that your appointment at the firm goes well before we leave."

The confirmation that I will be able to see them more often calms the anxiety that starts to build up inside of me. I may be nearly thirty, but I will openly say how much I love having my parents around and how much comfort it brings me. I'm glad he managed to push back important meetings to be able to come and make sure I was in the right frame of mind.

"At least we still have tonight with you. I'll bring a cake or something for us to have later; I know you'll appreciate that."

"I would love that, just don't let Lou know I've already eaten two cupcakes."

He looks at me sheepishly before he laughs.

"I won't, but I bet you she already knows. You always do it."

***

After going through with my father what I need to discuss at the appointment, I'm finally able to start assembling my friend's cakes. For the smash cake, I cut out a hole in the middle of two of the layers so they can hold some of his favourite squishy sweets. I love doing surprises inside of cakes, especially for children. The joy that takes over their face when sweets cascade around them is priceless. After they've both been assembled and are in the fridge, I place the choux pastry in there too, until I think of a spin to do on it tomorrow. I quickly go into the toilet and freshen up my makeup.

As I'm walking through the front of the shop, I give Ry a quick kiss on the cheek, telling him that I'll be seeing him later on as he's coming to mine for a meal before my parents leave tomorrow morning.

I jump into my car, type in the postcode for the address and follow my satnav until I come across a large glass building with the name in large writing. At the sight of the fancy building, I sigh in relief that I won't be overdressed. I know you can't be overdressed for a formal appointment, but I always have this fear, no matter where I go, that I'm too dressy.

I pull into the car park designated for visitors and make my way into the building. As soon as I walk in, I'm greeted by the receptionist.

"Hello, miss. How may I help you today?"

"I have an appointment today. I'm sorry, I'm not sure who with, but it should be under Evelyn Smith."

Just saying my true, full name out loud gives me the shivers. I never call myself Evelyn. As soon as I moved, I changed my last name to my grandmother's maiden name, Slater, and only went by Evie whenever possible. I didn't want Greg to find me, so I did everything I could think of to make sure I stayed as hidden as I could. I knew he didn't know my grandmother's maiden name, as when she married my grandfather, she changed to Smith and went by that until the day she passed. But I wanted to still pay homage to my family in some way.

The receptionist looks at the computer for a couple of seconds and then picks up a phone.

"Hello, Leanne. Mr. Kinsella's three o'clock appointment is here." She puts down the phone and directs her attention towards me. "His assistant is on his way to get you. You may make yourself comfortable in the lounge."

She waves her hand to an enclosed area with numerous armchairs. I wouldn't personally consider this a lounge, but I'm not about to question it.

The name Kinsella keeps repeating in my head. I know I remember that name being part of the law firm, but I remember it from somewhere else too. I don't know where, but the name sounds familiar. Seeing that I only knew the firm's name yesterday, after my father spoke to me about it, I know I must have heard it before.

Before I have a chance to think about it too hard, I see a tall, slender woman with shapely curves walking towards me. Her eyes instantly lock onto mine and she smiles. I figure out that she must be the assistant that was sent to get me.

My eyes are drawn to her mauve hair that catches the light as she walks. I wish I had the confidence to pull off a hair colour as beautiful as that. She's dressed in simple business attire, with black trousers and a short-sleeved shirt on, but I notice a tattoo of a hummingbird on her forearm. Once she's closer, I realise that it isn't in a traditional style. The entire hummingbird is in a watercolour style with a variety of bright colours. I also see that she's wearing a pair of killer heels that are to die for. If it's acceptable, I *must* ask where she got those from.

As she gets closer, her pretty hazel eyes draw me in, and when she smiles, she shows off her perfectly white, straight teeth. She reaches out a hand and I reciprocate.

"You must be Evelyn. I'm Leanne. It's lovely to meet you. Do you have an appointment with Trey?"

The sound of his name instantly makes my entire body freeze. I don't know how I hadn't managed to put it together beforehand; I *knew* he worked as a solicitor and was a partner at his firm. I instantly remember him telling me that his last name was Kinsella. I don't know how I hadn't put it together. A million thoughts start racing through my head. He will now know that I haven't been telling him the entire truth. He will know, from having access to my case files, what happened to me. *My* Trey will be finding out my deepest darkest secret. *My* Trey will finally find out how *tainted* I am. I won't blame him if he doesn't want to continue this—whatever *this* is between us—but I hope it won't stop. I have found somebody that likes me for *me*, who's managed to draw me out of my cocoon. I try not to dwell on the thought.

I want to leave, but I know I don't have a choice in the matter. I *need* to do this for me, for my family, and for my future. I decide to pull up my big girl panties and gain all the courage I have to go through with this.

Leanne is staring at me, now with question in her eyes. I quickly put on the fake smile that I have perfected over the years and try to find my voice.

"Hi, Leanne. It's lovely to meet you too. I must say that your shoes are killer. Are you talking about Mr. Kinsella?" She nods her head, giving me the confirmation that I needed, so I add, "Yes, I do."

She smiles and starts to lead me down the hall.

"Aww, thank you! I got them from this amazing little boutique on the high street the other day. It's called Mad Boutique. The name is fitting, as they have some really interesting clothing there. I get the majority of my clothes, shoes, and handbags from there. It's an amazing place. They have an array of these shoes, if you want to get them."

She winks at me, instantly knowing why I asked. Her attractiveness makes me wonder whether she and Trey have any sort of relationship ... I instantly shake my head, getting rid of that thought before it starts to fester in my mind. I don't want to dwell on who his past conquests are; besides, it doesn't matter as now he is *mine* and I am *his*. That is all that matters. I don't know how long that may be for after today, but I hope he can see who I *truly* am, and not the victim that I used to be.

I smile up at her, knowing that if it was possible, I could see a friendship with her.

"I may have to go and get myself a pair. I have an, umm, large collection of shoes and handbags. It's become an addiction, really."

I chuckle at the understatement. I have that many shoes and handbags that they've taken over my closet and underbed storage. I've even started putting some in the spare room as I don't have enough space.

Leanne laughs with me. "I may have to start stealing some then, especially if your clothing today has anything to say about your wardrobe. We should meet up sometime, go out for a drink or something."

"I would love that."

I smile, having not had a girlfriend since university. I can confidently say that that wasn't all Greg's fault. I had never been able to click with girls my age, especially in uni. They were always bitchy and stuck-up—as girls that age tend to be. They would slag you off behind your back but would act like your best friend to your face, and frankly, I had—*have*—no time for it.

I was always friends with girls who were older than me. When I was eighteen, one of my best friends was in her thirties. Even now, Teri is still my best friend, and even though she lives miles away, I speak to her every day. She is the only person who knows every single horrific detail of what happened with Greg. And as she is a single parent that went through something similar, she was there to help me when I needed her. I knew she wouldn't be able to move with me or help in that way, but she was there in every other way possible, and I will forever love her for that.

Obviously, Teri being the only person to know what happened will be changing after this appointment.

I'm pulled out of my head when I realise that Leanne has stopped. She turns to me and smiles.

"I'll be sitting over there." She points to a desk in the corner of the room by the hallway. "When you're finished, feel free to come over and we can organise a day to go out or something."

I smile and nod my head.

"I would really enjoy that. I'll make sure to come and find you afterwards."

She knocks on the door that we have stopped in front of, and in the depths of my mind I feel the urge to just run away as quickly as possible. But I know I need to listen to the fight part of my fight-or-flight mentality. I *need* to fight for this relationship and hope that he likes me just as much as I love him. *Wait, what?* I shake my head, knowing that it must be too soon to love somebody. Isn't it? Is there a certain time span on when it is acceptable to fall in love with someone? Is it after months of dating and being in a relationship? At that thought, I become more scared at what Trey will think when he finds out the truth.

I mentally shake my head and prepare myself for coming face to face with him in a couple of seconds, I hold my breath and wait until I hear his husky voice travel through the door.

"Come in."

Chapter Fourteen

Trey

I look up as Leanne opens the door for my next client. I've had my head buried in the paperwork, catching up on all that's gone on in the case. My firm put Greg Peterson behind bars in the first place, but I wasn't the solicitor in charge of the case back then.

He's a bastard, that guy. His rap sheet consists mainly of misdemeanours, until you see attempted murder sitting there staring back at you. Having read what he did to Miss Smith, I am angry on her behalf. Scum like him deserve to be imprisoned for the rest of their natural days. Maybe even sodomised with a broomstick, but that's not very professional of me to say.

Leanne ushers a woman into my office with a little gentle coaxing, and as she rounds the doorway, I am left standing with my chin on the floor. What the actual fuck?!

Standing before me is my beautiful girlfriend. Can I call her that? My gorgeous Evie. How in the world is she my client? I mean, I get it—Evelyn, Evie, it doesn't take a genius there. But her surname. There were photos in the casefile of her injuries, but never her face.

Evie walks timidly into my office and I immediately go to her. My heart squeezes in my chest like it's trapped in a vice. My palms turn clammy, and I feel sweat begin to bead on my brow.

I can't begin to fathom how she must be feeling. I think back to the case notes and the attempted murder charge glows in neon lights. I empathised with the victim—oh how I *hate* that word—before ever meeting her, but now I know it's *my* Evie, my heart races so fast I'm expecting to see it break out of my ribcage, leaving me hollow inside.

She looks beautiful in a red blouse and black pencil skirt, teamed with killer red heels that make her legs look like they go on for miles. I smile tentatively at her and get a sheepish one in response.

We've never discussed our pasts in great detail. I've never really told her what it was like to grow up in care. We've talked about her parents, but whenever she's tried to broach the subject of my parents, I've always avoided the topic.

And I know she's got a past of her own, skeletons in the closet and all, but we've never discussed the thing that seems to hold her back. I can always sense it in the way she acts. She's not all that confident, unless it's with Maya, Ryan or her parents, or when it comes to baking. When it comes to anything else, she seems a little reserved. I guess I'm about to find out why. It's selfish of me, but I don't want to hear what she's got to tell me. I don't want it to burst the bubble we've created—and I know it will. It will, because I'm already seeing red. I already want to throat-punch the bastard that hurt my girl. More than that, I want to tear him limb from limb, slowly, methodically and excruciatingly painfully.

This must be why those two toadies of his came to the store that night. It's all falling into place now.

"May I get you a glass of water?" I finally ask when I can form words. "Please."

She tries to smile at me, but it falters, and I know why. She's just walked into her boyfriend's office to discuss her abusive ex. An ex that tried to kill her. Why the fuck would he do that to such a wonderful woman? Because he gets off on the thrill of holding someone's life in the palm of his hand. That's what abusers do. My abusers tormented me and Leah because they were sick fucks who got off on hurting innocent children. My sister is now dead because of it. She turned to drugs to escape her reality, and they took her from me. The drugs and the bastards that hurt her.

This isn't about me, but I can't help the thoughts that tumble around in my mind. Our pasts are more similar than I previously thought. More than Evie would have thought. I guess, at some point, I should tell her my own truth, bare my soul the way she's about to. But that isn't a job for today. I want her to know me, all of me, including the sordid details of my youth. But it's a scary prospect, opening up, like slicing a vein and bleeding out. And maybe, if I'm lucky, the gravity of the situation she's in will give us a chance to really talk. Maybe she won't judge me as harshly as I previously thought. She doesn't seem a judgmental sort of person, but a nagging doubt has held me back from telling her the ugly truth.

"Take a seat," I say as I wave to a leather couch opposite the large glass coffee table.

She does as I say, and I take a seat opposite her. I try to keep my composure as professional as I can, but I can already feel it beginning to crack. If I'm not careful, the carefully crafted façade will crumble entirely.

I clear my throat and loosen my tie and top button on my collar. I pour us both a glass of water from the jug on the coffee table and pass a glass to her. She cradles it like it's something precious, or maybe it's for comfort.

"So," I begin uncomfortably, "what is it that brings you hear today, Evie? I believe it was to discuss an injunction, is that correct?"

"Yes," she replies as she looks everywhere except for directly at me.

I shift uncomfortably in my seat. I want her to feel comfortable opening up to me, but I can't approach this as her boyfriend. It has to be all business. But at the same time, I don't want to offend her and leave her feeling like I don't care.

"Okay, so let's start at the top. Tell me your story. Take as much time as you need, but tell me everything so I can help you. I've read the case file, but I always find it more useful to hear the words from the person's own lips."

"Umm …"

I watch her shift uncomfortably, smoothing out the invisible wrinkles of her skirt and pulling at the collar of her blood-red blouse.

"It's okay, Evie. This is a safe space," I say as reassuringly as I can.

"I-it's just … umm … it's hard to put voice to what happened. Especially as … you know … as it's you."

She takes a long gulp of the cool water, and I refill her glass as she places it down in front of her.

"Evie, if it helps, close your eyes and pretend it's not me you're talking to."

"Th-the o-only person that knows the full extent of my past is my best friend, Teri. E-even Ryan doesn't know it all. I don't w-want to be a burden on him. And it's hard to talk about, so I just try not to have to."

"It's okay, Evie. The privilege between a solicitor and client prevents me from telling Ryan, or anyone."

"Oh, no, I know you wouldn't tell him. I-I'm sorry, that wasn't what I meant."

"Look, take some deep breaths. In for the count of three and out for the count of three. Can you do that?"

She nods and I hear her take her first deep breath. I hate seeing her so vulnerable, and I consider asking another solicitor to take over from me. I don't want to recuse myself, but I want her to feel more relaxed.

"Would it help if another partner here took over your case? You could reschedule the appointment to give them time to go over the details and to give you some time to gather your strength."

"No," she shouts and then blushes profusely. "Sorry, I didn't mean to shout. I don't want anyone else. If anything, it might help that it's you, if I think about it. I mean, we'd need to have this discussion in a more personal setting anyway, so I might as well just do it now while I have the courage. All I've done before this appointment is talk to my dad and Ryan about the injunction and how important it is. I need it to be done now. I can't wait ... for my sake, for Maya's, and for those I love." She takes another deep breath and continues. "Sorry, I'm rambling. It's nerves."

Her nervous giggle covers how she's feeling inside, but I see right through her.

Sitting back, I unbutton my suit jacket and cross my legs in front of me, trying to give her the impression she can relax.

"Okay, s-so, umm ... the beginning ... He, *Greg*, he beat me, frequently. When we met, he was the picture of a perfect gentleman. But that façade began to crumble bit by bit, then all at once. He was a monster underneath. It was always there, waiting for you to scratch the surface. He was careful and methodical in his abuse. He hit me in places that wouldn't be seen when I was dressed. Nobody knew what he put me through until it was too late. I told Teri after he went to prison and she sobbed, begged my forgiveness for not being a better friend and knowing what was happening. But she isn't psychic, so I told her there was nothing to forgive. Anyway ..."

She takes a drink of her water and I see her elegant throat swallow before she continues.

"He ... the first time, he ... well ... we were in our bedroom arguing over something—something I can't even remember now. It was something small and petty. But the next thing I know, he has his hands round my throat as he throws me back against the bedroom wall. There was a vicious look in his eyes, but mixed with delight, like he gets off on the pain he inflicts. His grip tightened, and I found it hard to breathe, to swallow … I could feel myself on the brink of unconsciousness. I was teetering on the brink before he let me go and I ran past him.

"The next thing I know, he had me pinned to the bed on my back, his hands around my throat again, but this time, he was toying with me. He loosened and tightened his grip alternately. He loomed over me like … like he was going to kill me in that very moment. I was getting dizzy from the lack of oxygen, and I knew that I couldn't do anything. I was helpless. He was a black belt in ju-jitsu. He used his strength and knowledge to keep me awake, but not aware of my surroundings."

My heart thunders in my chest as I listen to her describe the monster that beat her systemically.

"H-he … he kept applying pressure until I couldn't breathe. The look in his eyes was sheer delight. Glee. He enjoyed my suffering. In a flash, I had an idea. I didn't know if it would work, but I had to try. I pulled my knees upwards and planted my feet on his chest, kicking with all my strength. It threw him backwards into the desk at the end of our bed. He didn't move, probably shocked to see me fight back. I ran and grabbed my mobile phone, dialled 999 and asked for the police. My voice was scratchy, but I managed to rasp out that I had been attacked and gave them the address.

"Greg sat on the landing at the top of the stairs and openly sobbed. He kept begging me. *Please Evelyn, please don't do this. I'm sorry. I'll never do it again. I'm not a violent man, I saw red and lost my temper, but I swear, I'm sorry. I'll make it up to you. Just don't involve the police.*

"I was still on the phone at the time, so I told them not to come, that I was fine. That was the first time I lied for him, but unfortunately, it wasn't the last."

Evie stops speaking, and I see the shimmer of unshed tears in her eyes. I want nothing more than to hold her, to console her, as her partner. But as her solicitor, I can't. My internal war battles on as she looks at me, with her heart on her sleeve and her need for someone to offer her comfort.

Before I can stop myself, I'm sitting next to her, pulling her into my embrace. I hold her and stroke her hair, whispering soothing words as she cries quietly.

When she moves her head to look up at me, I lean down and ghost a kiss across her lips. A silent promise that I'm still here.

I offer her the box of tissues on the table and she takes out a compact mirror from her handbag, dabbing at her eyes with the tissue.

"Can I get you a cup of coffee? I know you're a caffeine junkie like me. Maybe it will soothe your frayed nerves a tad."

"Th-that would be nice," she says as she sniffles and tries to regain her composure.

I buzz through to Leanne and ask her for two coffees.

"I know there's more you need to say, but it seems a good idea to take a break here. Tell me something. Tell me about Maya or something that brings you solace."

Evie nods and offers me a small smile.

"Maya is with my parents. They leave in the morning. I don't want them to go, but they've promised to visit more often. My father was the one who suggested your firm, and I didn't make the connection with your surname. Maybe it was nerves making me miss the dots. But when I got here, and Leanne called you by your first name, the penny dropped, and I almost wanted to run. I've never been one to burden people with my shit. I keep it bottled inside. Well hidden, controlled. But there are times when it feels like I'm going to burst from not being able to share this with anyone."

"You have *me*, Evie. *Always.* I'm *never* leaving your side. You can tell me anything, and I promise you no judgment, no belittling how you feel … I will never make you feel like your feelings don't matter. They matter more to me than my own."

"Thank you, Trey."

Leanne knocks at my door, and I call for her to enter. She leaves a tray on the coffee table and offers Evie a smile before departing, closing the door quietly behind her.

"She seems nice," Evie says.

"Leanne? She's lovely. I had an assistant before her, and when she went on maternity leave, Leanne was her cover, sent by a temp agency. When Alice didn't want to return after her maternity leave after all, I offered Leanne the job permanently. The stupid temp agency didn't want to let her go and made me pay them seven hundred pounds to sever her contract with them. But she was worth every penny. Still is. She's got a good head for the business. She's smart as a whip, funny, sarcastic … She gets the job done, though. She may have a playful nature, but when it comes to her job, she takes it very seriously."

"She's also gorgeous. I mean, jeez, I wish I could pull off such a bold hair colour. And her ink, *ohmygoodness.* I have always wanted something like that myself."

"She's pretty, I guess. Her girlfriend sure thinks so. And they make a hot couple."

"She's … *ohmygoodness,* you'd never guess."

"Yeah, Michele, her girlfriend, she's a solicitor here. I know you shouldn't mix business with pleasure, but I don't have any strict rules about it, and if they were to break up, then I'd just see if one of them wanted to transfer to one of our other offices. I don't want to lose my assistant, though, or Michele, because she's bad-ass at her job, so I hope they don't go down in flames."

I add sugar to Evie's mug before passing it to her. She accepts it with a smile, and I pick up my own mug before returning to my seat across from her. Her small smile slips, and she knows it's time to tell me more.

"It wasn't just me; there were others. They came forward at his trial and gave evidence, backed up by photographic evidence and a rape kit. It turned out he'd been married before we got together. I didn't know that, but he got married when he was still in college and divorced a year later. It was a little while after his divorce that we met. He was twenty-two and I was eighteen. He had a place of his own, and I'd often stay with him and eventually just moved the rest of my stuff in with him. He hid his past from me, never once revealing he'd been married or anything. He even had a kid. When he raped Lynne, she found out she was pregnant. But she couldn't keep a baby that linked her to Greg for the rest of her life, and as he wasn't on the birth certificate, she gave the baby up for adoption not long after she was born. He didn't know until his trial."

Of course, I knew all this before she told me, having read every little detail about Greg to be ready for this meeting. But reading it and hearing it are two different things.

"He systematically tore me down, piece by piece. He told me how to dress, how to act. If I wore something that he considered distasteful, he'd tear it to shreds and backhand me across the face. I learned the hard way. He bought me a whole new wardrobe of things he had chosen. He liked me to look like the trophy girlfriend if we went out together, but the few times I was allowed to go out alone, he made me cover myself from head to toe, which I had to anyway to cover the bruises. He was the master of manipulation and always had people watching me wherever I went."

She pauses her story to sip her coffee, sighing when it soothes her.

"He would call me from work. Whether he was on his lunch break or he'd gone to the toilet, every chance he got, he called. I couldn't get a job, because he was scared that I'd cheat. You wouldn't look at him and peg him for being insecure, but he was. And a complete control freak. He always wanted to know what I was doing, even if I was home doing the ironing. When I did get a job, he called me all the time, and eventually, they had to let me go because I wasn't being paid to talk to him all day.

"Greg played mind games. He made me text him photographs proving I was where I said I was. He made me cut all ties with male friends, and I didn't have many female friends except for Teri, who he thought he could fool, so he didn't see her as a threat. He came between me and my family. My mother, she hated him, wouldn't allow him in the house. She didn't know why she hated him, but she could tell he wasn't the kind of man I should be with. My grandparents, gosh, they hated him, but they wanted to see me, so they let him in the house so that they could spend some time with me. I hardly ever saw them alone.

"Greg made me believe that what we had was love. I was young and naïve, so I thought that's what love looked like. He told me nobody else would ever love me the way he did, that it wasn't possible. I left him more than once, staying with Teri and her son when I needed somewhere to run to. I couldn't go to my parents, because they'd be more intrusive and ask me questions. Teri let me stay, no questions asked. But he always made me come 'home'."

She air quotes the word for emphasis.

"He would call me at all hours, crying, begging me to come back to him. Made empty promises. Once, we went away for one of his ju-jitsu course things, where they have a display from people from all over the world, followed by gala dinners. We stayed with my aunt and uncle rather than a hotel, and he drove from theirs to Bournemouth. When we went for the dinner the second night, I think someone spiked my drink; I'd only had two glasses of wine, but I couldn't see straight, and I made him pull over for me to be sick on the drive back to my aunt and uncle's place. Anyway, so I fell asleep but woke in the early hours of the morning. I looked around, but he wasn't in the room, so I checked the en suite and he wasn't there either. I stepped back into the room and noticed my bags were there, but his were gone. I rang him, but it kept going to voicemail, so I left him frantic messages before falling back asleep."

Evie looks at me and our gazes lock as she continues.

"He called me back about six-thirty. I asked where he was, and he said he was on the beach in Bournemouth with some of the people from the course. I asked why he'd left, and he said it was because I had propositioned two men from his ju-jitsu club, asking them for a threesome. That was bullshit. I'm not that kind of girl," she adds quietly, her gaze breaking away from mine. "Long story short, he left me in Bournemouth with no way to get home, as he'd driven us. So, I stayed with my aunt and uncle for a week before returning by train. He rang me, telling me that when I got back we'd go and pick out an engagement ring. Little did I know I'd end up paying for that ring myself. I even went wedding dress shopping with my grandma, making her cry because she said I looked more beautiful than ever. But while we talked about marriage and babies, my heart felt like a balloon that had a small puncture, deflating over time."

"Oh, Evie …" I have no words to console her. She looks lost in her memories.

"I didn't want a baby with him. It would tie me to him forever, keep me in the seventh circle of hell. But one day, I found out I was pregnant. I'd been using the contraceptive injection, but they aren't one hundred per cent infallible. I had hidden that I was on the injection, but he called my doctors and found out, then he beat me and stopped me from getting it. He then tried everything in his power to get me pregnant without my consent, so I eventually fell pregnant with Maya. I'd only known about my baby for an hour before finding myself outside my parent's house. That was the day I never looked back."

She finishes her now cold coffee and looks at me with a bittersweet smile. The sadness in her eyes tears right through me, searing across my soul, leaving a scar in its wake.

"Maya was my *raison d'être*. I loved her more than anything. In that moment, finding out I was pregnant, I realised that if he'd succeeded in his attempt to kill me, he would have snuffed out her life too. I was tied to him for life by her existence, though that's what spurred me on to finally take him to court and put him behind bars.

"You've read the file, I know, but the photographic evidence I kept in a journal under a loose floorboard, that and the fresh bruises and contusions were enough to put him behind bars where he belonged."

"And you changed your name?"

"Yes. I'd always been Evelyn to him—any nickname was strictly forbidden, goodness knows why. So I just shortened it to Evie, not wanting to completely erase my birth name. And I legally changed my surname to Slater, a name he never knew. It was my grandma's maiden name. Anyway, what finally led me here today was his two goons turning up at *Queen of Tarts*. I knew he could still get to me from behind bars. So I came here hoping something could be done to … I don't know, add time to his sentence or take an injunction out against him. I already thought there was one in place."

"I'll do anything I can to keep that asshole where he belongs and keep him away from you. I'm just glad I was there that day."

"Me too. You saved me, Trey, and I am *so* grateful. More than you'll ever know."

I get up and move to sit beside her once more. Professionalism out of the window. I don't care. This woman owns my heart, and I'll be damned if someone tries to tell me I'm too close to this case, or it's a conflict of interest. I'm a named partner in this firm, and I'll do what I damn well please.

I take her hand in mine and trace lazy circles over the back of it with my thumb.

"You're so strong, Evie. You amaze me. How you've been to hell and back again, how you've survived a monster like him. How you've given your daughter the kind of life every little girl deserves. She's such a happy little girl. Smart, funny, sassy—like her mum—and, best of all, she's free. Does she …" I trail off, not wanting to ask the question.

"You mean does she know about him?" she asks softly.

"Yes. I don't mean to pry, but it's best if I know everything … for the case." And for the sake of my heart.

"She asked me once why other kids had a mum and a dad and she didn't. I'd kept quiet until then, not wanting to inflict emotional scars on her so young. I told her that her dad's a bad man and he's in prison for something very bad. I told her she wouldn't get to see him because I won't allow him to hurt her. She wasn't as fazed by it as I thought she would be. She kind of just shrugged her shoulders and said okay, and she has always been okay with just having me around. She wants for nothing and doesn't need a dad like him. He's not her dad, he's her sperm donor."

"Does he know about her?"

"Not to my knowledge. I've done my best to shield her from him. I don't want him trying to hurt her to get to me."

"What about his family? Do they know about her? Do they still speak to him?"

"I don't know if they talk to him or not. I've never cared to find out. To my knowledge, they don't know about Maya either. It's one of the reasons I was so scared on the night you saved me. I didn't want them to know about her and for it then to get back to him. I feel like he can still pull strings from prison."

"Evie, this is my solemn promise to you: I will make a statement to the police about that night. That way it goes into evidence. They already have enough on him to keep him in prison, but his scare tactics, they are just empty threats. He cannot hurt you. Will not hurt you. If he so much as tries, I will be there to protect you both. I will look into everything in your case and see what can be done. The prison monitor phone calls, they monitor mail, but they can't stop him calling his friends. They'll need to be more stringent now, after this."

"Thank you, Trey. Thank you for saving me, for listening to me go on about the biggest mistake of my life. Thank you for just being you."

"Don't beat yourself up, Evie," I say as I squeeze her hand gently. "You are not to blame. You are not responsible for the actions or reactions of another person. You didn't ask Greg to hurt you. You didn't do anything wrong. Nothing you could have done would ever have made you deserve what he did. He's an abuser, a manipulator. People like him get off on the power they feel when they hurt someone. Take it from me, they are the ones at fault. Greg is the lowest of the low."

"They?" she asks as she peers up at me through her eyelashes.

"Yes, people like him. They belong in the seventh circle of hell. Abusers like him don't deserve an ounce of energy from someone like you. He's tainted, but you, you're pure. You are raw beauty of the purist kind. You have the biggest heart of anyone I know."

She smiles shyly, and I lean in to wrap my arms around her, resting my chin on her head.

"You're something else, Trey, do you know that? I was so scared coming here today. I didn't want a total stranger quizzing me about my past. When I got here and realised it was you, I nearly ran back the way I came. I was so scared to bare everything to you. I didn't want you to know my darkness. Didn't want to taint you with it."

"Taint me?" I pull back to look her square in the eyes. "You could never taint me, sweetheart. I was tainted before you came along, and you brought hope into my life. You brought happiness in a way I had *never* felt before in my life. You are all the good in my life. You and Maya are so very special to me. I need you to know that."

She nods in silent acceptance of my words, but I wonder whether they've truly sunk in.

"You're too kind, Trey. But thank you."

I lean in and claim her lips with mine in a sweet kiss. There's so much I want to say, but sometimes words are not enough. More than words are needed when you want someone to believe what you feel is true.

***

After a long day of making calls and sending emails to various people, I made a statement to the police about the night of the attack. They told me that Evie would need to report it herself, so I called her and told her. She said she was scared, but I promised to go with her and hold her hand.

I make my way into the gym and mentally prepare myself for the rigorous workout I'm about to put myself through. I'm still running on excess adrenaline from when Evie told me her darkest truth.

When she left my office, she looked different. Head up, shoulders back, she looked like a weight had been lifted, and who knows, maybe it has. I hope it has.

Joe sidles up to me and smiles that goofy smile of his. Love looks good on him. I don't think they've exchanged those words yet, both scared of scaring the other one off. But I've known him long enough to know that it's more than just lust, or infatuation. He's fallen for Ryan, and I couldn't be happier for them. My best friend dating my girlfriend's best friend. It makes me smile.

"Are you ready for this?" he asks.

"The question is, are you?"

"Shut up, you wuss. I'm not a quitter."

He punches me playfully on the arm, and I grab him in a headlock before he can utter another word.

"Okay," he says as he taps my arm.

I loosen my grip and ruffle his shaggy hair before letting him go completely.

We decided to place bets on who would quit first. I am no quitter.

Joe might say he's not, but I'm not sure he can quite keep up with me physically. He hasn't been to the gym so much since he started dating Ryan. We'll see who's begging to quit by the end of our session.

The game, as they say, is on.

***

My heart pounds, and my body is slick with sweat. I pushed myself past my normal limits. So did Joe, but I won the bet. He quit just ahead of me, swearing like a sailor as he realised he was on the hook for paying for our drinks all night on Saturday.

I took a shower at the gym and then another as soon as I got home. I just didn't feel clean enough.

Now I'm showered and changed and am chilling with a horror flick and some microwave popcorn.

Evie has a meal with her parents tonight before they leave tomorrow, and I don't want to intrude.

I'm halfway through the new version of Stephen King's *IT* and, while I usually say don't mess with original films, don't remake them, I am actually enjoying the differences. It's slightly darker than the original, and Pennywise isn't such a "kid's party" type of clown.

My phone chimes on the coffee table, so I sit up and read the text.

>Hey, I know it's last minute, and you can feel free to say no, but would you like to come over tonight?

>I thought you were having a family meal?

>We are, but you're part of this family now … aren't you?

That right there warms my heart. The smile on my face could probably crack it in two.

I jump up and run upstairs to quickly change into something more acceptable than low-slung joggers and my university hoodie.

Realising I didn't answer Evie, I grab my phone.

>I am?

>You are … if you want to be.

>Oh, I do. I'm on my way. See you soon.

>Bring your appetite. I cooked enough to feed an army. Oh, and Joe is coming too. I couldn't say no when Ryan asked if he could tag along.

>Then you'll be eaten out of house and home. He's a monster.

I grab my car keys from the bowl by the door and lock up behind me before jumping in the car and speeding down my drive, eager to get there.

I've never really felt like part of a family before. There was only really me and Leah, then she died and left me alone. Joe is the closest thing I have to family these days. But the realisation that Evie is opening up in such a huge way, letting me into her life, her daughter's life, accepting me as part of her family … there are just no words for how I'm feeling … are there?

As I drive and sing along to "Hole in my Soul" by Kaiser Chiefs, it suddenly dawns on me. I do have the words. I'm just scared to say them.

My heart seems to skip a beat as one word plays on a loop in my head. *Love.*

Chapter Fifteen

Evie

After an emotionally draining day, I came straight home and just sat with Maya for an hour, basking in the comfort she brings. She was confused to start off with, but she could tell that there was something wrong, so she just snuggled into my lap while we watched the rest of *Mulan*. Afterwards, I had time to process how easy it was to open up to Trey, when I always found just discussing a *small* amount to anybody else extremely difficult. I had managed to fill my mum and dad in on what happened at the firm but hadn't managed to tell Ryan yet. I knew I wouldn't be able to properly discuss it with him until tomorrow, as Joe was coming with him, and I had invited Trey too.

I refused to sit there and wallow in self-pity on the last night that my parents were going to be here. I kicked my butt into gear and started the preparations for the meal I was doing tonight.

The sound of knocking on the door brings me out of my head. Just as I turn to the door, I hear it open. Three sets of male laughter flow throughout the house, and then I hear Maya's feet running from the living room towards the front door.

"Trey!" she squeals.

I manage to make it out of the kitchen in time to see her launch herself into Trey's awaiting arms. He spins her around while laughing as she squeezes his neck.

Ryan pulls Joe around them and makes his way into the kitchen.

"Well ... looks like I'm officially not the favourite anymore," he says in a joking manner, loud enough for Maya to hear.

Before he can say anything else, he stops, open-mouthed, at the platter of food that is lying on the table. I hear a quiet wow come from Joe's direction. My dad chuckles at their reactions.

"She said she made enough to feed an army; I didn't think she was serious."

I hear Trey's teasing voice behind me. Just as I go to turn around, his arm wraps around my waist. I feel Maya's arm wrap around my neck and, as I look to my side, I see that he's still holding her in one arm, while holding my waist with the other.

I giggle at them. I have to admit, my platter is impressive. I made everything—lasagne, chilli, pasta bake, salad and some garlic bread. As well as giving them the choice of either chips or rice.

I haven't had a chance to get the cake that I had promised my dad, so I had to ask Ry to raid the fridge at the bakery and grab what he could find. By the number of bags he and Joe are carrying, I think they brought the entire store with them.

"I don't know how we'll eat all the desserts that I've brought."

Ry looks worriedly at the table and then at the bags they're holding. I slip out of Trey's grip and make my way towards them. I take the bags that he is holding and peek in there. I gasp as I see the assortment of tarts, tortes, and cakes. I'm assuming Ry brought the honey cake in particular, because he knows it's Joe's favourite. What is it they say? The way to a man's heart is through his stomach.

"You've really brought the entire shop, haven't you?"

Ryan chuckles and looks slightly sheepish.

"I thought it was enough. Maybe I brought too much."

We place them all in the fridge, just about fitting them in.

"I'll take some home with us anyway."

My dad shrugs as he sees how much Ry brought. I know he will anyway; his excuse will be that he needs his fill when they go home.

We all take our places at the table. Maya sits between me and Trey, while Ry and Joe sit opposite us, with my parents at the heads of the table. We all dig in, chatting about random stuff and having a laugh. I realise how comfortable everyone is, and especially how accepting my parents have been of Trey. Neither of them liked Greg, but they've taken an instant liking to Trey. It warms my heart to know they approve.

When we've started on the dessert, my dad takes this moment to start bringing up old stories of when I was a child.

"This one year, it was the summer holiday …" He looks at my mum for confirmation and she nods her head. "We would go on holiday every year to a caravan that we owned by the coast. Now, there were always seagulls around, obviously because we were by the sea. We would always get something from the chip shop for tea on one of the nights and eat it on the beach. Seagulls would always swarm, waiting for some food. But usually one seagull would get really close and take a chip off you. We had managed to tell Evie that there was this 'one' seagull"—he emphasised this with air quotes—"that would follow our car around, all the way back home and then back to the caravan the next year *just* to try and steal food off her and to chase her around. She *believed* this until she was about ten and was confused when we told her that this seagull—which she named Scrappy—was actually multiple seagulls and that it wasn't possible for one seagull to follow somebody around for five years. She was distraught, and as soon as she could, she went to my mother's, her grandmother's, and told her how we lied to her. She spent the rest of that holiday baking with her."

I groan as everyone starts to laugh. Trey is the first to speak.

"You really believed that this one seagull would follow you everywhere you went?"

"I thought it was my friend and liked to see me go on little adventures! *The Little Mermaid* was my favourite Disney film at the time, and Scuttle was a seagull who was great friends with Ariel. That convinced me it was possible."

I try and hide behind my hands as I groan.

"I can just imagine little you calling this seagull to come closer for its seasonal chip!" Trey howls.

I stare daggers at my dad, who has tears running down his face. I look at Ry and Joe for some help, but Joe's face is red from laughing and Ry is sitting there silently convulsing. My mum is just sitting there shaking her head, holding back laughter.

"You're all bullies! I was only five when they told me!"

Maya grabs my hand.

"It's okay, Mummy, I would believe that too. I bet it was actually the same one. They don't want you to think dat though." she says as she beams up at me.

I lean down and kiss the top of her head.

"At least my clever girl understands. You're officially my favourite out of these goons."

I wink down at her and hear a collective gasp. I look up and see Ryan holding his hand over his chest.

"So you're saying that I'm *not* your favourite! You wound me, woman!"

Maya giggles at his dramatic voice,

"I'll always be *Mummy's* favourite because she letted me play with her hair."

She jumps from where she is sitting and goes to sit in Ry's lap, continuing their little squabble about who is my favourite. Trey takes this time to lean in closer to me. He places his arm on the back of my chair and leans into me, whispering in my ear.

"I think it's cute that you believed that seagull was your friend. At least it didn't bite off your pretty fingers in the process."

He winks at me and pulls back, grabbing another slice of lemon torte. I giggle as I turn and just watch my family.

I've grown to love this little dysfunctional family, especially Joe. He's quirky, and you can see the love between him and Ryan. I know they haven't said anything, as Ry would have rung me screaming as soon as it happened, but you can see the connection. Plus, the way he acts with Maya is lovely. He plays along with Ry and Maya's game, pretending to be on Maya's side while Ry acts offended.

I turn and study my parents. My dad's sitting there eating more orange tart, while my mum is watching Maya with soft eyes. It has been amazing having them over the last few days, just the way that they have helped me with everything that has gone on and made me realise all the love that I have around me and how I need to cherish what I have, no matter what life throws my way.

At the thought of love, I turn and look at Trey. He's looking at Maya with a slight—can I call it sadness?—in his eyes. I try and ignore the nagging feeling in my head that something is wrong, because as soon as I see it, it's gone. I just take in his toned body, and the realisation that he *actually* came—he's *here*—it hits me like a ton of bricks. He didn't run away. Even though he told me he wouldn't, there was this little nagging voice inside my head which just kept repeating *What if?* I don't know what I would have done. Letting Maya get so close to him was stupid on my part, because if he would have left, he wouldn't have just ripped my heart in two, he would have destroyed Maya's also.

But the fact that he came snaps my feelings into place. The realisation that what I'm feeling is *love*. What I had with Greg was just fatal attraction, but *this* is what love is. Wanting to share my life with somebody, wanting to make sure that they're happy. This is what it feels like to *actually* love somebody.

"What are you thinking about, gorgeous?" Trey's voice in my ear brings me back.

Goosebumps travel where his breath hits, and my breath hitches slightly.

"Oh, nothing, just away with the fairies."

I smile at him, trying to read his emotions. I wonder if he feels the same, or if it's too soon to feel anything like this. I've always thought that there was never a time limit to be able to love somebody, that it just happened when you were ready.

We all decide to make it into the living room to be more comfortable. My parents take the smaller sofa, while the guys and Maya sit on the floor. I sit next to Trey and curl myself into his side, feeling drained from today's events. I feel my eyelids become heavy, and I struggle to keep them open.

The feeling of being lifted and pulled against a strong chest wakes me slightly. I crack my eyes open and see Trey carrying me out the living room and upstairs.

"I didn't mean to wake you. Which one is your room?"

"The end of the hallway on the left." I yawn unceremoniously in his face. "Oh, my god, I am so sorry."

I try to cover my face as he pushes my door open with his foot. He chuckles and lays me gently on my bed.

"Don't be sorry; it was cute."

"It's embarrassing. I just yawned straight into your face. It's bad enough that I'm the host and I fell asleep halfway through the night."

He sits on the edge of my bed and brushes some hair off my face.

"It isn't. You've had a stressful day, and then you cooked. If you were running around like an energised bunny, then I'd be worried."

He smiles at me. I scoot over and make a gesture for him to lie down. The look on his face makes me speak up.

"Don't worry, you don't have to sleep, just lie down so we can talk. I feel awkward with you looming over me."

He smiles and lies on his side next to me. The sound of laughter downstairs makes me worry if it will wake Maya up, then a thought hits me.

"Wait, is Maya in bed?"

"Your dad took her up before I brought you up, and he's reading to her."

I smile, knowing that Maya would be asking for multiple books, as he will be leaving tomorrow.

"I, umm … didn't say thank you properly earlier. You need to realise how important it is that you still want to be here, to be with me after what I told you earlier."

"I wouldn't have pushed you away. I said to start off with that I don't date, so this is a large step for me. But you made me change my mind about my whole no-dating rule. Then when you came into my office and laid your soul bare … Evie, there's no way I could walk away from you. You have to realise what that man did was not your fault and that I will not judge you for it or walk away because you had something so awful happen to you. There are things I need to tell you about my life, things I've been scared would make you run a mile, so if anyone runs here, it won't be me. But that's a story for another day. I can see how tired you are."

I smile at him, trying to keep my eyes open. He notices my struggle and smiles.

"I'll let you sleep. I'll see you tomorrow. I've got a play date."

He winks at me then, leaning over, he kisses my forehead. I smile and snuggle into my blanket.

"I'll see you tomorrow."

By the time he's walked out of my room, I'm asleep.

***

The smell of bacon and eggs wakes me up from my slumber. Just as I make it out of my bedroom, I see Maya walking out of hers, rubbing her eyes. She silently takes my hand, and we make our way down the stairs. My mother is standing at the hob making breakfast, while my dad is sitting at the table reading the paper and drinking coffee. I notice that there is already an extra cup of coffee on the table waiting for me. Smiling, I sit down, pull Maya into my lap, and start sipping the caffeinated goodness.

My dad looks up at me and smirks. Confused, I raise my eyebrows at him.

"What's put that look on your face?"

"Just you, last night."

I then hear my mum giggle. I shake my head in confusion. My dad sighs.

"That is the first time I have ever seen you that comfortable with a man that isn't me or Ryan. As soon as you curled into Trey's side on that couch, you were out like a light. It was … nice to see."

"I was just tired, and it was comfy. I'm sorry I fell asleep last night. It was your last night here."

I groan and shake my head. My mum places a full English breakfast in front of me and my dad. I smile my thanks at her.

"It's okay, sweetheart." My mum's hand falls on my shoulder. "We'll be coming back in a month anyway. Seeing you happy was enough of a reward."

I smile up at her. She was the one who took it the hardest when she found out what happened with Greg. My dad managed to keep how he felt hidden from me, but my mum broke down. We had to have a long talk, as she felt guilty that she wasn't there for me when I needed her.

"I'm sorry that we have to leave so early, but your dad has got an important meeting with the CEO at two o'clock. We have to leave early so we can make it back in time."

I nod my head solemnly. I noticed the suitcases at the bottom of the stairs this morning but just wanted to pretend that they weren't there. I stand up and give them both a hug, with Maya following suit.

"Thank you for coming; I really appreciate it. I'll miss you guys."

I try and keep unshed tears at bay, not wanting to get too upset as they'll be back soon for Maya's birthday. I quickly pass my dad some containers which are full of his favourite cake and my mum's favourite tart. He smiles and kisses my cheek

***

I'm sitting at the till next to Ryan at the front of the bakery. I managed to get all the baking I needed to do early this morning faster than I thought. It was emotional saying goodbye to my parents, so as soon as they left, Maya and I finished breakfast and got dressed to come straight over.

I was in some serious need of company, so decided to come out to the front of the shop to speak to Ry and the customers. They were all so lovely, and I realise I miss that aspect of doing the front of the shop. I don't get the time to sit out here as often as I would like, especially with the amount of baking I've had to do lately.

"What happened last night then? Did you go back with Joe?"

Ry smirks at me and winks.

"Well, with little miss here"—he nods his head to Maya, who's sitting next to him—"I won't go into detail. But we did, and it was amazing. He's so sweet, Evie. He's just phenomenal. I don't know what I would do if this ended."

I feel my heart explode at the love he feels. It makes me happy that my friend has found somebody to love.

"I know how you feel; it's how I feel with Trey. It's weird, isn't it?"

Ryan beams at me, but before he can say anything, a throat clearing gets our attention.

We both turn, and I'm taken aback by how beautiful the woman standing before us is. She has long dark brown, almost black, hair. Her striking amber eyes are framed by long dark eyelashes. She's dressed in a pantsuit and has the face that screams *I don't need to wear makeup*. Before I can ask what she would like to order, her sharp tone cuts through the air.

"Are you Evelyn?"

I'm slightly taken aback by the use of my full name, as I haven't gone by that for the last six years, aside from in legal documents.

"Yes, I am. How can I help?"

I try and keep my voice calm, not letting her see how much hearing my real name has affected me.

"That's good. I'm Bobby. Do you know a Trey Kinsella?"

I trade a glance with Ryan, and he quickly ushers Maya to the usual table that she has when she plays with Trey. He helps Maya set up, with the promise that he'll be back in just a second. Trey should be here any minute, but I know the main reason Ry took her away was because he doesn't want her overhearing anything.

"Yes, I do. I'm his girlfriend. Do you need to contact him?"

At the sound of his name, I assume that she is one of his clients and needs help getting his number, so I grab my phone out of my pocket, ready to give it to her. I stop when I see her face screw up at the sound of me saying the word *girlfriend*.

"Well, I just thought you should know who he *actually* is. He doesn't care for you. He never has, and he never will. He only wants you for sex, especially because he's been seeing me as his side piece since the start. It's been a joke to him, as he wanted to see if he could get with the 'mysterious girl'." She air quotes the words she speaks in a scathing tone. "I just thought you should know that you will *never* have a chance with him. He is *mine*, and I don't need a worthless piece of trash trying to take *my* man from me. So I think you need to get this *girlfriend* nonsense out of your head. Trey doesn't do relationships, just plain old sex, no strings attached."

I sit there in shock; I can't find my voice to say anything back. When she realises that she won't get anything out of me, she turns on her heel and hastily retreats out of the bakery.

A million and one thoughts keep going through my head, but I'm too shocked to move. Am I that stupid to not see that he didn't like me, that it was a joke? I don't understand, because for me, it felt real, more than real. I thought I was in love with him, and that maybe he could feel that way about me. Anger instantly starts to seep into my body. How *dare* he trick me into thinking there was something in this. I sat there and told him my entire story, and he had the *nerve* to act like he gave a shit, when all he wanted was to get in my pants. But he already had, and he hadn't run away … I quickly throw that thought out. I don't want to go making excuses for *anybody* anymore. *Especially* somebody who has been screwing around behind my back, fooling not only me, but my family as well.

Chapter Sixteen

Trey

I'm sitting in my study, a tumbler of freshly squeezed orange juice on the desk in front of me, a sewing kit open in my lap. I've decided to do something I never thought I would. I went to the craft shop for some stuffing and a sewing kit, along with new glass eyes. Rabbit is undergoing reconstructive surgery, I guess you could say.

I may not have been taught how to sew, but you could say I'm self-taught, having sewn wounds up as a kid. I took many a beating that ended up with lacerations that needed stitching, but I never got taken to the hospital, because nobody cared enough. So I stole needles and thread and gritted my teeth as I painfully sewed my skin to heal the wounds.

It's time I fixed the last thing I own that reminds me of my beautiful sister, because I want to give it to the sweetest little girl I know, who happens to have a birthday coming up.

I swore I'd leave Rabbit in the condition he was in when I took him from the house and fled. His stuffing was lacking, and he had an eye missing. His fur was a dull grey from where he'd been through the washing machine countless times. Leah had owned him since she was a toddler, and even now, I can smell her on him. It's something ingrained.

I thought he was my last reminder of my sister, but I've come to realise that actually, I have my memories. They may not all be good ones, but until I was nineteen, Leah was the best thing in my life. We had good times, days at the beach, time spent playing in the park or drawing with chalk on the patio when we were with slightly better foster parents, or ones that had other kids they actually loved and felt they had to take us along with them. They're the things I cherish. My other memories stay locked in a box where they belong.

Feeling a pang in my chest as I think of my old life, a horrible memory surfaces.

***

When we finally moved in with our new foster parents, I was delighted. I was nine when Paul died of a heart attack. Leah was eight.

I was glad he died. Nothing could have made me happier than the day they told me he was gone. It's only a shame I didn't kill him myself.

His wife couldn't look after us alone, so we got a temporary placement with the Masons. They were good people ... until they weren't. At first, they treated us okay. But it soon turned sour.

Our lives seemed to have a pattern. We moved from one foster home to another because they couldn't look after us. We were too naughty—or that was always the excuse—and they ended up saying they didn't want us anymore, which was fine. It gave me hope. Until the next set of fosterers took that hope and crushed it in the palm of their hand.

The Masons were smarter than your average abusers. They just locked us in our rooms night and day.

Our lives with them consisted of going to school, coming home and doing homework at the kitchen table, eating our tea and then being locked in our rooms. There were no toys behind those doors. No colouring books or anything to pass the time.

The rooms were identical in layout. Stark white walls, a single bed, a small window that was kept locked, a wardrobe and a chest of drawers. Nothing else. The only thing that was different with Leah was that she had Rabbit. He was her one and only toy, something she could never sleep without.

The Masons never hurt us, never beat the hell out of us like Paul did. They just neglected us. When they had dinner parties with their friends, they dressed us up and paraded us around. They wanted everyone to think we were the perfect little family that had everything. In reality, we had nothing.

***

I shake my head and rid myself of the memory before I allow it to consume me.

As I'm unpicking the stitching along his side to add some extra stuffing, I feel something weird in his stomach. I pull at the stuffing in there to see what it is. I see a piece of paper. Goodness knows how it got inside Rabbit. What the hell is it?

Unravelling it, I begin to read:

Trey,

I hope you never find this note. I don't know why I'm even writing it, but I'm plagued with memories and I need to get this out onto paper, because those memories are invading my mind and I can't seem to shake them.

I can't take this life anymore. I'm just not strong enough, mentally or physically. I'm weak, so very weak. That's why I turned to drugs. I know you know by now about my addiction; it's consumed so much of me and I know you've noticed.

The truth is, the drugs make me numb, or at least they used to. These days it takes more to get me high, because I'm so used to them.

Life hasn't been kind to either of us, but I'm glad you managed to get out of it. You went to school to study law, and I know you were consumed by guilt for leaving me alone, but you had to study in order to fight for those like us that need someone strong enough to help them break free. I'm so goddamn proud of you for being strong enough to do that. I just wish I was like you. I long to put all this behind me, but I know by now that I never will. It's not my destiny. But it is yours. You're going to conquer the world one day, big brother, I know you are.

I guess I'm writing this to say goodbye. I've never been one for goodbyes in person. They hurt too much, and I know you wouldn't let me do this if you knew about it beforehand.

You need to know I love you, Trey. I love you more than anyone or anything in my life. But I don't have it in me to fight this anymore. The fear of what lies ahead of me, the haunting memories of the past … it's all too much to bear.

Please know I never did this to hurt you. I know your automatic assumption will be that I didn't love you enough to stay, but that is so untrue. You are the only good thing in my life. The only thing that's kept me going as long as I have. But I can't rely on you for the rest of my life. It isn't up to you to be my caretaker. You need to go on and live your life and it's better for you if you don't have a drug addict sister holding you back. But I'm not doing this because of you, I'm doing it because of ME. The cycle is too hard for me to break. The memories are more than I can take.

I don't remember the last time I was happy, truly happy. A time when I was sober. Were there any good things in our lives? The only good thing for me was you. But I can't remember anything else that made me smile.

The beatings you took in my place, the times you had to get a needle and thread to sew a cut … the times you held me in the night while I cried myself to sleep … these are the only things I can remember.

When I had leukaemia, I thought that I would die. And honestly, I was more than content to pass into the next life. Because maybe the next life will be better than this one.

But I got better and that was because of you. Your bone marrow made me strong again. Physically, at least. But mentally, there was nothing anyone could do for me. Not even you. The truth is, Trey, that I kept a tally scratched into the wall of the amount of times he raped me. I gave up the tally when it reached twenty. That was when I knew something had to end, and it wouldn't be him, so it had to be me.

That's why this has to be my last goodbye. I'm hiding this note inside Rabbit because I don't want anyone else to find it. I truly don't want you to find it, but at the same time, I want you to read my words and know that none of this was your fault. Like I say, something had to end, and it wasn't going to be Pete.

Did you know he found me after I aged out of foster care? Well, he did. He came by several times a week. He liked to make out like it's because he cared, but it wasn't; it was so he could get his rocks off. He fucked my broken body even when I lost consciousness because of the heroin in my system. He was sick, depraved, abhorrent. I couldn't take the torture anymore. I'm so, so sorry. I'm the reason he's dead. I guess I shouldn't confess to stabbing the bastard, but what can they do to me once I'm gone?

I don't know how to say all the things I wish I could. I'm just hoping you can understand why I had to go. Not because I killed Pete, but because he killed me. He took my innocence. He took what wasn't his to take. So, the only thing left for me to do is abandon this body that holds me prisoner. I'm hoping I go on to some kind of afterlife where I can be with our parents and grandparents.

I love you, Trey. I know I've said that already, but I can't say it enough. I love you, but this is where I must leave you.

You need to go on to really make something of your life, show anyone that ever hurt you that they can't hold you back from realising your full potential.

Sadly, I'm not going to be there to see it myself, but be sure I'll be watching over you for the rest of your life. Wherever I end up, I'll be keeping watch over you, making sure you stick to the right path.

This is where I say goodnight, Trey, because goodbye is too final.

I love you, brother.

Your little sister, always,

Leah xoxo

I watch as my tears wet the page, almost smudging my little sister's writing. How could she take her own life on purpose? I thought it was an accidental overdose. What a goddamn fool. Why couldn't I see it for what it was?

I couldn't save my sister, and this note is like a sucker punch in the gut. I feel hollowed out by her confession. I'm not bothered that she confessed to killing Pete. Even working in law, I will never reveal that piece of information. It's long since been a cold case, and this note might wrap things up for them, but I will never let them besmirch my sister's name, call her a murderer. Because she wasn't. Whatever she did to him, he had it coming. It was self-defence, nothing more.

I put Rabbit down and walk outside with a cigar. Leah's note is crumpled in my hand, and I know what I must do. I take my lighter and touch it to the corner of the page. Her confession will go with me to my grave.

Watching as the flames lick at her words, I feel tears trailing down my cheeks. Why didn't I find this note sooner? But I guess it doesn't matter. What's done is done now.

I know Leah loved me, and now I know she doesn't want me to blame myself for her death, but I always will. If I'd gone back to see her that day instead of going out to celebrate after hearing I'd got into my chosen university, I might have caught her and stopped her. But the thought hits me that she would have gone down the same path eventually.

I leave the note to burn in the ashtray on the table on my deck. Turning to head inside, I wipe my eyes and take some deep breaths.

Walking back to my study, I pick Rabbit back up and go back to fixing him. Leah would be pleased to know I've found love and that this cute little bunny is going to a very special girl.

Evie might not know I love her ... yet, and she might not even feel the same way. But I know for certain now that love is the feeling, unnamed until now, that has been building to a crescendo inside me.

Once Rabbit is fixed and looking as good as he can, I place him in the gift box I bought and filled with crepe paper. Placing the lid on, I look at it and smile. Leah would have loved Maya. Had she been able to get clean, she would have doted on her so much, the same way I do. That little lady has worked her way into my heart, and she resides there along with her mother. If I had any reservations about dating a single mother, they evaporated when I realised I would never let anything, or anyone, hurt Maya. I'd take a bullet for her. She'd never end up knowing the world that I grew up in. My darkness will never taint her innocent light. I'd never allow that.

I grab my keys, get in the car and turn on the radio. It seems in tune with my melancholy feelings as "Like You" by Evanescence plays.

Pulling up outside the bakery, I cut the engine and wipe the tears that fell as I listened to the haunting lyrics of the song that reminded me of Leah. Grabbing the bouquet of calla lilies from the passenger seat, I make my way to the doorway. I have a play date with Miss Maya, and then I'm hoping I can talk Ry into babysitting for Evie tonight.

Not watching where I'm going, I bump into a woman as she rounds the doorway.

"I'm so sorry, I wasn't watching where I was going."

My heart jumps into my throat the second the scent of expensive perfume hits me. What the hell is she doing here?

"Bobby?"

"Oh, Trey. Hi."

"What are you doing here?" I ask, my tone brusque.

"Nothing, just a friendly little visit to young Evelyn."

"Her name is Evie," I say with a hint of warning in my voice. "What the hell would you want to see her for? You don't even know her."

"Well, that's why I'm here. To get acquainted. Now, if you don't mind, I really need to be going."

"Not so fast," I say as I slip one hand around her upper arm.

I haven't seen or spoken to her since I fucked her and called her Evie by mistake. It's no coincidence she's here.

"Let go of me," she shrieks.

"Not until I know what you've done."

I drag her inside the bakery with me as I juggle holding the flowers and opening the door.

Evie's head bobs up as the bell over the door jingles, and if looks could kill, both Bobby and I would be dead in an instant.

I look at Bobby and she just smiles, unaffected by the vibes coming from Evie.

Ryan stands with his hands on his hips and looks at me as if I'm something he stepped in. What the hell has Bobby done? Only one way to find out.

"Ryan, could you take these please?" I ask as I hand the bouquet to him.

He tries not to take them from me but has to catch them when I let go. He puts them on the counter and tuts at me as Evie's heels click-clack on the floor as she walks to where I'm standing.

"Get out, both of you," she seethes, rage rolling off her in waves.

"No. I'm not going anywhere. And neither is she until I know what went down in here."

I stand defiant as she tries to stare me down. I let go of Bobby's arm as I roughly push her to one side.

"Who wants to be the first to tell me what the—"

I see Maya at a table not too far away and stop myself from swearing. Lowering my voice, I continue.

"What went on here?"

"Maybe you guys should take this elsewhere, you know, little ears and all," Ry says.

"I'm not going anywhere with him," Evie says, her voice laced with disgust.

Her words hurt me, because I haven't done anything here.

"Evie, babe, you need to hear him out. I know, I know what I said"— he holds his hands up in surrender—"but every story has two sides."

"Fine." She huffs as she turns on her heel and walks in the direction of the decorating room.

I grab Bobby's arm and drag her with me as I follow hot on Evie's heels.

Once the door is closed behind us, I don't have a chance to speak as a hard slap rocks my head to the side. *Fuck, that hurts.*

"What the hell, Evie?" I ask in shock.

"You had it coming you … you pig," she spits.

"What am I supposed to have done here?"

"You've been stringing me along like some … some … tart. You've been screwing this little slapper all along and playing me for a damn fool. How could you, Trey? I thought I meant something to you. You gained my trust; I trusted you with my heart and Maya's. But you aren't worthy of that trust, you two-timing prick."

"What the—"

I look at Bobby and see her eyes alight with glee. She's caused this, and she'll damn well fix it.

"What the hell have you been saying, Roberta?"

"Telling your little *girlfriend*," she says, air quoting the word, "that she doesn't mean anything to you."

"And what on God's green earth gave you the right to lie like that?"

"Pfft! The right? I have every fucking right after you fucked me seven ways from Sunday and then called out *her* name. You think that didn't hurt? Well, think again, asshole."

"So, let me get this straight … you came here to destroy my relationship because you're jealous? You're upset that I didn't choose to settle down with you? To *love* you?"

"Love? Don't make me laugh. You always come back to me. No matter what. You're incapable of monogamy, much less *love*."

I see Evie watching our exchange with a confused expression furrowing her brow.

"Roberta, you are one psychotic little bunny boiler. I'd be surprised if you knew how to spell love. You're only capable of being psychotic. You're fixated. I don't get it. You and me, we were only ever fuckbuddies. That's it. Nothing more. Never have been, never will be. And I stopped fucking you long ago. I have been nothing but faithful to Evie. I haven't even seen you or spoken to you since that afternoon. You're right, I fucked you and called you Evie. Why? Because she'd worked her way under my skin without my permission, and I needed to fuck you to relieve the ache. That's all it was. I wanted to be buried inside Evie from the instant her grey eyes looked at me for the first time."

I pause to take a deep breath, and I look directly at Evie and instead talk to her.

"Evie, it's true that Bobby and I used to be intimate." The word leaves a bitter taste on my tongue. "But that stopped before you and I started dating. I meant every word when I told you I don't date. And Bobby and I have never dated. We've fucked, but nothing more. I've never felt anything for her. Except the disgust I feel right now.

"Bobby and I haven't slept together since before I got up the courage to ask you out. It's true, I screwed her, and I called out your name. She's come here today to try and ruin what we have because she's jealous. She can't take it that I want you and only you. But that's her problem, not ours. What we have is far too precious for me to ever fuck it up or let it go."

"What? You realise this is all a lie, don't you, Evie? He's lying through his teeth."

"Don't make me laugh, Roberta. You're a jealous whore," I bark.

Evie looks between us both but doesn't speak.

My mouth gets the better of me as I confess the truth in my soul.

"Evie Slater, you are everything to me. You and Maya are my world. I need you to look at me and know I am speaking the truth. I would never cheat on you; I wouldn't even dream of it. You are all I want, all I *need*. Why on earth would I build a relationship with you, with your daughter, if I didn't really care about you both? Why would I risk breaking your heart? For some floozy like her?" I cast a disgusted look towards Bobby, who is now standing with a look of shock on her face. "Do you truly believe I'd do that? Look into my eyes and see the truth in my words. I didn't think I was capable of ever building a lasting relationship, but you showed me that I am capable. I want us to have a future together, the three of us. You, me and Maya, that's how I see my future."

"You see a future with her, but you couldn't with me?" Bobby asks, interrupting me. Her voice is pained, and the look on her face is crestfallen.

"I do, Bobby. I'm sorry that you can't handle that, but it doesn't make it any less true."

"W-why?" she asks, her bottom lip quivering and unshed tears glistening in her eyes.

I look at Evie and reach for her hand. She doesn't resist as I take it in mine.

"Because I love you, Evie. That's why. I've never said that to another living person besides my sister, but I mean it with all my heart and soul, everything that I am now and everything that I will ever come to be. You've taught me to live instead of just existing. Piece by piece, you've fixed something in me that has been broken since I was nineteen years old. This isn't how I envisaged telling you, but every single thing I said is true; I *love* you, Evie."

Bobby runs for the door, barging past me with tears rolling down her face. I truly never meant to hurt her, but I've never felt anything real for her, and she needed to hear that even if she didn't *want* to.

I stand before Evie; her silence is deafening. It speaks volumes, telling me I've screwed this up and that regardless of me loving her, she doesn't reciprocate my feelings.

"I'm truly sorry, Evie. For all the pain I've unintentionally caused you. I know I don't deserve you, and I don't deserve to ask a favour of you ... but please ... let me say goodbye to Maya. It isn't her fault, and

I know better than a lot of people how it is to feel unloved as a child. She doesn't deserve to shoulder the doubt about how I feel about her. Truth is, I love her too. I love her as if she were my own. I don't want to say goodbye." I pause to take a shuddering breath as tears begin to cascade down my face. "I-I'm so sorry, Evie. So very, deeply sorry. What we had—"

A sob chokes me as I use the word in the past tense

"What we had meant the world to me, and I will cherish my memories of it fondly. For what it's worth, I don't think I'll ever love another woman again. You were it for me, sweetheart. You were my world."

Chapter Seventeen

Evie

His revelation repeats in my mind. I want so desperately to scream back how I feel, but I can't seem to make my brain, or my mouth, cooperate. I watch as he scans my face desperately, and upon seeing the blankness reflected back at him, his face crumbles and he turns on his heel, walking away from me. From *us*.

I continue the internal fight in my body, desperately trying to make it do what I want it to do. I manage to spur my body into action. I spring forward and grab his arm, and he spins around with a pained look on his face. Shock at me reaching for him flashes through his eyes momentarily, but they quickly fade back to a haunted expression.

I can't blame him. He bared his soul, told me everything in his heart, and then I just stood there, mute.

I take in a deep breath, trying to think of how to approach this. What do I say? How do I tell him how I feel?

"You have never caused me any pain. None. You haven't done anything that I haven't been constantly thankful for. You've brought love and happiness into my life. Honestly? I have felt like I have been falling in love with you since day one. I thought it was too soon and that it wouldn't be reciprocated." I take a deep, shuddering breath. "I once thought that what I had was love, but I figured out that it wasn't. He broke me, systematically put me down and hurt me; he made me believe that I would never be capable of loving somebody, and that I'm not *worthy* of love; he made me feel *worthless*, both inside and out,"

I pause, and at the mention of Greg, Trey's eyes look like he's capable of murder. He instinctively takes a step towards me.

"But then you came along. *You* made me feel special, like I *was* worthy.

I never knew real love was until you came along. What I had with Greg wasn't love, it was just me being scared to be alone. But you brought out *something* in me, and I want—no, *need*—to explore this more. I don't want *you* to leave *us*, and *I* don't want to leave *you*. I want you to be part of this family. You haven't just helped me become more confident, you've helped Maya too. She's doing things that she wouldn't usually do. She's speaking more to people; she's come out of her shell. I would *never* take that away from her. *I* love *you*. *Maya* loves *you*. I'm sorry for slapping you in the face." I wince as I see the red mark on the side of his face. "When Bobby told me that, it just made me so … upset, which then turned into anger. I'm really sorry."

"There is no need for you to be sorry," replies Trey. "You were upset. Bobby came in here with one intention—to jeopardise everything I hold dear. It wasn't even about you. You were only her target because I've been ignoring her, so you were her way of getting to me. So if anyone's to blame, it's her. She came in and decided to mess up something good, because she is jealous. There hasn't been anything going on between us for a long time; it's only been you. And you don't understand how relieved it makes me feel hearing those words come from your lips. I thought it was just me, and that hurt in more ways than one. I felt hurt that I laid everything out only for you to reject me, but it also took me back to a childhood lacking in love. That's a story for another day, but I just flashed back to painful memories, a lot of loss and regret."

He pauses for breath before continuing.

"I'm used to losing the people I love. I'm used to protecting my heart and not even allowing love in. I didn't mean to fall in love with you. I don't mean that to sound harsh, it's just true. You were something unexpected, Evie, and when I realised I loved you, that was a momentous thing for me. But the look of utter shock on your face … that was like a sucker punch that sucked all the oxygen out of my lungs. I thought you didn't feel anything for me and that this has all been one-sided, that I've imagined you feeling the same connection I feel."

I place my palm where I hit him on the side of his face. I lock eyes with him, and see unshed tears, but his handsome face is now stretched with a huge grin residing there. His arms sweep around my waist and he pulls my body into his. I take a deep breath, inhaling his masculine and comforting scent. In that moment I realise something—he smells like *home*.

I slowly reach up and claim his lips with mine. I feel the kiss travel through me, making my stomach do somersaults. Before we have a chance to let it go any further, the decorating room doors burst open. We turn, and I see Ry standing there with a huge grin stretched on his face.

"So, you've sorted it out, then? I don't need to castrate anybody?" He gives Trey a pointed look.

I laugh at his attempt to appear mean. That's something my soft-hearted friend doesn't have it in him to be, unless someone really hurts me or Maya.

"I'll be right back and let you two macho men fight it out to the death." I pat Ry's chest as I walk past, watching him pretend to puff his chest out. I see Maya sitting at the same table she was at earlier. I look around and notice that Ry has closed the bakery, which is why he was comfortable to leave Maya out here to check on us. Probably to make sure I hadn't killed him.

I stand there and watch her for a couple of seconds. She's sitting on a chair, swinging her legs back and forth while colouring. I realise that Ry has left his phone on the table, and it has Disney songs playing in the background while Maya hums along. I smile. It isn't very often that I get to just stand here and watch her; she usually goes on high alert when she is left alone, even if it's just for a second. A calmness washes over me as I come to the realisation that there isn't anything to be afraid of, that I *can* let myself be happy and enjoy the rest of my life.

Maya's head whips up when I get closer, and she looks up at me, a grin etched into her face. She runs over to me, and I kneel just in time to reciprocate the hug she wants to give me.

"You okay, Mummy?"

Her eyes keenly scan my face and body language. Ever since she has been old enough to walk, she has been able to tell that something has happened by just how I act. I know it's because of how scared I was when she was younger, so it has rubbed off on her to check if I'm okay constantly. I'm glad that this time, without lying, I can confidently tell her that *everything* is fine.

"I'm great, baby. Come with me a second?"

I stand up and take her outstretched hand, leading her into the decorating room. By the time we get in there, Trey and Ry are sitting on stools, laughing and joking around. Maya instantly drops my hand and runs towards Trey. He reaches down and picks her up, sitting her on the table in front of him. The relationship that they have created in the short time they have known each other has shocked me. I've never seen her let somebody get this close to her in such a short amount of time. She has always been hesitant to let people get to know her.

I walk up and lean into Trey's side. Just as I do, his free arm wraps around me, pulling me closer.

I take a deep breath, wanting to let Maya know what is going on, but not knowing how to properly go about it. Before I have a chance to figure out what to say, Trey starts to talk.

"I want you to know that I may have only been friends with your mum for a little amount of time, but we have decided to be boyfriend and girlfriend. Do you know what that means?"

Maya instantly starts to smile, nodding her head to tell him she understands.

"That means you love Mummy, right? Like, more than lemon tart?"

She looks at Trey with big eyes, waiting for him to answer her. He chuckles at her question and takes a deep breath.

"It means I love you *both*. Not just your mum, but *you* also. I definitely love you more than lemon tart, and that's saying something, because it's my favourite."

As he says this, his hand tightens on my waist. I can feel the nerves radiating off him as he waits for Maya's reaction to his words. She looks up at him, her bottom lip wobbling as she tries to keep unshed tears at bay. Trey looks up at me with shock all over his face.

"Only Mummy, Uncle Ry, and my nanna and grandpa has only tolds me they loves me more than lemon tart. I loves you too. I love how you play with me and make me laugh, and how you make my mummy smile and laugh."

She smiles shyly at him and opens her arms, silently asking for a hug. Trey smiles and let's go of my waist. He leans forward and gathers her in his arms, and she winds her arms around his neck.

I quietly move away, letting them have their moment, I bump into Ryan who, while they were talking, stood up and made his way around the table towards me. Maya lifts her head, which was nestled in the crook of Trey's neck, and looks up at me and Ry.

"Group hug?"

She beams up at us, and we laugh and make our way over. As I get closer, I notice that Trey's eyes are glistening with unshed tears. I wrap both my arms around them, kissing Trey's cheek in the process, and Ry takes the other side, doing the same. We stand there for a couple of seconds, just basking in the love that is radiating off each other. Ry is the first to talk, bursting the bubble that we are encased in.

"I am unbelievably happy that you guys are finally telling each other how you feel, because it's been driving me insane how you haven't acknowledged it."

He shakes his head in mock annoyance. We all laugh at him.

"I love you too, Ry."

***

Standing outside Maya's room, I try to be as quiet as possible as I listen to Trey read her a bedtime story. I have to stifle my laughter at the different voices he's managing to pull for all the different characters while he reads *The Cat in The Hat*. For as long as I can remember, Maya has been obsessed with Dr. Seuss. She has a small bookshelf in the corner of her room, which is filled with a complete boxset of the entirety of his books. She also has the majority of the original Disney books, my old collection from when I was a child.

I quickly make my way downstairs when I notice he is coming to the end of the story. I go about making us both a coffee and cleaning the kitchen while I can.

After the events earlier, the rest of the day was one of my calmest and laziest. Trey came back to ours after we made sure *Queen of Tarts* was shut up properly. We ended up watching some Disney films, and Maya spent the entire time telling Trey who was who, and what she loved about each character. I enjoyed just sitting there and watching them interact.

There's something about watching her and Trey build their relationship and squabble over who is the best Disney princess. They got into quite a heavy debate as to whether Moana is classed as one … I refused to get involved. The bond between the two brings me so much happiness. The one thing I wanted from a man was that he could accept that I am a single mother and that Maya comes first, before me and before anybody. And Trey just strolled up and accepted it all from the word go. He understood that she was my main priority without me having to tell him directly. We've never even discussed his love and acceptance of Maya, because it's evident for all to see that she means as much to him as I do.

Being a single mum is hard work, but it's ultimately so rewarding, seeing her grow into the little lady she's becoming—headstrong and feisty, just like her mother—and that brings me more pride than anything else in the world.

Bringing someone into our little bubble wasn't something I thought about doing, thanks to Greg. Trey wasn't even a remote possibility, until all of a sudden, he was. Something about him was different and he made me let my walls down. I allowed him to develop a bond with my daughter, which came easier than I ever thought possible.

I always knew that no matter who I dated in the future, they needed to accept we come as a package. But I come with baggage, and I didn't expect someone like Trey to come in and knock down all my walls. But here he is anyway. And my walls have crumbled to dust.

We ended up squashing ourselves onto the one sofa and snuggled under a throw blanket; it actually felt like we were a proper family, having a regular night. It all felt just so *natural*.

I was too lazy to cook, so we ended up ordering in. I usually don't like ordering takeaway too often, but after the course of today's events, I was too emotionally drained to stand in the kitchen and cook for the next hour. Maya was happy, as she usually is when she finds out we're ordering Indian.

The sound of Trey walking down the stairs brings me back to reality. I turn and smile at him.

"Is that mine?" he asks as he points to the cup of coffee on the side.

"Yup, I've already drank mine. I basically drink it as soon as it's in the cup."

He looks at me, taken aback by the fact I drink it scalding hot.

"I don't understand how you can drink it that hot; that just seems like torture."

"My dad says the same. My mum does it too, and he said it must be a female thing. Something about us being closer to hell, so we can handle it hotter."

I shrug and make my way back into the living room. As Trey follows, he laughs. We both sit back on the sofa and cuddle under the blankets. He channel surfs and stops when he comes across reruns of *Friends*.

"Do you mind? *Friends* has always been this secret addiction of mine. I've lost count of how many times I've watched it from start to finish."

"I don't mind; I love the show. I can't remember either, but it just doesn't get old. I've got the entire boxset on the shelf over there, and I usually find myself reaching for it more than not. The one episode that I can't watch very often is the whole Rachel and Ross fiasco; it just grinds my gears."

I grin sheepishly at him. He chuckles and settles in. We find ourselves watching hours of the show, laughing from start to finish. By the time the reruns have finished, with the promise of them returning tomorrow, I look at the time.

"Oh, my god. It's half eleven! I don't know how I've stayed up this late."

"I should probably get going. I completely lost track of time; I didn't mean to stay this late."

He starts to stand up to leave, and a sudden wave of sadness washes over me at the thought of this bubble having to end.

"Umm ... I know it may be soon, but then we've told each other we love each other and, umm ..."

Trey laughs, breaking my rambling.

"You ramble when you're nervous. Has anybody ever told you that?"

I groan and try to hide under the throw. He pulls it away from my face and smiles.

"*Everyone* tells me that. I think it's one of my worst qualities."

"It's cute."

"*Cute?* Cute is what you call an animal. It's *embarrassing.*"

He bursts into laughter.

"Okay, it's endearing. Is that better?" he asks with a laugh. "What were you saying anyway?"

"Oh, I was just wondering if you would, umm ... stay for the night?" He gets a look on his face that I can't quite place, so I try to quickly backtrack. "I mean, you don't have to feel like you have to. It was just a thought, you know."

I shrug my shoulders, instantly feeling self-conscious. He instantly smiles. Why is he smiling? Didn't he just try to reject my offer?

"I thought you would never ask. I would love to stay the night. I'll have to leave early, though, because of work. I was trying to calculate what time I would have to leave."

I relax at his statement and shrug off the feeling of not feeling confident.

"You're getting awfully familiar with the word love, aren't you?"

I bump his hip with mine as I walk past him, letting him know that I'm joking. He chuckles and silently follows me up the stairs to my room. I suddenly realise he has no clothes here. He notices that I've stopped by the cupboard and I'm just standing there. He comes behind me and wraps his arms around my waist.

"What's going on in that pretty little head of yours?"

"I've, umm … not actually had anybody in my bed aside from Maya, like *at all*. It's weird, but then not weird either, does that make any sense?"

He starts making lazy circles on my stomach, and his touch starts to stir something inside of me.

"I understand what you mean. I don't have to stay if you don't want me to. All you have to do is say the words."

I groan as a sensation builds between my legs.

"No, I want you to stay."

I feel him move my hair from my neck and, as he trails kisses from my shoulder and up to the base of my ear, goosebumps appear in his wake.

I try to contain a groan as my need for him builds. He spins me around to face him and captures my lips in a soul-crushing kiss. He sweeps his tongue against the seam of my lips, begging for entrance. I gladly concede and part my lips for him. His tongue dances with mine as he kicks the door closed with his foot. He guides me back until the backs of my knees smack against the bed. I fall back, not expecting the bed to be so close.

He hovers over me, continuing his exploration of my body as he trails kisses over the swell of my breasts, moving my vest top and bra in the process. My nipples pebble as he briefly swirls his tongue around them, before kissing his way down between the valley of my breasts. He continues down to my abdomen until he reaches the top of my leggings.

He gently pulls them down, along with my thong, but before he has a chance to do anything else, I sit up and reach to take his shirt off.

He shakes his head at me.

"Tonight is for you, and for you alone."

I try to argue in some way, but he takes advantage of the upright position I'm in and pulls my taut nipple into his mouth again. I groan and comply when he gently guides me back down to the bed.

I try to control my breathing, but I shudder and gasp when he gently eases his finger inside me. My hands subconsciously grip the sheets. He builds a steady rhythm and leans down to suck my clit, making the euphoria that I'm feeling skyrocket. His finger hits my G-spot multiple times and my hips buck. I try to stifle my moan of pleasure as I reach my climax.

"Oh god …"

I moan as the wave of pleasure travels through my body. I try to gain control of my body once again, but I fail. Little aftershocks continue to course through me.

Trey stands and strips down to his boxers, his erection obvious, and climbs into bed beside me. He pulls the covers from under me, then pulls them up over us. He pulls me into his chest and tucks his arm under my head.

"That was the sexiest thing I have ever seen," he whispers in my ear. "There's just something about watching your orgasm tear through you and you riding the crest of the wave."

"Let me do something to repay you."

"No. We can do this for forever. We have time to properly explore each other's bodies; I have just been getting acquainted."

"I like the sound of that."

I try to stifle a yawn but fail miserably.

"Go to sleep. I love you."

I feel my body relax as he curls around me more, my body fitting against his perfectly. I don't think I will ever tire of him saying that, just knowing that this could be my forever. I don't think I could ask for a better way to live this life. I feel my eyes start to droop as tiredness consumes me.

"I love you too," I manage to mutter, before falling into a blissful sleep.

Chapter Eighteen

Trey

I get to work a few minutes late after taking a shower with Evie this morning. I have a stack of files that need putting away, so I call through to my assistant, Leanne, to ask her to file them for me.

I have a nagging feeling lingering in the back of my head. I need to tell Evie about my past. She doesn't know all the skeletons in my closet yet. Whilst a lot of people don't air their dirty laundry so soon into a relationship, I know that the sooner I tell her, the better. I want her to know what she's getting herself into before we get in too deep.

Having already told her I love her, I know that I'm in so deeply that it will hurt me if she runs when she finds out. It will be like her reaching into my chest and tearing out my heart, using it as a trampoline and then pushing it back into my empty chest cavity, battered and bruised and barely beating.

I pull a file out of my drawer, needing something to keep me occupied, but this isn't strictly work. For a while now I've had an idea in the back of my mind but meeting Evie and hearing her story has really brought it to the forefront. Add to that the suicide note from Leah and it makes it all the more important.

There's this abandoned building I've come across through work, and it would make the perfect place to build the foundations of my idea. What started as a little seed planted in my mind has grown over time. I've seen all these women when I do our firm's pro bono cases, and people like them need somewhere to feel safe. There isn't anywhere for them to go that's actually local, so they end up moving miles away from everything they know because there's no other choice.

I've called the building manager, and I've taken a look around the place. I've even used my work contacts to put other things into place. Now more than ever, I know I need to do as much as I can to help people. It's what I've worked so hard for all through my adult life. I live to help people. Sure, I work plenty of other types of cases in my job, but it's helping abused women that gives me the most satisfaction, knowing I am making a difference in their lives.

I've spoken to the holder of Leah's trust fund. Our grandparents left us both money when they passed away, maybe because they knew that we'd need it one day. Maybe they knew foster care wouldn't really pan out for us. Or maybe they just prepared for that eventuality.

When Leah died, her money became mine. Our grandparents stipulated that if something was to happen to one or the other of us, then the surviving one would get all the money. Perhaps they assumed I'd die, and Leah would be able to make something of her life with the money. But they got that wrong. Instead of me, my innocent little sister was the one who died.

We both escaped our lives, but in totally different ways.

When her money became mine, I didn't want to touch it, so I left it in the trust fund. But now, I need a bit of extra cash to purchase the building I want to turn into a shelter. As the money is technically mine, there's nothing stopping me from using it. It's just that I haven't wanted to because it felt like I was betraying Leah.

But now, well, now I'm not betraying Leah, I'm honouring her. I intend to name the shelter after her in some way.

I know that I've never told anyone Leah's story. To be honest, that's partly because I'm a private person, and partly because there was always a piece of the story missing. Since finding her note, that piece has finally fallen into place. So, now, armed with all the facts, I want to do something, even if it means having to tell her story ... and mine.

Before I do all that, though, Evie needs to know.

***

I invited Evie over to my place and said I'd cook. Ry is watching Maya, because I told him there are things I needed to say to Evie without Maya hearing. He was cool with it, although he did give me a look that said if I hurt his friend, he'd hunt me down and nobody would find the body.

The sauce smells great, and I'm just waiting for the tagliatelle and garlic bread to finish cooking. I cheated and bought a garlic baguette, but the sauce for the bolognese is made from scratch.

The doorbell goes, and I turn the gas ring down slightly, so it doesn't boil over.

"Hey, beautiful."

"Hey, something smells good, even all the way out here."

I take her small hand in mine and guide her through to the kitchen.

"I might not be able to bake, but being a single guy, you learn to cook, or you live on a diet of ramen noodles."

Evie giggles, and damn if it doesn't make my heart flutter at the sound.

"So, what are we having?" she asks as I pull two glasses out of the cupboard.

"Bolognese, but because I don't like spaghetti very much, I've substituted it with tagliatelle. Is that okay? Oh, and there's garlic bread, but I'll admit I didn't make that from scratch. It's care of Waitrose."

"Mmm. Sounds good and smells delicious."

"Red or white? Or are you a rosé kind of girl?"

"Ooh, white would be good, thanks."

I pour two glasses of white wine and continue to stir the sauce as Evie takes her glass and comes to stand next to me.

I dish up and carry our bowls through to the dining room, where I've set the table with candles and fresh flowers. Stargazer lilies are so beautiful, and they brighten up any room. When did I become so girly?

"This room is beautiful, Trey. So much natural light filters through. I love it."

"Thank you. It's one of my favourite rooms."

We make small talk while we eat which helps calm my nerves a little, but I can't deny how nervous I am to open up to her properly.

As I load the dishwasher, Evie pours some more wine. Once I'm finished, I take her hand and lead her into my study.

I pull the gift box from my bottom drawer and put it on my desk.

"This is something for Maya for her birthday, but there's a story behind it, a story I need you to hear."

I clear my throat and then take the lid off the box. Carefully pulling Rabbit out, I hand him to Evie.

"This belonged to a very special person in my life, one I didn't do enough for, and she was taken from me too soon." I choke back a sob. "Her name was Leah, and she was my little sister. This, here, is Rabbit.

He's seen better days when he was full of stuffing and wasn't so faded. But I recently fixed him; he needed new eyes and more stuffing if he was going to belong to Maya."

"It's beautiful, Trey. Maya will love him. And I'm sure it will mean more, knowing that it belonged to Leah."

"I've bought her something new too, I just wanted her to have this. It's been with me for many years s-since Leah d-died." I swallow around a rising lump in my throat. "Leah sadly died when she was just eighteen, but she'd had Rabbit since she was a toddler. He was her favourite thing, and she couldn't sleep without him when she was younger. I know I haven't told you much about my past, and that's one reason I asked you here tonight. You need to know before getting in too deep with me, and if you want to walk away when I tell you, I swear I won't hold it against you."

Evie looks at me as she traces small circles on the back of my hand. Her eyes are full of curiosity, but I see no trace of the worry I thought I'd see.

"Leah and I grew up in foster care. Our parents were so young when they had us. If the information I have is correct, my father was sixteen and my mother was fifteen when they had me, then they had Leah a year later. Apparently neither of the pregnancies was planned. Their parents argued over what was best for us. My paternal grandparents wanted them to give us up, give us to a couple who could give us a better life. Their argument was that our parents hadn't had their lives yet, they were just beginning, but another couple who were stable could offer us a good home.

"Anyway, my maternal grandparents wanted them to keep us. They said they were doing a good job with me, and they'd cope now they had Leah too. But they couldn't make our parents' minds up for them. Eventually, we went into foster care, with the hope that a loving couple would adopt the two of us.

"You hear stories about children who fall through the cracks in the foster system, less so now than back then, but we ended up falling through the cracks and into a pit of darkness."

I stop and take a sip of my wine, my mouth feeling as dry as cotton wool.

"We were bounced from home to home, never staying in one place too long. I tried to protect Leah like any big brother should. I looked out for her the best a boy of my age could.

"I would goad them into hurting me instead of Leah. All of our foster fathers were abusive. They would whip me with belts—using the buckle end—and beat me so badly. Leah would do something they thought was wrong, and I would try to shield her from the beatings, making them angry at me to take the attention away from her."

Evie still says nothing, but I can read her thoughts as they flit across her face. She's sad for the children Leah and I were.

I grab my bottle of whiskey and pour myself a generous amount. I offer Evie some, but she shakes her head. Taking a large gulp, I feel the burn ease down the back of my throat, and it offers some relief to the pain I'm feeling at bringing up all these old memories.

Telling Evie the rest of our story is the hardest thing I think I've ever had to do, but I do it because she needs to know the boy behind the man I am today.

"Rabbit is the only thing I have of Leah's now, except memories. As I was fixing him, I found a piece of paper rolled up inside him. I'm not sure whether Leah wanted me to find it or not. Maybe she'd given up caring; I don't really know. But I found it and read it before burning it. She told me she loved me, and she didn't blame me for not being there to protect her when I went off to study law.

"The truth is, she's the reason I studied law in the first place. Well, because of both of us, but mainly Leah. But I wasn't home enough to see what she was going through. Our last foster father before we aged out of care, he … r-r-raped h-her." A sob tears through me at having to say those words aloud. "Geez, this is so hard. Umm … so, he didn't stop raping her after we moved out of their home. He would find Leah and r-rape her repeatedly. She … she kept a tally scratched into the wall of the amount of times he did it.

"I should have been there, Evie. I should have saved her. She overdosed, and I wasn't there to stop her. I got there too late. She was already—"

I take a few deep breaths before continuing.

"She was already dead when I arrived. I called an ambulance, but it was futile. She was gone."

"Oh, Trey," Evie says, making me look her in the eye.

I see tears trailing down her face and reach to wipe them away with the pads of my thumbs.

"Don't cry, Evie. Please."

"Trey, this is obviously too painful to talk about. You can stop. You don't need to say more."

"But I do, Evie. I'm responsible for my beautiful sister's death, and you shouldn't want to be with a man like me. My darkness, my poison, will taint your innocence. It will taint Maya. And that's the very last thing I want. I should have thought about that before getting too close to you. But for a man who doesn't do relationships and has never experienced love … I was selfish, and I got close to you, to you both. I understand if you want to walk away, I really do. I'm a disgrace. I didn't save the person who meant the most to me in life."

"Trey, don't you see? It isn't your fault. Leah's demons were too much for her to bear. She was eighteen, and she'd been beaten, abused, neglected … r-raped." I watch her throat bob up and down as she swallows. "She used drugs as an escape, and from what you've told me, she couldn't break the cycle she was in. That is in no way, shape or form your fault. You did what you could."

"But it wasn't enough."

I crumble in my chair, my shoulders drooping and my head falling to my chest, as I cry openly. The loss of Leah feels so fresh right now.

"Trey, listen to me. Look at me, please. You need to see the truth in my words."

I look up, and it takes all my strength to hold her gaze as she continues to talk.

"You were enough. You did more for her than anyone else in her life. You were her one constant. She was lucky to have you. Maybe you don't see it, but I do. I didn't have anyone except Greg. I would have been lucky to have someone like you fighting my corner, shielding me from the hurt he inflicted. Leah had that. Leah was lucky.

"I am so sorry that she took her own life. Trust me, I've been where she was, in the sense that I too took an overdose once upon a time. It didn't work. I wished like anything that it had, because he came to collect me from hospital, and when he opened the curtain to the cubicle, I screamed at him and told him to get away from me. I told him I wasn't his possession, his little toy, but he grabbed my clothes and threw them at me. He pulled the curtain shut and helped me pull on my clothes, then he signed discharge papers to get me out of there.

"When we got home, he made me some soup because I couldn't

swallow, but later beat me so badly that I ended up back in hospital with broken ribs and a laceration on my scalp. He told them I'd tripped down the stairs because I was still woozy from the tablets, and they were gullible enough to believe him.

"So, whilst I didn't have the *same* life Leah, there are some parallels. She was beaten, so was I. She took an overdose, so did I. Luckily for me, it didn't work. It sure didn't feel lucky at the time, but look where I am today; I own my own home and my own business, and I have a beautiful daughter.

"Sadly, life didn't work out that way for Leah. Her demons were too strong for her to resist. But you, Trey, have nothing to be ashamed of. You were her brother, her protector and she loved you so much. You said she felt like she held you back, but she didn't, did she? She spurred you on to help women like her."

"But I couldn't help her. I had my head buried in my studies. I was blind to her pain."

"You weren't blind. You saw it. You did what any brother would. Okay, so in the end, it wasn't enough to save her, but that isn't your fault. It's nobody's fault. If you'd saved Leah that fateful day, she would have found another time and place to do it when you weren't around. Why do you think she waited until you were gone? Her overdose wasn't a cry for help. She wanted to die. That's heartbreaking, but it's also the truth."

I pick up my glass and swirl the amber liquid round, watching as it moves.

"You're amazing, Evie." My words are a barely audible whisper, but I know she can hear me.

Standing from her chair, she places Rabbit on my desk and comes to stand in front of me. She stands between my legs and I look up at her. I place my glass on the desk and put my hands on her hips. I pull her towards me, and she comes willingly.

"I need you, Evie. I need you to help me forget, just for a few minutes. Will you help me forget?"

I don't know if she knows exactly what I'm asking, but I can't explain. I want to lose myself in her, because I love her, and she can help wash away the darkness I feel like I'm drowning in.

She leans down to kiss me, and I slide my hands up under her dress, finding the material of her thong and pulling it down over her knees. The material pools at her feet and she kicks it aside.

I toy with her clit and she moans into my mouth as I kiss her. Sliding my finger back and forth between her wet folds makes her gasp.

Her warmth is deliciously inviting as I slide one finger inside her. Her back arches, and she holds onto my shoulders, her head thrown back in ecstasy as I slide my finger in and out, while using my thumb to toy with her clit.

Evie falls back against my desk and I push everything behind her to one side with my free hand. I push her back, and she lies on my desk. I watch her breasts rise and fall with her rapid breaths.

Sliding another finger inside her makes her cry out my name. My heart races and my cock throbs, begging to be buried inside her. I work her harder, and she grips the edge of the desk, her knuckles turning white.

"Harder, Trey, please ..." she moans.

A growl reverberates through my chest as I give her what she needs. Her legs wrap around my waist as I slide my fingers in and out of her in a relentless, almost punishing rhythm. It doesn't take long for her to cry out her orgasm. She rides the waves of the delicious little aftershocks coursing through her as I suck her juices from my fingers.

I quickly undo my jeans and pull them down, along with my boxers. Without giving her warning, I align myself with her and push inside in one swift move. Evie cries out as I slam into her over and over.

I unbutton the top of her summer dress, exposing her breasts, covered only by her bra. Reaching behind her as her back arches, I unclasp her bra and pull the straps down her arms. I discard the material and lean over her. Swirling my tongue around her nipple until it's a stiff peak, I look up and see her pleasure written on her face.

I do the same to the other nipple, then bite down gently as it pebbles under my tongue. I slow down my movements, not wanting it to be over too soon.

Toying with her clit with one hand, I reach up and cup her breast with the other. Her moans spur me on, driving me crazy with lust, desire and an overwhelming feeling of love. Her hands reach up and grasp at my hair as I fuck her slowly, pulling almost all the way out of her before driving back inside.

Her long legs wrap around me and her heels dig into my ass. I didn't realise she still had her high heels on, but the sting only increases my desire.

I reach my hands up under the hem of her dress and grasp her hips tightly.

"Evie."

She looks up at the sound of her name.

"Look at me."

Her gaze stays level with mine as I build a steady rhythm, driving in and out of her and driving myself out of my mind in the process.

This. This right here is what I need to forget my troubles. I want to drown in her love.

"Touch yourself for me, Evie. Reach up and cup your breasts. Toy with your nipples as if your hands were mine."

She complies, her eyes still trained on me.

"I love you, Evie Slater. My mind, my heart, my soul and my body, they are all yours. Forever."

Her eyes mist over at my words, and I lean in to place a chaste kiss on her lips before climbing higher and higher, chasing her orgasm before my own.

It isn't long before she crashes over me in a tidal wave of ecstasy. I don't relent as she cries out at the sensation of being pushed beyond her climax. I grip her hips harder and fuck her faster, now chasing my own climax.

Her walls clench around me, coaxing my orgasm out of me. I fall over the edge of oblivion as I see stars in her eyes.

Collapsing down on top of her, I claim her sweet lips with mine, and the taste of her mingles with the whiskey on my breath. Her nails rake down my back, no doubt leaving red marks in their wake, but I don't care. I kiss her with every ounce of energy I have left.

***

"You are it for me, Evie Slater," I admit softly as she lies in bed next to me.

Her head is resting on my chest, my heart pounding underneath her. We came up to shower, but instead ended up in my bed.

I reach down and toy with her nipple. It pebbles under my touch and I smile like a loon. I love the reactions I draw out of her.

Reaching my hand down further, I grasp the base of my budding erection. We might have lain here to rest, exhausted from our escapades in my office, but now I'm getting hard again. I can't help it. Her naked body pressed against mine is of little help in stopping how I feel.

I work myself over, knowing she's watching what I'm doing. I can hear and feel her breaths coming faster.

Sliding down my body, Evie takes my cock in her hand and my hands fall to the sheets as she pumps her hand up and down at a steady pace. As she increases her speed, my breaths come sharp and fast. My body reacts to her touch, and the smile that spreads across her face tells me she knows what she's doing to me.

I lock eyes with her beautiful grey gaze, and she leans down to suck and lick at the tip of my cock. Her lustrous hair falls around me, so I gather it in one hand, pulling it out of my line of sight.

She takes me further into her mouth as her hand keeps the pace. Her tongue swirls around me, and I can feel my balls begin to tighten, a warning that my orgasm is imminent.

"Fuck," I cry as she increases her pace. I'm so close. I can't hold out much longer.

Reaching her free hand down, she cups my balls and I can't help my body's reaction as I come in hot spurts down the back of her throat. She licks me clean of every drop before coming up to meet my gaze. Her eyes are filled with lust.

She brings out the devil in me, and I have a feeling that our kind of love does something to her that she's never felt before.

"I love you, baby," I say as she crawls up over me and lies beside me once more.

"I love you too, Trey. So, so much."

Those are the last words I hear before drifting off to sleep.

***

I watch Evie leave, and my heart squeezes in my chest. I wish she didn't have to leave. I wish we could be together all the time. Just the three of us—me, her and Maya. Maybe one day it could be the four of us. That would be the ultimate thing to make my life complete, a baby that is part Evie and part me. Not that I would treat that baby any differently to Maya, of course. I love the bones of that girl.

Going back into my study, I return Rabbit to his box and then place it back my drawer. I grab my whiskey glass and the two wine glasses, make my way to the kitchen and leave them there as I head back to my study to look over the paperwork that I brought home.

I didn't mention my plans to Evie. Truth be told, I was a little hesitant, unsure what she'd make of it all. Then there was the whole

Leah conversation, and although I could have brought up the subject of a shelter in her name then, I couldn't. I couldn't form any more words. Instead, I chose to lose myself in her.

It seems to be a recurring theme that it's only when I lose myself in Evie that I actually find myself, the real me. The me I want to be all the time.

I pull open my top desk drawer and look at the box. The silver shines in the soft glow of my study. I open it and look at the two-carat diamond in a princess cut, set into a band of eighteen-carat white gold.

A smile takes over my face as I imagine what it would look like in its rightful place. But that's something for another time … a time in the not-too-distant future, I hope.

Fuck! Love has turned me into something I never knew existed within me. It's turned me into the man that wants the whole nine yards. Two-point-four children, a white picket fence, a dog running around in the garden … Hell, I can picture it now.

Closing my eyes, I rest back in my wingback chair. Grey eyes swirl in my vision, and beautiful dark hair blows in the breeze. There's a porch with a swing, a French bulldog barking as it chases butterflies in the garden … a little girl, a little boy… I see my future in an instant.

That's the last thing I see in my mind's eye as I drift off to sleep.

***

Waking, I feel a crick in my neck. While massaging it with one hand, I look at the time. It's past one in the morning. How I slept in the chair that long, I don't know.

I grab my phone and head to my room, setting my alarm and plugging it in to charge. I take a quick shower, and another orgasm tears through my body as I close my eyes and picture Evie kneeling in the shower with her lips wrapped around my wet cock. If she were still here, I'd bury myself inside her and maybe even toy with that puckered hole that I haven't dared touch yet.

I don't know much about her sex life with Greg—and truth be told, I don't want to—but I don't think he ever took her in that way. My heart races in my chest as I think about being her first … and her last.

I want to be her last everything. I want to be her lover, her friend, her confidante and, one day, her husband. I want to wake up next to her every morning and fall asleep with her by my side every night.

What was it about Evie that made me start to think this way?

Honestly, I'm not sure. I just know that it's what I want to do with my life. I want to make her my wife and the mother of my child.

When I was younger, I made Leah a promise I'd never have children until I was ready. And I've never been ready. Until now.

Life is a funny thing. Our future isn't set in stone; the end goal is always changing. All my life, I've been blind to a future where any of what's in it now was possible. But for the first time, my eyes are open, and so is my heart.

Evie Slater buried herself under my skin without me even noticing. She burrowed deeper until she became inextricably part of my soul. How it happened, I honestly don't know.

Things have already been sent to test us. Our first date started with two assholes trying to hurt her but ended so much sweeter. I found a friend in Evie before anything else, and our love blossomed from there.

I never thought about dating, never mind dating a single mum. But thoughts of her being a single mum have never even entered my mind. I see her as Evie, and I know if I want her, Maya comes as part of the package deal, and I wouldn't have it any other way.

There were times when I thought I'd inadvertently hurt Evie or perhaps Maya. I thought my past would poison their present and future. But now all I can see is a life filled with love.

I thought telling Evie my darkest secret, that I couldn't save Leah, would make her see me differently. But it didn't. She still loves me, and that's enough to make my heart triple in size. She surprised me when she didn't run after hearing Leah's story and its tragic ending. I guess it was all in my head that she'd scare easily, that her flight or fight instinct would kick in and she'd ultimately choose flight.

I head to bed, dressing in a pair of low-slung lounge pants before burrowing under a blanket that still smells like Evie.

Resting my head on my pillow, I close my eyes and inhale her intoxicating scent. I revel in thoughts of her touching me, tasting me. She's truly incredible, and I can't imagine another woman ever being able to make me feel this way. There's something about her, something I can't quite name, that has me all tied up in knots. I'm hers, she's mine. Our souls are entwined in a way that can never be undone. Our bond is sure to be tested over time, but the one thing I know for sure is we will always come out on top.

Love is something I never thought I'd experience. My past taught me that people weren't to be trusted. But my past also had a hand in shaping me into the man I am today, and while there are things I would change if I could, I have become a better man because of all that has happened.

Most of all, I became a better man when I met Evie and began to change without noticing I was doing it. She did something to me, cast some sort of spell over me, making it so that I could never go back to be the man I was before. She makes me want things I'd never have wanted without her. Her love makes me a stronger man. A loyal, loving, fiercely protective man. A man that would give her the world, if only it was his to give.

Chapter Nineteen

Evie

Trey, Ry, Joe and I wanted to make sure that Maya had the best birthday this year, wanting to go above and beyond to make sure she enjoyed her seventh birthday. Ry says I always go over the top for her birthday, but I don't think I do. In my eyes, she's my baby, and I like to make sure she has a good day. I always have this fear of her thinking she is missing out on something as she only has me in her life, aside from Ry and my parents of course. I don't want her to feel like that, especially since I refused to let *any* man be in our life until Trey came along. I wasn't expecting him to just appear in our lives out of thin air, but I'm grateful that there is somebody else to love and cherish Maya just as much as I do. I knew this year had to be special, as we have expanded our once little family, and I wanted to make sure everybody was involved, even if I had to be sneaky about it.

All four of us took Maya to her favourite restaurant and decided to surprise her with my parents. She thought that they couldn't make it as they Skyped her a couple of days before and said that they had "important meetings" to attend to. She was sad that they couldn't make it but understood when they told her they would see her the weekend after.

Her face was the reflection of joy and surprise when she saw them sitting there at the table with bags of presents around them.

After we made it back home, she stood there and explained every single present to them and told them who brought it and how much she loved it. She nearly brought Trey to tears when she proudly stood up and said that he had given her Rabbit, and how her auntie Leah had wanted her to have it in her care. She had been carrying it around with her all day and refused to put it down. I could tell that it shocked Trey when she called Leah her auntie, but you could see how proud he was that she loved something that reminded him of his sister so much and held such a special place in his heart.

He ended up staying that night, having brought a bag with a change of clothes with him. He told me that we would be leaving early for Maya's other birthday present. He wouldn't tell me what it was as he said that it was partially a gift for me also.

So, at half six this morning, we were on our way to this *secret* destination. Maya spent the entire ride asleep as she isn't a morning person and woke up when we were close to the destination.

"Are we there yet?" Maya asks in a sleepy tone.

Trey and I lock eyes while laughing, both sharing joy that she had been asleep so she couldn't ask that question a million times, like all children do.

"We're nearly there, sweetheart. I was just about to ask your mum to wake you up, otherwise you would miss it."

I look at him confused.

"Miss what?"

"You'll find out soon enough. You really don't like surprises, do you?"

"No, I don't. I *hate* surprises with a passion. I like having everything planned to the most minute detail. Ry jokes that I have OCD."

"I think I'll have to agree with him there."

I feign shock and disgust, but I can't disagree, because for as long as I can remember I've always wanted to be in charge, for fear that it won't go the way it has to.

I've always planned for the smallest inconvenience. No matter how unlikely it is, I make sure it doesn't have a possibility of happening. I even control what happens on my birthday—I can't stand having a surprise birthday party. I'm always involved. Ry tried to plan a surprise party once but decided to tell me and get me involved because he noticed how stressed I got not knowing. I think it's partially due to Greg doing things completely out of the ordinary and, if something didn't go his way, he would punish me for it, so I like to make sure that everything is going a specific and set way.

I know with Trey that there will be surprises, because he's really enjoyed pulling this together for Maya's birthday and knew that she would love it. I have all my faith in him, and I know that what he does, he does out of the goodness of his heart, and I'll love it anyway.

"Maya, look to your left."

Trey speaking pulls me out of my head, and I turn to see what he's pointing out to Maya. We pull into a car park with a sign displaying *Warner Bros Studio Tour: The Making of Harry Potter.* I try to hold in my squeal of delight, Maya doesn't manage to, and her squeal travels through the car. My mouth hangs wide open as I realise that he's brought us tickets to go on the Harry Potter tour. I told him months ago how obsessed we were with Harry Potter, and how I have always wanted to take her to the studios but haven't had the time or the money to do so.

A muted *Oh my god* travels from my lips as I try to contain my excitement. Maya is still squealing and laughing while bouncing in her car seat, while Trey is just looking at us and laughing at our expressions.

"I knew you had planned something big, but … not something like *this.*"

I stare at him in wonder. It's weird having somebody do something like this for us. I'm used to doing everything by myself and having to make sacrifices to make sure that Maya's birthday is perfect, so she does feel like she's missing out. It's not like I'm unwilling, or I hold it against her that I make those sacrifices—I would gladly do *anything* for her, and it's worth it to see her face light up when she gets something she has been asking for.

But having somebody else wanting to make sure that she's going to have the best time shows me how I don't have to be alone in this, that Trey will make sure that we are cared for.

"I knew you wanted to bring her here, and I thought Maya's birthday was perfect timing. I couldn't help myself, and with that reaction, it's totally worth it."

He smiles sheepishly as I shake my head at his logic. We all get out of the car and make our way to the entrance. Maya's curious eyes try to take in every tiny detail.

"Oh, my god! Mummy, look! There's a poster of Sirius!"

Maya is pointing to a large, what I'd assume to be a concrete, wall, with paintings of multiple characters' faces in wanted posters. We all walk forward as we all marvel at the large chess pieces scattered around.

"Look, Maya, it's me!"

I stand in front of a wanted poster of Bellatrix Lestrange.

"You as Bellatrix? You're more like Hermione." Trey looks at me, confused, as Maya laughs and nods her head.

"Ry started a joke years ago of how I remind him of Bellatrix, because I can be a little weird at times, and now whenever we watch any HP movie, he always says it's me instead of Bellatrix."

I shrug my shoulders at Ry's logic. I never questioned it, especially since I do have my weird—quite psychotic—thoughts at times. We continue our way into the entrance, wanting to make sure we get our time slot.

I'm shocked that Trey managed to get tickets at such a short notice and keep it a secret. I can *never* keep a secret and must *always* tell *somebody* because it kills me on the inside not telling anybody.

We make our way through security, and we all stare in awe as we walk through and see the doors to the Great Hall. A lady in uniform approaches us.

"Are you Maya?"

She bends down to speak to her. Maya nods while backing into my legs. She may have come out of her shell more, but she gets especially taken aback when somebody knows her name when she hasn't told them.

"Well, I heard that it is your birthday, so you get a special badge, and you get to help me open the doors to the Great Hall."

Maya instantly perks up at the thought of being special and smiles at the lady. She looks up at me for confirmation and I nod my head. She follows her over and holds one of the door handles while a couple of other workers ask more children from the crowd to help open the doors. Trey's hand winds around my waist as we both watch.

***

After walking around the first half of the tour and going into the Forbidden Forest shop and buying our weight in merchandise, we come across a small restaurant.

Trey stands waiting for food while we try and find a table in this packed place. We finally find one at the back of the room. I place all our bags carefully on the floor and sit down, sending him a text so he knows roughly where we are.

"Mummy, this is just the bestest day everrr …"

She draws out the word as she looks outside, marvelling at the life-size house, which is made to look like Privet Drive.

"Oh my god, Mummy! It's Harry's house. Do you think he stayed in there? Because if he did it would be so cool!"

She looks at me wide-eyed as she starts to get excited again. Trey's laugh booms behind us as he stands there with food in his hand.

"I got you a Corona with that. Thought you would appreciate it."

He smiles at me as he places the food on the table. I start adding up how much the burger and hot dog for me and Maya would cost.

"How much did it cost you?"

He smirks at me, knowing my intentions.

"Nothing for you to worry about. Today is about Maya and you, so don't worry."

I go to argue, but he shoots me a no-nonsense look. I smile at him and watch as he starts talking to Maya about her day and asks if she's enjoying it.

I feel bad not paying for any of this, but thankfully he didn't have a chance to say no when we were in the gift shop. I rushed Maya over and paid for everything we wanted before he had a chance to realise.

I'm extremely grateful, more than anyone can understand, I just don't want him to feel like I'm with him for the money aspect, because I'm not. I can support myself, and that's something I've always had pride in. I've never felt like I need a man to bring money into the house. I know I can do it by myself and live more than comfortably, while also running a successful business.

I know this is for Maya's birthday, and he has truly enjoyed spending the time to make sure she has a great day, while wanting to spend the money and not make me feel guilty about it … it makes me feel confident. He accepted that we come as a package deal, and that to love me, he must love her, which he has proved time and time again. It shows me that he *truly* is in it for the long run, and that this isn't just some fling.

***

The sound of the front door slamming into the wall behind it jolts me from my sleep. I jump out of bed and notice that I'm the only one in the bedroom. I turn to the clock and see that it's five in the morning. I hesitantly make my way through the bedroom and into the living room. As I get closer, I hear cupboard doors slamming open and shut. As I round the wall to the kitchen, I see Greg slumped against the counter, drinking vodka straight from the bottle.

I wince, noticing how drunk he already is. He can't stand up straight, but he obviously doesn't care and just continues downing the bottle.

"Babe?" I quietly walk towards him, not wanting to startle him. "How about you come to bed, huh?"

He looks through me, his eyes glazed over, and nods his head, finishing the bottle and then flinging it on the floor. The sound of the glass shattering jolts me, but I keep a poker face and help him into the bedroom. As I near him, I notice red lipstick covering the entire side of his neck, and the smell of cheap perfume assaults my senses.

I knew he was angry when he left earlier. I finally fought back, but the realisation that he let somebody else near him disgusts me. I place him in the bed, not even bothering to undress him, and get on with cleaning the kitchen, not wanting to be anywhere near him.

***

I shake my head, not wanting to ruin a perfect day because of Greg. I *refuse* to let him mess with my head anymore. I push him to the *furthest* corner of my mind and place a million *mental* locks around the file, finally pushing it away. I want to start a new life, with people that I actually love and that I know love and cherish me for me.

I look at Trey, catch his eye and give him the widest smile I can muster. He reaches his hand across the table and grasps mine for a second then carries on eating and talking to Maya.

I know the reason why I struggle with trusting somebody wholeheartedly is because I'm terrified of being cheated on. It made me want to do something with my life, to have a backup plan, just in case things didn't work out how I intended them to and I had to move.

I ended up taking a crash course in counselling as I knew that, in the future, I wanted to be able to help somebody who was in the same predicament that I was in. So I passed and got a certificate stating that I was a licensed counsellor. I've never done anything about it, but I like having the choice to do something about it if I ever want a career change, or if I come across somebody who needs my help. I like having multiple options and gateways if I need to.

"Hey, Mummy, can we go into Harry's house?"

Maya looks up at me with her doe eyes. I smile down at her.

"Of course, sweetheart. You don't even need to ask. Today is for you, and we will do whatever you want."

She beams up at me and grabs mine and Trey's hands. We finished our lunch not that long ago but wanted to finish our drinks and rest before carrying on with the end of the tour.

***

We finish the tour just a couple of hours later, and we come across the last gift shop.

"Oh, wow! It's huge."

Maya stands there, mouth gaping as she looks at all the things you can buy. It's a child's dream … okay, I'll be honest, it's *also* an adult's dream.

"This day has honestly been amazing; I don't know how I can ever make it up to you."

I lean into Trey's side, watching as his keen eyes never leave Maya as she stands at a rack, looking at all the badges they have on display.

"Just seeing how happy you two have been today is enough. The smile on Maya's face as she's been walking around, and the awe on yours, is a reward."

He kisses the top of my head, then makes his way over to Maya as a family appear next to her. I giggle at his over-protectiveness. For the entire day, if she wasn't holding his or my hand, he's kept his eyes on her and been as close to her as possible. He reminds me of my father. If we were ever at an event where there were loads of people, he would be as close to me as he could and wouldn't let me go far for fear of something happening to me.

I make my way over as I hear Maya's voice get higher. I rush over, as she only usually does that when she's in pain or extremely excited … I'm praying she's excited. I come up behind her and see her holding a pin badge in the shape of Hedwig. I instantly breathe a sigh of relief.

"Look! It's the last one, and he's my favourite." She beams up at me and Trey. "Can I have him pleeeasee?"

She draws out the last word, while giving her large doe eyes. Trey's face instantly softens as he's sucked into the charm that is Maya-Rose. I chuckle, knowing the response that will be coming.

"Of course you can, especially since he's the last one. He obviously wants to come home with you."

Trey smiles while he reaches down and picks her up, placing her on his shoulders. I laugh at the goofy expression on both of their faces as they roam around, trying to find the "best toys possible".

I trail behind them, picking up things and placing them in my basket as I go. I stop as I see figurines of Buckbeak and a Dementor. I place them in my basket, hiding Buckbeak as I know Trey is obsessed with him, and I just love Dementors. Just as I turn around to leave, I see a Dobby figuring in the same style. I look at him—he's standing there holding the book that Harry placed the sock in for him to be free. I grab it, knowing that Maya loves him and cries at the scene every time.

I make my way back to Trey and Maya, making sure the presents are hidden as well as possible. I know they won't pick them up as they went past the only display case which holds them.

I find them standing by the back wall, which is covered in stuffed toys of all the characters and animals. I stand beside Maya, who's staring at a plush Hedwig and marvelling at the fact you can make his head move.

Trey wraps his arm around my waist. "Do you mind if I just run to the other side of the shop for a second? There's something I want to get."

I nod my head, confused as to why he wants to go back the way we just came from. He gives me a quick peck and ruffles Maya's hair before turning around and making his way through the shop. I focus my attention back on Maya, who grabs my hand and tries to pull me to the other side of the plush toys. She stops in front of a plush Fawkes, pulls one out and gestures for me to lean down.

"Do I have enough birthday money for this?"

She looks at me and dances on the balls of her feet impatiently.

"You can have whatever you want. You don't have to use your birthday money; I'll buy it for you."

I don't want her to feel like she has to buy her own things with her birthday money that was given to her so she could buy something in a shop. Today is part of her birthday.

"No, Mummy, it isn't for me, silly." She huffs at me in annoyance. "I know that Fawkes and Buckbeak are Daddy's favourite animals from Harry Potter. I wanted to get him this as a thank you. Plus, I can't get Buckbeak because you have one in there."

She points to the basket, but I'm too shocked to even look and realise that he has appeared when I crouched down. *Daddy*. She called Trey her *dad*.

I feel my eyes fill up with tears as they cascade down my face. Maya looks at me shocked, and instantly comes up to hug me.

"What's wrong, Mummy? Have I done something to upset you? I'm sorry."

She looks up at me with worry all over her face. I smile, and her face becomes confused. I'm not surprised. I think seeing somebody with tears streaming down their face while smiling is probably a weird sight.

"No, baby, you haven't upset me. I'm just happy. Of *course*, you can buy that for—"

I look at her and realise something. It doesn't matter whether he is her biological father or not; he has shown her so much *love* and *compassion*; he's been showing her how to care for something deeply. He's showed her not to be afraid of anything, and to *follow* her dreams. He has done things that a *father* should do and teach.

The fact that she called him Dad shouldn't surprise me. It took me off guard, yes, but he *deserves* to be acknowledged for everything that he has done for her over the past couple of months. She should be able to be open to love, especially to someone who she would have never usually opened up to in the first place.

The fact that she is calling him that shows me how deep their connection is, and how much she *truly* cares for him. I always wanted her … blessing, in a way.

If I know that Maya is one hundred percent sure about him, I know that there will be no problems in the future about who I care for the most. I didn't want to have to make sacrifices when it comes to her feelings—they're like sponges at this age, and I don't want anything to affect her mental state badly. I also didn't want to lead Trey into feeling like I was going out with him for a test. He is it for me.

Having a man come into my life while I'm a single mother is hard. I knew it was going to be difficult, but trying to make sure that my child is happy and doesn't feel left out or threatened in any way, and then also making sure that I can get that relationship with my other half—it's needed. The balance *has* to be just right, especially because Maya, who has *never* had that father figure in her life, needs that stability just a little bit more.

Okay, yes, she has Ry, but he's always been more of an uncle that she can play with. She needs that figure in her life to be able to go to if somebody bullies her. Someone to go to if she feels threatened and wants to be protected. Something that I *can't* give her. That's something *I* have to come to terms with—there will be things that *I* won't be able to give Maya, things that *only* Trey can.

A bond with a father and daughter is *crucial*; it's something to be *cherished*. I've always wished that my daughter would have the same bond with her dad that I have with mine. So Maya calling him Daddy, without even thinking, is the best thing that could *ever* happen.

"Daddy's coming," I say. "Do you want me to hide it in my basket?"

Her eyes scan behind me and widen. I turn and see the top of Trey's head in the crowd as he makes his way back over.

"Yes please, Mummy. Hide it good though."

She places Fawkes in the basket and grabs a Buckbeak one, throwing him on top.

"Buckbeak is for me though."

She giggles at my expression and launches behind me, landing in Trey's waiting arms. I turn and see him standing there with Maya resting on one arm, but with an extra bag in the other. I eye the bag and raise my eyebrow at him.

"What you got?"

He chuckles at my instant need to know.

"I'll show you when we're in the car. Have you got everything you want?"

He looks at Maya first, and she nods her head in approval. He turns to me and holds out his hand, wanting the basket that I'm carrying. I grin mischievously and pull it closer to my body.

"Umm … I believe so." We turn and make our way to the till, when I remember something. "No! Wait, give me two ticks."

I turn, jog to the candy section that I saw in the furthest corner and grab three chocolate frogs. I hastily make my way back and see Trey still standing there, in the same position with Maya, looking at me like I'm crazy.

"Now I know why Ry calls you Bellatrix."

We all laugh as he looks at the boxes in my hand.

"What did you go back for?"

I laugh at his inquisitive stare and stick my tongue out at him as I repeat what he said to me.

"I'll show you when we're in the car."

I hear his laughter as I walk to the till, followed by the two people I love.

"You wicked, wicked woman."

***

I finished paying for the monstrosity that we brought in the last gift shop. I swear they add the smaller gift shops scattered in to ease you into spending all your money, making you think that you can't possibly buy anymore. And then you suddenly appear in this gigantic gift shop and you realise that there are so many more amazing things that you can get.

We lug it all into the car, with Maya holding the "special" bag with

Trey's present in. I grab the couple of bags that I want to give them right now, not having the patience to wait until we get home. I let Maya sit on my lap in the front, knowing that there is no point in strapping her in the back as she wants to give Trey her present.

Trey sits in the driver's side and looks at us weirdly. Maya is sitting on my lap with a bag on hers, and I've got extra bags at my feet. He grins and pulls out the extra bag that he got earlier.

"Looks like we all got the same idea huh?"

We all laugh as we realise we're all too impatient to wait until we get home to give them to each other.

"Can I go first, please?" Maya asks while bouncing in place.

We both nod our heads. She reaches into the bag and pulls out Fawkes, looking at Trey as she does so. She reaches over and passes it to him. His face morphs from shock, to disbelief, and finally to awe, all within a couple of seconds.

"Is this for me?"

He looks at her and down to Fawkes and back at her again. She giggles at his reaction.

"Of course it is. I bought it for you because you gave me the best birthday present. You've also been the best daddy … and, umm, I've never had one before but you're super nice to me and tell me you love me, so …"

She shrugs her shoulders, instantly getting shy at calling him her dad, even though she was so confident about it earlier.

His eyes glisten with unshed tears as he processes what she says. He reaches over and grabs her from my lap, placing her in his as he hugs her. I feel tears slowly trickle down my face as I witness the first time he has ever been told this … I know how much he struggled after Leah's death. And I think telling me about her, giving Rabbit to Maya, and then her calling him Dad, was just a roller coaster of emotions for both of them. Maya leans back and cups his face in both of her tiny hands.

"I am honoured for you to call me your dad. I hope you know how much I love both you and your mum. And the best birthday present? I think your mum's cake was quite amazing, don't you?"

He tries to lighten to mood after seeing Maya's face still wet with tears, and she laughs through them.

"I mean … Mummy's cake was awesome. But I just loved today so much. Sorry, Mummy."

I laugh at her as she winces when she looks at me.

"If you didn't say today was the best, I would have been surprised, sweetheart. Can I give you guys your presents now? I can't keep it a secret any longer."

Trey looks at me confused.

"You got us presents as well? Well, now it's becoming a competition." He pretends to be annoyed as he tickles Maya's sides.

I pull out the figurines and pass the correct ones to them.

"It's fitting really, because Maya got you Fawkes and I got you—"

"Buckbeak."

His voice cuts mine off as he stares at Buckbeak enclosed in a glass casing. He leans over and kisses me forcefully on the lips. He pulls back and stares at it again, then puts it back in the box to help Maya's with hers.

"Dobby!" she squeals.

We laugh at her as she recreates the scene.

"Thank you, Mummy! You know Dobby is my favourite."

She gives it to Trey to put back in the box while she climbs back over to give me a hug. She kisses my face as she giggles.

I lean back and stare at the amazing little girl she has become.

The sound of a camera going off gets our attention. Both my and Maya's faces lift, and we stare at Trey. He's sitting there with his phone up—the sound of a camera going off must have been him taking a photo.

"What did you take a photo of?"

He grins as he turns his phone around. His background is now a photo of me and Maya, staring at each other so intently you can see the love shining in that one gaze.

"I just had to; the photo doesn't do it justice, but at least, whenever I'm missing either of you, I can look at my phone and see your smiling faces."

My breath gets caught in my throat as I stare in wonder at how amazing one man could be.

"Can we take a photo of all of us?" Maya pipes up.

Trey doesn't say anything, just pulls us closer and takes multiple photos of us, some with us pulling funny faces, and some with us smiling. I make a mental note to ask him to send those to me so I can print them off and frame them to go in the living room.

"Now it's time for your mummy's present. You ready, sweetheart?"

He looks at Maya, who nods her head. I look at both of them, confused.

"What do you mean my present?" I ask hesitantly. "Is that why you told me you had to go and grab that thing?"

Things start clicking into place as I realise he went off to buy me something *sneaky*.

He smiles and nods his head as he passes Maya something out of the bag. I open the box and gasp as I pull out a glass display case. As I look in, I see a replica of the Time Turner hanging inside.

"You didn't have to get me that. Thank you, it's beautiful."

I look up at both of them with a smile on my face. I place it back into the box, not wanting to break it, so I can put it on my shelving unit at home.

"We wanted to. It was Maya's idea; she said she knew you would love it."

Maya looks up at me and I lean down and kiss the top of her head.

"I do, thank you. I love you both. So, so much."

"I love you too, Mummy. And I love you, Daddy."

Trey's face transforms into a bigger smile than before as we shower him with the love he deserves. He wraps either arm around me and Maya, and we all lean together in a mishap of a hug.

"I love you both too, dearly."

Epilogue – Part One

Trey

Two years later

I won't deny that life has been hectic lately, but I'm glad it's all slotting together nicely. When I first had the idea, I didn't know if I could pull it off, but with Leah's trust fund money, a little of my own, and a lot of hard work from all involved, it's finally time to cut the ribbon.

The Leah Kinsella Foundation is now officially ready to be opened. The press is here—photographers, TV cameras, and a local newscaster to give us the coverage this place deserves.

Evie has been amazing, and I couldn't have done this if it weren't for my wife by my side. Closing my eyes, I picture her in her wedding dress: a sweetheart neckline with lace above it that morphs into lacy sleeves, a small diamante belt at the waistline, and the rest of the dress clinging to her in all the right places. She looked stunning. My eyes had filled with tears the instant I saw her standing at the top of the aisle with her father.

Maya had walked down the aisle ahead of her, scattering rose petals. Her lavender-coloured dress was so beautiful, she looked like a little angel.

It was one of the best days of my life. I only say "one of", because the day my son Jace entered this world was probably the only thing that could match my wedding day. Well, except for the day Evie agreed to be my wife, that is.

My family mean the world to me, I only wish Leah was here to see it and be part of it. She missed out on so much, her own chance at a future like this cruelly stolen from her when she was forced to feel like the only thing left for her was to take her own life.

That's one of the reasons today is so important. There's insufficient help out there for women today, women who are abused, whether as a result of domestic violence or otherwise.

The Leah Kinsella Foundation is a charity that stands in the local community to help women become survivors instead of victims. Whether they've been raped, attacked or abused. Whether it's their partner who is abusive or a family member. That's what we want to try and change.

Evie had trained to become a counsellor and now, as well as working her main job at *Queen of Tarts*, she is also going to start working here as of today. Having the traumatic kind of past that she did has led her to want to help women get out of similar situations. She's given Ryan more responsibility at the bakery, and he's only too happy to step up. He can't bake, but he can run front of house while an experienced baker comes in on the days Evie is here.

I slip an arm around Evie's waist and pull her close. Her perfume smells floral and sweet, a perfect combination for her. She's dressed demurely in three-quarter length black trousers, a soft pink cashmere jumper I bought her for Christmas, and black court shoes.

"I can't believe we're really doing this." I whisper against her ear and watch her shiver in delight.

It's nice to know that, after all this time, I still affect her, even in the smallest ways. I can't help but imagine her nipples pebbling beneath the lacy bra I watched her put on this morning. God how I'd love to bite them and make her climax with wanton abandon. Maybe later. No, *definitely*.

"It's really happening, Trey. You did this."

"No, *we* did this Evie. I couldn't have done this without you."

"You were already making plans for this before I came along, Trey. It's all you."

"Don't be so goddamn stubborn and modest. I had the plans all laid out, but you helped me bring it to fruition."

"I have helped a little, sure, but—"

"No buts." I cut her off with a finger to her lips.

I lean down and claim her lips in a soft, sweet kiss. The shoulder of her jumper slips down, showing her rose tattoo. She got two tattoos done recently for our children. This one is because Rose is from our daughter's name, Maya-Rose. The other one is Jace's name, date of birth, weight, length and time of birth, all surrounded by some elegant dot work and a small footprint taken from Jace when he was born.

I also recently got a tattoo, a phoenix on my upper back, between and over my shoulder blades. It's to symbolise re-birth from the ashes, and I feel that's what both Evie and I have done—risen from the ash to be something beautiful once more.

Apart, we are good. Together, we are phenomenal. I wouldn't be half the man I am today if it weren't for my beautiful wife.

Looking down, I see the sunlight glint off her engagement ring and white gold wedding ring. I hold my own left hand up and look at my matching ring. The inside is engraved with our initials and the date of our wedding. It wasn't a big affair, due to me not having any family to invite. But our closest friends were there, along with Evie's parents. Joe was my best man and, breaking tradition, Ryan had been Evie's maid of honour. I don't know what you'd call it when it's a man in that position, but whatever. We shared an intimate and special day with those who mean the most to us.

Jace was our honeymoon baby. We'd decided to start trying for a baby just before we got married, and although we didn't expect it to happen so fast, we were delighted that it did.

Ry has the kids today. He's somewhere in the crowd beyond us. A large gathering of people has come to watch us finally open this place, and I won't deny how nervous I am.

My palms begin to sweat as I think about the fact that this day is finally upon us. How we got here is a long journey, full of ups and downs for each of us. But since getting together, we've definitely outweighed the downs with a million and one good things.

They say everything happens for a reason, and I can say I wholeheartedly agree. Having read a book recently, I have a new tattoo idea that's planned to happen next week. It's a saying that is really quite profound: *wyrd bið ful aræd*. It's translated as "Fate is wholly inexorable".

Fate threw Evie in my path for a reason. It brought us together because, somehow, we make each other whole. There was something missing from my life that I didn't fully understand until I met Evie: love. Love was missing. Sure, my sister loved me, and Joe does too, but the love of a wonderful woman like Evie came like a bolt from the blue.

"Looks like you're up, handsome," Evie says as she stands in front of me, one palm flat on my chest. "You've got this, Trey. Don't sweat it."

"Nuh-uh, we've got this. You're coming with me," I reply as I fold her hand into mine and pull her along with me.

We come to the steps as the mayor's car pulls to a stop.

"Mayor, it's a pleasure to meet you. I'm so grateful to you for being here today."

"It's a wonderful thing you're doing here, Mr Kinsella," she replies as she shakes my outstretched hand.

"Mrs Kinsella, it's a pleasure to meet you. I hear wonderful things about you," she says as she reaches out to Evie.

"Please, call me Evie."

I feel Evie's calm soothe my frayed nerves like a balm to my soul. We turn to the gathered crowd as a microphone is handed to me.

A hush falls as I take a deep breath and ready myself to speak.

"Good afternoon, ladies and gentlemen. Welcome to the opening of The Leah Kinsella Foundation. We wouldn't be here today if it wasn't for one very important woman in my life. A woman taken too soon through her struggles with abuse: my sister, Leah. Without her, this foundation would probably never have happened. It was her life that inspired me to open this shelter and found the charity. It was her untimely death at the tender age of eighteen that put me on this path.

"Now, I don't speak of Leah and her struggles often, apart from with my family. But as you are gathered here today, it inspires me to tell you a little of who she was.

"Leah Kinsella was the brightest, most beautiful young girl, and I was lucky to call her my sister. But growing up in foster care took its toll on us, and it seems Leah more than me. I won't go into too much detail here, but she was abused by one foster father after another. I used to coerce them into beating me instead of her. I used to protect her, shield her from as much as I possibly could. Unfortunately, that wasn't enough. She was beaten, neglected and sexually abused. This led to her taking her own life all those years ago.

"It is in memory of the woman I knew and loved that my wife and I are here today. We honour the life she had cruelly torn away from her. We are here as a beacon of hope, a light in the darkness, for anyone who has suffered in any kind of way. Whether they're trying to escape an abusive partner, needing to talk to someone about awful things like sexual abuse, we are here to listen.

"My wife, Evie, is one of our counsellors. It has been a lifelong passion of hers to help women in their time of need. She's an inspirational woman, without whom this foundation could not have happened."

I take a deep breath as Evie squeezes my hand gently, reminding me she's here, keeping me grounded.

"So please, ladies and gentlemen, if you or someone you know needs help, please remember we are here. We implore you to seek help, to come to us and speak out. Everything you say will be held in the strictest confidence.

"As well as offering counselling services, we offer shelter. We have several rooms here and planning permission to build more if needed. When we set out to bring this foundation to life, we wanted to give shelter to people who need it, to give them hope in the very darkest of times. We have space for single parents fleeing their home, and we work with other professionals to get them into a new home of their own.

"We also offer legal services, provided by the law firm I am proud to be a named partner of: McDonough, Kinsella and Lloyd. We invite you in today during our open day, so that you may see some of that which will be provided for those who need it.

"Our mayor is here and will be helping cut the ribbon momentarily. But before she does that, I just want to say thank you. To my best friend Joe for being my moral support, my shoulder to lean on, the best friend a man could wish for. Joe, you have been amazing, and I wouldn't be here if not for your support.

"To Joe's fiancé, Ryan, for being there for Evie these last few years. For helping her become the strong woman she is today.

"To my beautiful children, for giving me hope in the vast chasm of darkness that encompassed me for many years. Maya and Jace, you are my *raison d'être*, just like your beautiful mother.

"To Evie Kinsella"—I pause and turn to face her, looking straight into her swirling grey eyes—"for being the love of my life, the beat of my heart, the very thing my soul needed when it was adrift. You are the brightest light in the dark. You are the best thing ever to happen to me, except our amazing children. I love you, and I couldn't be prouder of you for overcoming your own obstacles to be here today by my side as I start the biggest venture. We wouldn't be here without you. I know Leah would love you so very much, just as I do.

"And last, but by no means least, thank you to each one of you and all the people that helped make this possible. The builders, the decorators, the volunteers—gosh, there are just no words. A simple thank you is not sufficient for any one of you. From the bottom of my heart, thank you for all your continued hard work.

"Now, Mayor, if you wouldn't mind helping us cut this ribbon and open the doors to The Leah Kinsella Foundation."

"If I could just say something first," says the mayor as she looks to me and then out at the crowd. "Mr and Mrs Kinsella, we as a community must thank you. You think everyone else is worthy of thanks, but the two of you deserve it the most. Without your generosity, this wonderful charity and this building right here would not exist. Without your dedication to the cause, many women would continue to struggle. But it's with much hope for their futures that I cut this ribbon today. I want them to see this place as the beacon of hope you intend it to be, their anchor in the storm. So, thank you both for being here and giving so much to our community at large.

"Ladies and gentlemen, it's with great pleasure that I can now declare The Leah Kinsella Foundation officially open."

She cuts the giant ribbon attached to the front doors, and the crowd bursts out into a round of applause.

***

After an exhausting but happy day, the children are in bed, and Evie and I have the chance for some time alone.

"Thank you for today, sweetheart. You were amazing. And the photographers loved you. Not as much as I do, though. I love you more than words can ever express. You are my life, my love, my friend, my wife, my everything."

"Trey," she says with a dreamy sigh. "You are a man both worthy and capable of so much love and so much more. Leah would be so proud of you today. You have done something truly remarkable, a feat not many would be capable of. You turned an abandoned building into a safe haven for women with troubled pasts and presents. They will now have somewhere to go to escape that hellish life that holds them captive."

"We finally did it, Evie. With the firm giving me more freedom to take on pro bono cases, and the foundation up and running, I will be able to give these women some hope. When they turn to the firm for advice, I will be able to point them in the direction of the foundation, providing them, as you say, with a safe haven."

Evie leans into me and captures my lips with hers. Her gentle touch coerces me into opening my mouth to her. Her tongue explores my mouth and guides mine in a dance that makes my heart beat wildly in my chest.

I reach down between us and cup her breast over the soft cashmere of her jumper. Her soft moan makes my cock twitch, so I slide my hand under the material of her lacy bra and tease her nipple with my thumb and forefinger.

Evie's back arches, pushing her ample breasts closer to me. Without breaking our kiss, I manoeuvre us so that she straddles my lap. She groans deeply as I undo her trousers and slip my hand under her lacy panties. Teasing her clit with my thumb earns me a gentle bite to my bottom lip. She kisses away the small sting before kissing her way down my neck.

My cock hardens as she rubs herself against my hand. I slip a finger inside her with ease, thanks to how wet she already is for me. She growls as I push in and out of her, and fuck if that isn't the sexiest thing, her purring like a kitten. My little sex kitten.

Our sex life has vastly changed during the course of our relationship. Where she was once timid and unsure of herself, she now oozes confidence. Our love has made her blossom, and her willingness to open herself up to me has shown her that love and trust go hand in hand. She trusts me with her body as she does her heart.

Evie pulls back and discards her jumper in a flash. Then her hands go to the buttons of my shirt. My mind flashes back to us on our wedding night, Evie needing help to undo her dress so she could peel it away and expose her sexy lingerie to me. She'd unbuttoned my shirt, then my trousers, as she stepped out of her dress that left a big pool of cream-coloured material on the floor.

As she'd pulled down my trousers and boxers, my erection had sprung free and she'd knelt before me, taking my cock in her hand and guiding it into her mouth so she could lick and suck her way to help me reach my first mind-blowing orgasm of the night.

That was the night Jace was conceived, and that memory is imprinted on my heart as well as my mind.

Straddling my lap in her lacy bra, I watch her glorious breasts bounce as she continues to ride my hand. I slip a second finger into her, making her cry out. Kissing my way down her neck to the hollow of her throat, I continue to thrust my fingers inside her. As I dip my head down to kiss the swell of her breasts, Evie grasps the long strands of my hair, her hand pulling my head closer to her, her silent encouragement to bite her the way she craves.

Pushing aside the material of her bra with my free hand, I lean down and capture her nipple between my teeth. I pull back gently before letting go. Repeating my actions twice more, Evie cries out, and I feel her walls clench round my fingers. She's teetering on the brink of her first orgasm and I can't wait for her pleasure to coat my fingers.

I unclasp her bra and slip the straps down her arms. She throws it to one side as she pants, climbing higher towards the peak of her climax.

"Trey," she whispers in a shaky voice.

"Yes. baby?"

"I … I need to …"

"I know, baby, let yourself go."

Her walls clench me tightly as I fuck her fast and rough with two fingers. She cries out my name as her orgasm tears through her.

An adorable little mewling sound leaves her lips as she rides out the little aftershocks. I reach out and cradle her head in my hand before pulling her to me, my lips crashing against hers in a passionate, urgent kiss.

Lifting my fingers, I break our kiss and drag them over my lips before sucking them into my mouth. Her grey eyes are glued to my movements. They darken with lust as she pulls my fingers from my mouth and slants her lips over mine. Our tongues dance together as she tastes herself on me.

I lift her so that I can slip her trousers down over her hips.

"Evie," I say as I pull away, needing to breathe.

"Yes, baby?"

"What would you say if I said I wanted another baby?"

Shock registers on her face but is quickly erased by a smile. She says nothing as she reaches to undo my trousers. She frees my cock and works me up and down, earning her a nearly feral growl.

"Evie, stop, I'll come too soon," I urge as she works me faster.

She comes to a halt before guiding my cock into her wet heat. I watch as my cock slides into her with ease. If there was ever a more erotic sight …

Grinding herself against me, she rocks her hips as she grips the back of the couch behind my head.

I grip her hips as she pulls herself up, my cock sliding out of her. My eyes are glued to the sight as she lifts herself up and down repeatedly. I lift myself to match her thrusts and she pants as I slam into her. Her walls clench around me, milking me for all I'm worth.

I'm unable to hold back much longer, my need to come inside her is all-consuming. We've been careful to use protection, only forgetting in the heat of the moment once or twice since Jace was born, but the way she slipped herself down on my cock without use of a condom is all the answer I need to my earlier question.

Nothing could make me happier than to think we might be making another baby tonight.

I so desperately want for us to have another child. In the past, I wasn't sure I wanted children because of how I grew up. But our family means the world to me, and I would never allow harm to come to them. I would never let them slip through the cracks the way Leah and I did.

Riding me hard and fast, Evie moans with each thrust. Her breasts bounce and her hair falls over her shoulders as her head falls back.

Leaning down, I suck her nipple into my mouth. Her cries are the only encouragement I need as I bite down.

"Evie," I pant out.

"Uh-huh?"

It sounds like a question.

"I need to …"

I grip her hips and lift her until my cock slides free of her. She moans at the feeling of loss, but I push her down onto the couch and realign myself with her, slipping back in with ease. I don't hold back as I fuck her hard and fast, her moaning only fuelling me on. I slip a hand between us and play with her clit. Her head sinks back into the cushion beneath her as she cries out her orgasm.

Without relenting to allow her time to ride the climax out, I fuck her as hard and as deep as I can. The thought of her carrying my baby takes over my mind as I thrust into her again and again.

I love Evie and our children with all my heart, and tonight I feel like she's claiming yet another piece of my once broken soul. Who knew I'd meet someone who would not only make me whole again, but breathe new life into me at the same time?

My rhythm changes as my balls tighten, and I thrust into her once more, crying out her name as my orgasm tears through me.

As I carry my beautiful wife upstairs, she buries her head into the crook of my neck, and I smile to myself. My heart beats that much harder because she gives it a reason.

Laying her down on the bed, I lie by her side and pull her into me. I pull the duvet over us so we can get some sleep.

***

I don't know what time it is. It's dark outside, but our curtains are still open. I must have forgotten to close them.

Looking to Evie's side of the bed, I see it empty. Suddenly, the light from our en suite pours into the room. She's standing there wearing nothing but a smile, and I feel my cock begin to stiffen at the sight of her curvaceous body and her voluptuous breasts.

"About the question you asked me earlier …" she says as she walks over to me with an extra sway in her hips.

"What about it?"

"Well, I was thinking, now I've got Jace back off to sleep, we could maybe try again."

So that's why she wasn't in bed when I woke. I must have slept through his cry because I was exhausted, but it was meant to be my turn to get up. *Wait, what?* The end of her sentence takes me by surprise.

"I was thinking we could make the most of the time we have before he wakes again."

Her sultry smile and her sexy body are all I can see. Another baby is all that I can think of. What has become of the man I once was?

I was alone, scared of commitment, afraid of having children. Then a whirlwind named Evie blew into my life and rocked the very foundations I'd crafted for myself. She and Maya changed my life irrevocably, and now with Jace, I have everything I never thought I wanted, never knew I needed. And I crave nothing more than to bring another baby into this world with my beautiful wife.

Our gorgeous little Frenchie, Diesel, barks at the bedroom door. Shit, now I have to go and let the dog out. Perfect timing as ever, Diesel.

"Hold that thought, baby," I say as I plant a kiss on top of her head, before grabbing a pair of jogging bottoms from my drawer.

I pull my bottoms on quickly as Diesel lets out another quiet yap. Somehow, he's learned that he has to be quieter at night because of the children. They say dogs are intuitive, after all.

As I let him into the back garden, the security light comes on and I see him run off. As he takes his sweet-ass time, I think about how I pictured my future when I got with Evie. A home of my own? Check. A beautiful wife? Check. Children? Check. A dog? Well, that was at Maya's insistence, but yes, I love our little Diesel.

Locking up behind him, I head back upstairs to make the most of the time we have left until Jace wakes again. I'm now wide awake and raring to go. I only hope Evie hasn't fallen asleep waiting.

I walk into our room and slip the little lock across, so that if Maya wakes, she has to knock. I look at our bed and see my wife lying there looking like the last meal of a starving man on death row. She is utter perfection.

Stalking over to her like I'm a predator and she's my prey, I climb on the bed and work my way up to hover over her.

Her arms wrap around my neck and she pulls me in for a kiss. I'm momentarily lost in her kiss until her hand reaches down and wraps around my cock. It hardens under her touch and I growl at her playfully. I love the little vixen she's become in the last couple of years. I truly marvel at how open and adventurous she's become.

My life has never been the same since meeting Evie Slater. Making her Mrs Kinsella was the best thing I ever did. She's beautiful, compassionate, loving, and a devoted mother and wife. She's passionate about the things that matter most to her and loves nothing more than her family. We're her everything, and she is ours.

All coherent thought leaves my mind as Evie pushes me down onto the bed and straddles my waist.

Epilogue – Part Two

Evie

The sound of laughter jolts me awake. I look to my side and don't see Trey lying there. Groaning, I roll out of bed and rub my eyes. The sound of Maya's laughter along with Trey's floats up from downstairs. Their bond has only solidified in the past two years. I knew she was a little bit scared when we had Jace. I can't hold it against her; she had been an only child for just over eight years, so having a sibling was scary for her. But she was *amazing*. As soon as I had Jace, she took on the big sister role with ease, and the amount of love that she shows him is phenomenal. Everything that she feared instantly went out the window, and we've constantly made sure that she knows how much she is loved, and that there are no favourites.

I make my way into the nursery. Jace is awake, and he's just lying there and cooing at the ceiling. I sit in the rocking chair in the corner; it's my favourite part of the nursery, mainly due to it having such sentimental value. This was the rocking chair I had for Maya, and that my mum had for me. It's always stayed the same—a pure white, but with small Winnie the Pooh and Friends as characters on the backing.

I love Jace's nursery. We struggled with what we wanted it to look like, especially since they told us that Jace was a girl to start off with. They couldn't tell us his sex from the scan itself, as he was stubborn and kept his legs closed. But the sonographer said that his heartbeat sounded like a girl. I didn't even know they could determine the sex due to their heartbeat, it's not something that has any scientific evidence to back it up, but they were wrong anyway. We went neutral with colours and everything just to be safe, as they told us that they can't be one hundred percent sure of the gender from the heartbeat. We were all quite surprised when we found out Jace was, well, a boy.

We didn't change the nursery when Jace came into the world; it was too beautiful to change. There are three plain white walls, but with the last one being a feature wall. On one of the plain walls, there's a large photo of all four of us in the hospital, just after I had Jace.

On the feature wall, there is a large tree in the corner, the branches and roots travelling the entire span of the wall. The part closest to the tree is set in winter, with snow encasing the entirety of it, a couple of squirrels dancing in the branches, and a hare going back into its burrow. There is a frozen lake in the corner, and you can just make out a fawn on the ice, with a rabbit and a skunk sitting next to him. Maya gave us that idea, to add in something Disney, and we thought Bambi was fitting, as it shows growth and finding a family that they never thought possible.

It then goes to spring, with some flowers blooming, the leaves starting to come back on the tree, and a deer standing in the middle. Where spring and winter meet, the sun shines and the snow looks like it's melting away, with the lake slowly starting to thaw.

Then it travels into summer. Fields of flowers encase the setting, with the sun shining brightly. The squirrels are still in the branches, making it look like they're travelling from one season to another. Rabbits, deer and fawns are spotted throughout the floor, dancing through the flowers. The lake glistens in the sunlight, and you can see faint hints of fish under the surface.

And then my favourite season, autumn. The leaves from the tree slowly turn from green into orange and red and then fall off to cover the floor once more. The squirrels are carrying nuts and stuffing the into the other end of the tree in the other corner, while a deer and fawn are curled into each other, with a rabbit and skunk lying next to them.

We hadn't left the ceiling out, painting it a bright blue with clouds to look like the sky. There are a couple of birds flying around also. The ceiling seems to be Jace's favourite thing; he'll lie there for ages just staring and giggling to himself.

It took me and Ryan weeks to complete. We brought specific paint that wouldn't give off any harmful fumes, so it was safe for me to use while I was pregnant.

I've loved painting and drawing since I was a child, and that was one of the many things that pushed me to decorate cakes with the detail I do, and Ry is just an amazing artist anyway. While Ry and I painted the wall, Trey and Joe built all the furniture to go in here. The cot is off-white to contrast with the rocking chair and walls, along with the changing table and chest of drawers on the other side of the room.

There's a faux off-white rug in the middle, breaking up the hardwood floors and tying everything together.

The love that was put into this room is what makes it what it is—*special.* I find myself sitting in here all the time; it's comforting. It's sad that Jace is outgrowing his cot and will be going into the room next to Maya's, but at least we will have another child to fill this space with.

I haven't told Trey yet, but I can't wait. I've made sure to keep it quiet this time. He knew I was pregnant with Jace before I did. He dragged me into the bathroom and told me to take a pregnancy test, telling me he knew because my "boobs were getting bigger". *Men.*

Jace starts to get fussy, so I get up and look at him as he pulls himself up into a seated position. He's grown so fast. I don't remember Maya growing this quickly; it's like I blink, and he's grown. It seems like only yesterday that he was a light in my eyes, and now here he is.

I pick him up and smile at him. he giggles at my expression and reaches up to touch my face, and the softness of his hand melts my heart. There is nothing more perfect than a baby and how they react; there's nothing more rewarding either. Watching them grow is just fulfilling.

I place him on his changing table and grab the bag with the presents that I brought specially to tell Trey I was pregnant again.

"Maya!"

I call her, knowing that she'll be able to hear me. The sound of her feet pounding on the stairs makes me smile. She's become so free since Trey came into our lives; he's truly brought the best out of her, out of *all* of us.

"Yes, Mummy? Is it time?"

The one thing that I love, and that I hope will continue, no matter how old she is, is that she will *always* call me Mummy. It has so much meaning to it, that one word. It was the first word she ever said for a very long time, and I'm glad that even though she is nine she doesn't care what others think and will continue to call me that. She's even taken up teaching Jace how to say it, much to Trey's chagrin.

She beams as she watches me finish putting a top on Jace, which on the front reads *Youngest Middle Bear.* I give Maya hers; it reads *Oldest Bear* ... again. I'm already wearing mine; it has *Mummy Bear* on the front. I pass Maya Trey's top, which reads *Daddy Bear.* I grab the box that is at the bottom of the bag and I pick up Jace.

"You ready, sweetheart?"

I look down at Maya. I knew she would be excited when I told her yesterday, but she pinky-promised that she wouldn't tell Trey, as I wanted it to be a surprise.

She nods her head at me as she laughs.

"I love you, Mummy. And I can't wait. Hopefully, it's a girl this time, though. We need more girls in the house."

I laugh. She was excited when we told her Jace may be a girl, but she told us she didn't care whether the baby was a girl or a boy. I think now it's worn out; she loves holding Jace and playing with him, she's an amazing big sister, but I think she wants a sister to be able to play with. Honestly, I don't mind. People always say that it's impossible to not decide what gender they want, that people always have a preference. But I have both, so it doesn't matter to me. As long as they're healthy, I'll love the baby either way.

"I love you too, sweetheart. Let's go. Otherwise your dad is going to run around the house asking what's taking us so long."

We laugh at the thought of him doing that again. He's very protective of all of us, in a good way. He understands how my relationship with Greg made me feel when I fell pregnant with Jace. Yes, I was happy, but because of the way that I had to flee when I fell pregnant with Maya, and how bad the pregnancy was due to stress, I struggled. It was weird. To have somebody there to care for me when I was having those two o'clock cravings, and when the morning sickness hit, which shouldn't be called morning sickness because I *never* got sick in the morning. He likes to know that we're all okay, especially since we decided we wanted another baby. It's like he goes into full dad mode.

At the mention of his name, Trey's voice travels throughout the house.

"You okay, babe? Maya? Do you need any help?"

"We're fine, honey. Stop worrying yourself."

I look at Maya, and we both laugh at the same time. We make our way down the stairs and see Trey sitting at the island in the kitchen. We both sold our old houses, wanting to get one for the both of us, to celebrate our growth as people *together*, not separate. We decorated it together and made sure that it had all of our tastes in here. So it's *our* home. The wall on the stairs and the hallway is my favourite part of the house; weird, I know. But it has framed photos lining the entire stairway and hallway.

It starts with a few photos of me as a child, and a few that I had managed to find of Trey and Leah. It took me ages to find some, especially since he thought the only thing he had left to remind him of Leah was Rabbit, which Maya keeps on a shelf in her room.

But I wrangled my uncle to have a look in the database, and he managed to find a few. Then there's photos of Maya as a child, then growing up, with some photos of me with Ry, and of Trey with Joe mixed in, signifying our life apart. Then there's the photos of all three of us from when we went to the Harry Potter studios. The two largest photos were taken on our wedding day: one of the three of us, and then the other with all of our family in it. And then it goes to photos of me pregnant with Jace, all of us standing together. And then the odd one with Ry and Joe, and my parents.

It shows our whole life, from when we weren't together to when we found each other. It's our life story, and I love it. It shows our growth as people and how, together, we make a whole.

Trey looks up at us all and smiles. His eyes go to my top and then flit up to mine, confusion swirling in them. His eyes instantly go to Maya, and he notices that we're wearing similar tops.

"What is this?"

I smile as I hand Jace over to him and his eyes scan the top Jace is wearing. A choked sound comes out of his mouth as he looks up at me with unshed tears in his eyes.

"Are you serious? Like, really, truly serious? This isn't a practical joke? It's not April Fool's Day, is it?"

I smile at him and nod my head. I push Maya forward, and she hands over his other top. He reads it and laughs.

"Seeing as though I didn't have a chance to surprise you last time, I had to be really careful. I found out a couple of days ago and saw these online, so I had to order them. But there's something else that I have got for you."

He looks at me confused as I pull out the box and pass it to him.

"What's this?"

I jump impatiently on the balls of my feet.

"Just open it, or I'll open it for you."

He tears in, and a huge smile spreads over his face. At the top is a

Babygro that says *Baby Bear* and my pregnancy test. He looks up at me with tears slowly cascading down his face, then he laughs and pulls me towards him with his free arm, the other holding Jace. He places his hand on my stomach and smiles. He nods to me to grab Jace, and he motions for Maya to come over. He picks her up and places her on his knee. We all grab onto each other in a group hug.

"Are you serious? You aren't playing a joke on me, are you?"

He looks at me and back at all of the tops we are wearing. I laugh at him. Not only was me falling pregnant the first time hard on me, but it was hard on Trey too. When he was young, he promised Leah that he wouldn't have a child unless he knew for sure that was what he wanted, and seeing that he had spent the entirety of his life just having flings, I knew when I came along it changed his life.

When I fell pregnant, we had a long talk. I knew he was scared that something would happen to him, or to me, and he was worried about what would happen to Maya and this baby. I assured him that it would be fine, and I knew the moment that I had Jace, when he was standing in that hospital room with me holding my hand, as soon as he saw our baby enter the world, all of those thoughts would leave his head. And they did.

"Of course I'm not joking. We're having another, making our family whole."

He looks at Maya and gives her a wide smile.

"How do you feel Maya? Are you happy?"

"Of course I am, Daddy. I can't be happier. I hope it's a girl though."

I see him visibly relax at the sound of Maya being okay. He laughs at her, and they start making jokes and talking about school.

***

"We've got one more present for you."

I look at Trey, who looks sexy in his tailored suit. Our wedding has been amazing; I couldn't have asked for a better day. With there only being a select few of us, it's a lot more personal than having hundreds of people attend. We both wanted something personal, and neither of us really had that many people we wanted to invite.

Trey, my husband, looks down at me in confusion,

"We weren't meant to be getting gifts."

"Well, you broke it with the flowers you sent to me this morning, so I get to break it too." I stick my tongue out at him as he laughs. "I'll be right back."

I kiss his cheek and walk away, finding Maya with my parents. My dad looks up at me and smiles.

"You enjoying your day, sweetheart?"

"Yes, thank you, Dad. Thank you for walking me down the aisle."

He smiles at me and clears his throat; he's been emotional all day, and he hasn't wanted to admit it. He became teary-eyed when he walked me down the aisle and refused to acknowledge it when I asked if he was okay. I know it's because his only daughter has got married, and he must understand that I'm not much of the little girl he remembers me to be.

I look down at Maya and smile.

"You ready, sweetheart? Are you sure you still want to do it?"

"Yep, I'm ready, Mummy. Are we doing it now?"

"Yeah. Let's go then."

I hold out my hand towards her and she grabs the piece of paper that my mum is holding out. Everyone is in on it aside from Trey, as this is his surprise after all. We make our way to Trey, and he suspiciously eyes what is in Maya's hand.

"So, it isn't a present from me per se, but it's from Maya."

I smile and nod down at Maya, giving her the encouragement that she needs. She takes in a deep breath and walks up to Trey. He's sitting down, and he picks her up and places her on his lap, I notice that everyone has come towards us and are either sitting or standing as they watch.

"So, I, umm … I asked Mummy the other day, and she said it was okay and that I should ask you. I've never had a dad, I only had Mummy, Uncle Ry, and my nanna and grandpa. But you came and you love me, and I love you. And because you and Mummy are gettings married and Mummy now has your name, I wondered if you could a-dot me? So, you will be my daddy, and thens I won't be the only Slater. Mummy said that I will have your last name, so we can all be a family. This means you'll be my proper daddy too."

She smiles shyly up at him. His face quickly transforms from being intrigued to shock, and then tears start to cascade down his face. Maya looks up at him confused and looks at me worriedly. She reaches up and cups his face in her hands.

"I'm sorry, I didn't mean to make you sad. You don't have to if you don't want to."

Unshed tears instantly fill her eyes at the thought of upsetting Trey. He smiles at her and shakes his head.

"No, no. I do want to adopt you. I would love to. I never thought I would hear those words. A piece of paper doesn't validate what you are for me; you

are my daughter, and I would like to think that you view me as your dad. But, yes, I would love to adopt you, then we will be a true family."

He smiles down at her, wiping away the few tears that managed to escape. She beams up at him and squeals, then she passes him the piece of paper and he places it on the table to hug her. Maya's arms wrap around his neck as she burrows her head there, and his arms sweep around her.

I keep my unshed tears at bay, not wanting to ruin my makeup, but knowing that it is such a huge step for both of them makes me happy. I slowly walk closer to them, not wanting to ruin the bubble they have encased themselves in. When I get closer, Trey's head lifts up and he smiles at me. He lifts an arm that was around Maya and pulls me closer. Maya looks at me and pulls me in, squeezing me into their hug.

I hear everyone cheer and we all look up. Maya beams up at Trey, and Trey laughs.

"Were you all in on this?"

They all laugh and a chorus of yesses travels through the room. He looks at me and smiles, and I lean over and capture his lips in mine. Butterflies travel through my stomach at the feel of his soft full lips. I never thought that after all this time he would still affect me in this way, but instead of fizzling out, it's become greater. I pull back and kiss Maya on the top of her head.

"I love you both."

Trey looks us both in the eyes.

"I love you too," says Maya, "and I love Mummy."

She smiles at both of us, Trey saying yes to the adoption has lifted off a great weight off her shoulders.

"I love both of you, always."

***

Trey laughing pulls me out of my memory. That was one of the best days of my life, and I will cherish it forever.

"When is everyone coming over?"

I instantly turn to look at the clock, and my eyes widen at the time.

"Oh shh—" I look at Maya and grin sheepishly. "Sugar. They'll be here in like an hour. I think Ry and Joe said they'll be coming earlier, though."

We're having our weekly dinner. Every Sunday, we alternate whose house we're going to, and have a large Sunday dinner. Just to have a catch-up and spend some time together as a whole family. It's nice, and this week it's at ours.

Just before my wedding, my parents moved into our little town, claiming that they were fed up of the long distance and wanted to be closer. I can't moan; it's nice having my parents only down the road. They love popping in to see how we're doing and to take Maya and Jace to the park if we've both had a long day at work. They love their grandchildren.

"I'm going to put on the shirt that Maya brought down," Trey says. "It'll be a nice way to tell them."

"That's another reason why I bought them. I thought it would be funny to act all nonchalant about it until they ask."

He laughs at me and winks. "See, you're a wicked woman."

I place Jace in his play pen in the living room, Diesel lies in his bed next to it and looks at me as if he's telling me he'll protect him. I laugh and pat him on the head.

Trey helps me in the kitchen, helping me prepare the chicken while Maya stays in the living room with Jace. We've started to give her small responsibilities like looking after Jace while we're cooking tea. She's great at it, and she's learning how to be responsible and do things the correct way. Thankfully, we have a baby monitor set up in the living room, so while we're cooking, we can see what's going on. It isn't like we don't trust her; I just like to know how everything is going. It's always good to keep an extra eye just in case. My anxiety has never fully left me. There'll no doubt always be some *residual* effects, but luckily, Trey has always been understanding of that.

The front door opening gets all of our attention.

"Why, hello, darlings!" Ry's voice booms throughout the house.

Trey and I look at each other and laugh. Ry and Joe walk through the kitchen door and smile at us.

"Hey, guys, how are you all doing?"

Joe's hello is a lot more subdued than Ry's, but you can see the happiness on his face. Ry walks up to me and gives me a hug, then he looks down at my top and smiles.

"Hey, darlin'. That's a cute top. Where did you get that from?"

"Oh, just a clothing website. I saw it and had to buy it."

Joe disappears into the living room, trying to see where the kids are. He's also taken on the uncle role; he loves the kids, and I know he wants his own. He and Ry have been discussing adoption after they get married. I hear a gasp coming from the living room, and I see Joe running from the living room into the kitchen. He's got Jace on his hip and Maya holding his free hand.

"Please tell me you're not joking."

Joe looks between me and Trey, while Ry stands there looking at all three of us, confused.

"What's going on, babe?"

Joe turns Jace around so Ry can see his top, while motioning for Maya to stand in front of him. Ry looks at the lettering and squeals.

"Oh, my god! Really?"

I laugh and look at Trey, and we both nod our heads.

"Yeah, I found out the other day. I told Trey this morning."

Ry jumps up and down and squeals again. Diesel runs into the kitchen and starts yapping at all the excitement. Ry reaches down and fusses him.

"I can't believe this. I can't wait. We're going to be uncles again."

Ry looks up at Joe and they both smile at each other. Joe turns to Trey and starts to congratulate him, while Ry walks over towards me. He encases me in his arms and sways us from side to side.

"I told you that I would help you find the right man, didn't I?"

I smile and laugh as I squeeze him.

***

When my parents came in, they had the same reaction as Ry and Joe. My dad shed a couple of tears. Even though he will deny it for as long as he can, he's become more in tune with his emotions in his old age. My mum is so happy for us, and she proceeded to do a happy dance with Ry.

These are the moments that I live for, seeing my family all together and happy. It may have taken me a long time to open up my heart to somebody new, but when Trey came along, I knew. I knew he was the one for me; he was what I needed in my life. The way that my dad and mum have taken Trey under their wing shows they truly view Trey as their son. Just watching the way that they interact with each other shows the bond they have.

"How long until the potatoes are done sweet pea?"

My dad eyes the oven, and then looks at me with a sheepish grin. I laugh at him while rolling my eyes.

"They have five minutes left. What's with that look? I know how to cook, you know. Plus, potatoes won't give you food poisoning."

I bob my tongue out at him and dodge his impending poke to my side. I laugh as he grabs a towel to try and swat my legs, then I turn and grab a spatula.

"You can't hurt a pregnant lady! That's just cruel."

I feign horror as I continually dodge his attempts, then I hear somebody coming in through to the kitchen, probably to see what all the commotion is about. I see Trey and smile, knowing that he will come to my aid. Before I can make it towards him, he gives me a devilish grin and grabs the extra towel on the side.

"My own husband and father! Tag teaming me, how cruel."

We laugh as the timer goes off on the cooker. I smile and grab all the trimmings for the Sunday roast. Everyone hears the cooker and makes their way into the kitchen, helping to make sure everything is prepared.

We all sit at the table and start to dig in. I look at my family and realise everyone I love is right here. I have a husband who is so amazing, caring, and passionate; he's stirred a fire inside of me that I thought didn't exist. I have a beautiful daughter who is so loving and has such pureness in her heart that I can't fathom it. And I have Ry and Joe, who are like two peas in a pod. They share the same energy and can show even the most broken thing the love they deserve. And my parents, who showed me how to love until I couldn't love anymore, who taught me how to be compassionate.

This is the family that I *deserve*; this is the love that I *deserve*. There is no such thing as being undeserving. It may have taken me a long time to understand that, but I do now.

She may not be here, but my grandmother taught me how to love people, and how to forgive. She told me that "no matter what happens in your life, you *deserve* the love you will feel in the future. No matter what happens, you *will* pull yourself up. Even if you fall in hell, you will keep on going."

The End

About the author

Keren Hughes

Keren is a bookworm whose bookshelves groan under the weight of her obsession, but she believes there's always room for "one more book."

She lives in the UK with her son and when she isn't reading or writing, she's nurturing the reader and writer in him as he's currently writing his own book.

Keren loves to connect with her readers. You can reach out to her on social media. She loves to talk anything books, movies and TV.

Her other obsessions include Disney, Marvel, and she's a Potterhead for life.

Jodie Harrold

Jodie is an avid book worm, who also enjoys writing, cooking, art and snuggling with her cat, Casper. She lives in the UK and has always enjoyed reading since she was little when her family read her classics at bedtime.

When she is not writing, she is studying at university to become a counsellor, but she also intends to keep writing.

You can contact Jodie through social media where you will be given sneak peeks of upcoming books, and pictures of her cat.

More Black Velvet Seductions titles

Their Lady Gloriana by Starla Kaye
Cowboys in Charge by Starla Kaye
Her Cowboy's Way by Starla Kaye
Punished by Richard Savage, Nadia Nautalia & Starla Kaye
Accidental Affair by Leslie McKelvey
Right Place, Right Time by Leslie McKelvey
Her Sister's Keeper by Leslie McKelvey
Playing for Keeps by Glenda Horsfall
Playing By His Rules by Glenda Horsfall
The Stir of Echo by Susan Gabriel
Rally Fever by Crea Jones
Behind The Clouds by Jan Selbourne
Trusting Love Again by Starla Kaye
Runaway Heart by Leslie McKelvey
The Otherling by Heather M. Walker
First Submission - Anthology
These Eyes So Green by Deborah Kelsey
Dark Awakening by Karlene Cameron
The Reclaiming of Charlotte Moss by Heather M. Walker
Ryann's Revenge by Rai Karr & Breanna Hayse
The Postman's Daughter by Sally Anne Palmer
Final Kill by Leslie McKelvey
Killer Secrets by Zia Westfield
Crossover, Texas by Freia Hooper-Bradford
The Caretaker by Carol Schoenig
The King's Blade by L.J. Dare
Uniform Desire - Anthology
Safe by Keren Hughes
Finishing the Game by M.K. Smith
Out of the Shadows by Gabriella Hewitt
A Woman's Secret by C.L. Koch
Her Lover's Face by Patricia Elliott
Naval Maneuvers by Dee S. Knight
Perilous Love by Jan Selbourne

Patrick by Callie Carmen
The Brute and I by Suzanne Smith
Home by Keren Hughes
Only A Good Man Will Do by Dee S. Knight
Secret Santa by Keren Hughes
Killer Lies by Zia Westfield
A Merman's Choice by Alice Renaud
All She Ever Needed by Lora Logan
Nicolas by Callie Carmen
Paging Dr. Turov by Gibby Campbell
Out of the Ashes by Keren Hughes
A Thread of Sand by Alan Souter
Stolen Beauty by Piper St. James
Mystic Desire anthology
Killer Deceptions by Zia Westfield
Edgeplay by Annabel Allan
Music for a Merman by Alice Renaud
Joseph by Callie Carmen
Not You Again! by Patricia Elliott
The Unveiling of Amber by Viola Russell
Husband Material by Keren Hughes
Never Have I Ever by Julia McBryant
Hard Limits by Annabel Allan
Anthony by Callie Carmen
Paper Hearts by Keren Hughes
The King's Spy by L.J. Dare

Our back catalog is being released on Kindle Unlimited
You can find us on:
Twitter: BVSBooks
Facebook: Black Velvet Seductions
See our bookshelf on Amazon now! Search "BVS Black Velvet
Seductions Publishing Company"

Black Velvet Seductions